Erik the Navigat

CW00507153

Book 5 in the New World S

By

Griff Hosker

Published by Sword Books Ltd 2021

SWORD
BOOKS

Copyright ©Griff Hosker First Edition 2021

Cover by Design for Writers

Contents

Prologue

I am Fótr of the Clan of the Fox. We live in the Land of the Wolf and we are content for we helped Sámr Ship Killer to regain his lands from the Norwegian King. This land is a good land and we are happy but sometimes, where there is a particularly fine sunset over the sea then Bear Tooth and I sit staring west. Bear Tooth is a Skræling and was born across the western sea. My clan fought the sea to return to the land of our birth and Bear Tooth helped us. He would never return to the worlds of his birth. He has a wife and he has children but a fine sunset made both of us think of the land we left. Bear Island was good to us but more than that we thought of the brother I left there. Erik the Navigator had been the reason we had managed to sail to the new world of Bear Tooth but the three sisters had been spinning and he was meant to stay there.

"Do you think that he lives still, Bear Tooth?"

The man I now regarded as my best friend shook his head, "Who can know for certain but I believe that the world is in balance. I was born there and live here. He is the reverse. So long as I live here then he will be happy there." He gave a sad smile, "There are no certainties, my friend, and all that we are left with are our beliefs. Look in your heart and listen to the voices in your head. Do you believe that he lives?"

I did as he asked and stared with my mind instead of my eyes. I saw a man, but he was dressed as a bear and I saw him with the Skræling we had found, Laughing Deer. I saw a young child holding his hand and I knew, beyond any doubt that it was my brother. I opened my eyes and I smiled, "Aye, Bear Tooth, Erik the Navigator lives, and I am content. When the sun burns the western sky I shall return here and watch the west with my mind!"

North

Griff
2021

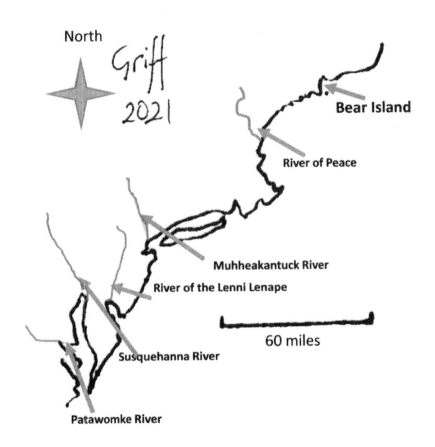

Bear Island

River of Peace

Muhheakantuck River

River of the Lenni Lenape

60 miles

Susquehanna River

Patawomke River

Chapter 1

I was named by my people Erik the Navigator but the clan who adopted me call me Erik, Shaman of the Bear and I am happy to be accorded that title. I sometimes wear a bear's head and skin over my helmet for I was born on Orkneyjar where every man becomes a warrior. Our islands lay to the north of the lands of the Saxons. Those who feared us called us Vikings but that was not our name nor was it Norwegian as King Harald tried to make us. We were just the Clan of the Fox. We valued our freedom and we left to sail the seas and discover a new home. We had found one, but I was the only one who remained when the rest of the clan took our drekar and sailed east. I had a mail byrnie, a spear, sword and seax. The weapons made me a mighty warrior but I knew that when they broke I would have no way to repair them. I also had two tools, a hatchet, and an axe for felling trees. Along with the few belongings we had recovered from Bear Island they were my last link to my family. I am happy here for I have a wife, Laughing Deer and two sons, Bear and Cub. The blood of Lars, my father has been planted in this new world. Since I defeated the Penobscot warrior, Wolf's Tooth, I had not needed my weapons. The gods had destroyed the treacherous tribe by destroying their boats when they fled south, but we were still watchful.

Each autumn we had left the coast and returned to the winter home the clan used. It was strange to have two homes and homes that were totally different from anything I had ever known. The dwellings that the Mi'kmaq used were left when they headed to the coast each summer and the first thing they did was to repair them. Laughing Deer and I were a new family and so the clan helped us to build our home. It was cosy and private, but I was used to a longhouse. There were neither tables nor chairs. These people did not work wood. It seemed to me that they changed nature as little as possible. The winter homes were warm for we hunted the animals with fur and buried ourselves beneath them at night.

Life in the winter camp was peaceful. The time for war and that was rare, was when the clan were in the summer camp overlooking the bay and Bear Island. That was when conflict might arise, but I learned, as I sat with the other men around the fire that war with the Penobscot had been rare. They were enemies but until they had tried to attack us it had been skirmishes and individual combats which had been endured by the naturally peaceful clan. I had seen that when we had prepared for the battle. The real warriors had stood out and they had been natural fighters. Most had not. I did not say those words to them but I thought that had Arne and our men met them and made peace instead of heading off to fight the Penobscot then my brother might not be dead and we might have had a home in the new world. *Wyrd*.

I could see why the clan had chosen this patch of land which was shared by other Mi'kmaq clans. There were large patches of open water, they were like the larger tarns we had back in the east. There were fish to take and animals to hunt. The Mi'kmaq clans each kept to their own area and as the land and waters were so fertile there was no conflict. Life in the village followed a pattern. The women collected wood, berries and food every day. The men went hunting or fishing. These were not farmers. The village sheltered in the clearing they had made and the rest of the forest in which we lived was our hunting ground. I was not as skilled with a bow as most of those who had returned east on the drekar but my strength and the better metal tipped arrows I knew how to make made me more skilled than most of the Mi'kmaq. The warriors liked to get as close as they could to their prey before they released. I was able to use my bow from a longer range and often when a herd took flight early, I was still able to bring one down. We hunted fish with spears as well as using fish traps. My metal headed spear was superior to the stone ones of the clan. I got to know the men of the clan

4

better as we hunted. I could speak their language easily now. I no longer had to struggle to find the word I needed and as we headed to hunt or fish I would speak with the men.

The one part of this new life I did not like was that I was Erik the Navigator and yet, in this sea of trees, I could not navigate and I missed the sea. I found the winter life easy, but I was always waiting for summer when we could return to the east and I could see the sea once more. I yearned to sail the birch bark snekke, *'Ada'*. I could not help it for within me was the desire to find new places. When I sat with the other men around the winter fires and we talked, I asked them about the land to the west and the south.

"Why do you wish to know about those lands, Shaman of the Bear? Do we not have all that we need here and at our summer camp?"

Black Bird and his brother Runs Far were my closest friends amongst the men. I asked them the question when we returned from the hunt which had yielded four good deer but where we had also strayed to the very edge of their land. The river which marked the boundary was filled with fish and called the Alesstkatek or river of rock shelters. The far bank was Penobscot land and that was as far west as we ever went. It was as we headed back with our bounty, including the red-fleshed fish we had speared that I had asked about the lands to the west.

I saw the other warriors waiting for my words. I shrugged, "I came with my brothers from the lands to the east. We sought what was in the west. When we reached here, we found a perfect place. Your clan is lucky, but I was the one who first found this land for my clan and I wonder what is over the next ridge. The river we saw, the Alesstkatek, has hills beyond it. Is there another sea there?"

Long Sight shook his head, "I have travelled more than the other men. I walked for four days, once, beyond the river and all that I saw were mountains rising in the distance."

Black Bird was thoughtful, "There may be a sea to the west, Erik, for when we held a gathering of the tribes once there was a warrior, a Mohawk, who spoke of great seas in his land which took days to cross."

I shook my head, "When we came west it took moons to cross the Great Ocean. What you describe sounds like a larger version of the waters close to our winter home. One day I would like to travel to the western edge of this land and find such a sea as I crossed."

Runs Far asked, "Are you not happy with the clan?"

I could tell that I had offended them, and I shook my head, "Of course not. I have my wife and my children, and I have my friends but in here," I tapped my chest, "there is a worm which gnaws at me. It makes me wonder what is over the next line of hills."

5

Black Bird nodded, "I had such a desire when I was young but as I got older the fire burned less fiercely. I am content."

Over the next years, I came to understand their viewpoint. Indeed, when we headed back to the coast and I saw Bear Island once more I wondered why I had been so restless in the winter camp. I had made a Mi'kmaq version of a snekke with a sail and sailed back to the longhouses we had built. We had taken all of value, but the graves of the dead were still there, and I honoured the dead by kneeling close by them and speaking to the spirits. The buildings had been well made but I knew that in a few years nothing would remain. Nature would reclaim them. This would not be like the Romans in the land where we had lived. There would be no lines of stones to mark where they had trodden. My clan had been like the Mi'kmaq, we drifted over the land and when we were gone so were the signs of our existence. I took my eldest son, Bear, with me when we travelled there, and I told him the tale of the Clan of the Fox. When he grew and had a family then he would pass the tale on.

I held a place of honour amongst the clan for I had been instrumental in them defeating their enemies, the Penobscot. Often the chief, Wandering Moos, would ask my advice or my opinion. They seemed to believe that I really was a shaman. I was not but I knew that some of the things I had brought with me gave me almost magical powers. I had announced myself as such when I had first spoken to them as we believed that they would be less likely to kill a shaman. Simple things impressed them. By using my knife and my flint I could make fire far faster than any of the others. Even when I explained how I did it and allowed them to use my knife and flint they still ascribed magical powers to me. The skills of sailing were also a mystery to them. They could paddle and navigate that way but using the wind to move quickly seemed a gift from the gods. I eventually came to accept all of this and cease trying to make light of my skills.

Life went on like this as my family grew. My second son, Cub, had been born when Bear was four and could now help Bear and his mother and me when we foraged and gathered food. I now had two sons and I enjoyed teaching them both. It must have been as it was for my father with my brother Arne and myself. I was content although, each year, I looked forward to our summer migration. The flies and the heat from our winter camp would have been unbearable and we moved to the coast each spring to enjoy cooler, fly free air. My skin had now darkened, and Bear found it amusing that I had white lines on my face from where I had screwed up my face and the sun had not burned it.

When I came from the steam hut and he saw the white skin in the middle of my body he would giggle.

Life was good for the clan and my family and I were content. When we returned to the summer camp the women and children would repair the salt pans. All summer we would let the sun burn the sea water in the mud and stone-lined enclosure and then collect the salt. The salt would help us preserve the meat and fish we collected in winter. Men would both hunt and fish every day while the women and children would forage in the forests and gather shellfish. The bay we used teemed with the creatures we had called lobsters in the east. They were found in the rocks but unlike the crabs had to be hunted with spears for they lived too deep to be caught by hand. A few hunters had devised a sort of trap with was weighted on the bottom and tethered to the land with a vine. They were clever hunters for all that they had to do was draw up their traps each day and empty them. The clan had, at one time, hunted the moos on Horse Deer island but when they had tried to drive us away they had slaughtered them all. I knew that Wandering Moos regretted that decision for it had upset nature. Now we still hunted them but that was harder to do on the mainland where they could be frightened by the noise and flee. We used everything we took from the moos and the deer we hunted. Antlers and bones became tools and weapons. Hair became ropes and their skins could be made into a variety of things. I now wore a deer skin vest and had a pair of very short hide breeks. I saved my seal skin boots for the times I was at sea and wore instead, mockasins which I made. For three days each week, I would sail *'Ada'*. Bear came with me and we fished the waters around Bear Island. Sometimes I left him on the beach with his mother and brother while I went into the deeper waters beyond the island. I would not risk my son yet. There I caught bigger fish than the ones who fished using the birch bark boats. My two hulled snekke meant I could carry fish which were as long as I was. My hatchet and spear meant that they did not thrash around for long. When we hunted it was Bear who came with me and carried my spare weapons. He was learning to be like his father and when he was old enough, Cub would too. Our life had a pattern, and I was content.

My two sons meant that the thoughts of wandering again were hidden deep within me and I contented myself to living with the Mi'kmaq. The Norns were spinning, however, and one day, a warrior came from the south. He, too, was a Mi'kmaq but from a different clan and when he entered our camp, I felt a sense of unease. The tribe was a large one and spread out over many hundreds of miles. From the direction he entered our camp he had come from the south and his clan might have come from the land of the Peace River which marked the boundary between the two tribes. The Penobscot had an even greater area of land that they controlled.

It was late in the afternoon when he arrived and Bear, Cub and I were gutting the fish we had caught. He looked at me as he walked towards the dwelling of Wandering Moos. I thought I dressed and looked like the other men, but Black Bird had told me that my face had different features to theirs and I was different. I had a beard and that marked me as someone not of this land.

Black Bird came for me. "There is a visitor and Wandering Moos needs you to speak with him."

I handed my seax to Bear and rinsed my hands in the pot of water, "Here, use this and continue to gut the fish. Do not cut yourself!"

I knew he would not for that would mean he would not be offered the blade again, "I will be careful!"

I followed Black Bird and entered Wandering Moos' home.

"This is Long Walking of the Clan of the Otter. Their summer camp is a long march south of here. This is Erik, Shaman of the Bear. He will understand your words."

The warrior began to speak, "When we reached our summer camp Penobscot warriors were waiting for us. We live close to the Peace River, but it is an uneasy peace we enjoy. They told us that a clan of the Mi'kmaq had captured a demon and he had slaughtered many of their warriors. They said that unless the demon is handed over to them then they will make war until the Mi'kmaq tribe is just a puddle of blood seeping into the sea. Our chief sent men to travel to the other clans to find this demon. I have walked for seven days to find you. As soon as I entered the village, I saw the demon with the fiery hair upon his face and head. I see you now, but, close up, you do not appear to be so terrible."

I nodded, "I am no demon but a man such as you, Long Walking." I turned to Wandering Moos. "I do not wish to be the cause of such bloodletting. I will go with Long Walking. I would not want others to die because of me."

Wandering Moos was a wise man and he shook his head, "What do the Penobscot wish of Erik, Shaman of the Bear, for the battle took place some years ago. Why now?"

Long Walking shook his head, "We know not. I confess that many of us were curious about this demon and having seen him I wonder if the Penobscot have made a mistake. He does not look so terrible."

Wandering Moos smiled, "This warrior slew more than twenty Penobscot including their champion, Wolf's Tooth. He was stuck by their poisoned arrows and did not die. Do not underestimate this warrior, Long Walking. Erik, this is not your decision to make. We will meet the other warriors and decide what we must do. Long Walking, you will have to stay the night and we shall give you our answer in the morning."

He nodded, "I would hear more of this tale, Wandering Moos."

I was troubled for whilst I did not fear the combat I did not like the danger it brought to my new family and people. This was a blood feud, and I knew from home, across the seas, that such things could be passed from generation to generation. The sisters had spun, and I was like a fly caught on their web. I could do nothing about this. I was unable to sail back across the seas. The birch bark snekke I had built was fine for the coastal waters but would last just days, at the most, on the open sea.

We ate, as we always did, in the open area before the dwellings we used. The women brought the men their food as we talked. I could see that Laughing Deer was troubled, but she knew better than to interrupt the talk of the elders of the tribe. I knew why Long Walking thought so little of me. My weapons, byrnie, helmet, all the accoutrements of a warrior, were in my home. While I was slightly broader and taller than most of the rest of the men I was hardly imposing. I had noticed that the other warriors, Black Bird, Runs Far, Screaming Hawk, all had scarred bodies. The tribes did not fight regularly but when they did then the conflict would be bloody. My body looked like the body of a man who did not fight. Others told my tale. Black Bird knew me the best and it was he who told the tale from the first attack on Deer Island by the tribe through to the battle which had seen the Penobscot destroyed. I saw Long Walking's eyes widen as he heard of my skills.

"I can see now why the Penobscot wish this man's death. He has hurt their clan."

Wandering Moos nodded, "And they do not know of the treachery of Laughing Wolf. Their hidden archers with their poisoned arrows might have not only killed Erik but also many of our tribe."

Screaming Hawk, whose name belied his quiet nature, said thoughtfully, "Perhaps when the tribe hears of the treachery, they may reconsider this."

Long Walking nodded, "That may be true. Perhaps blood need not be shed."

Black Bird broke the silence which followed, "But it still means that Erik will have to travel with Long Walking. He would be the one paying the price for our peace."

Runs Far smiled, "With due respect to Long Walking and his clan, we need do nothing. Long Walking took several days to reach us, and we know that the last time the Penobscot came they travelled in boats.

Even if Long Walking tells them where we are, by the time they can come here we will be back in our winter camp. Even Long Walking and his tribe do not know where that lies."

Wandering Moos was a thoughtful man, "And is that honourable?"

"You speak of honour, Wandering Moos, in the same breath as you mention the treacherous snakes that are the Penobscot!"

Runs Far had raised his voice and that was not the way of the clan. Wandering Moos looked troubled and Black Bird said, "Brother! If you cannot behave like a man, then join the women and fetch food!"

I could see that I was dividing the clan. I closed my eyes and sought guidance. When we had been in the winter camp, I had often tried this but failed to reach Gytha. Now I was closer to her grave and her voice came to me or I thought it came to me. Perhaps this was just my own voice and I was taking solace in believing it came from a spirit. Her words confirmed what I planned, she told me to go with Long Walking.

"I will return with Long Walking and I will speak with the Penobscot. I cannot have brother quarrelling with brother and I cannot be the cause of further bloodshed."

Laughing Deer was approaching with more of the ale I had taught her to brew, and I saw the terror on her face. I gave her a weak smile, but I did not know how I would explain my decision to her.

Wandering Moos nodded, "You are wise, Erik, Shaman of the Bear, and you have honour. I do not like what you do and do not want you to risk your life. You do this for the clan and so I will only consent if Long Walking swears now, that his clan will do all that they can to protect you."

The warrior nodded, "We do not like the way that the Penobscot have behaved. This threat does not sit well with any of our warriors. Will they make more demands when we have acceded to this one? I swear that if there is treachery then the Clan of the Otter will act."

Wandering Moos nodded. Before he could speak Black Bird said, "And you shall not go alone, my friend for I will walk the warrior trail with you."

"And I." added Runs Far.

Wandering Moos held up his hand, "Before every warrior in the clan chooses to follow this path, I say that I consent to the brothers going with Erik, Shaman of the Bear, but none other! That is my decision."

The elders of the clan all nodded, and it was decided.

Laughing Deer and I did not speak of it until Bear and Cub were asleep and we cuddled and whispered for we did not wish Cub to be woken. He took time to be quietened when woken! "Is this our future life, husband? Will men constantly seek to fight with you when all we want is peace?"

"Do you regret the choices that you made?"

Her head shook, "Of course not but this is not fair! You did not bring this on us, it was the Penobscot."

"Then perhaps this visit will end it. They wish to speak with me, and I might be able to explain to them."

She sighed, "They are not like our tribe. They like war and see death in battle as noble. They are also like the sand upon the shore. Their lands are vast, they live to the south of us and they hunt and raid as far south as the Lenni Lenape and they live many hundreds of miles from here!"

They were more like my people for they enjoyed war. I knew of many Norse and Danes who also wished for a life of war and raiding. Fótr and the rest of the clan could fight but more often chose not to. We had left for the new world to avoid unnecessary fighting and bloodshed. Once more I was brought back to Arne and his wish for war.

"Let us see. There is a circle here and I may be able to break it." I was not confident I could, but I had to try.

We left the next morning and I was laden for I carried in a sack my byrnie, helmet and my weapons. I hoped for peace but was prepared for war. The others carried the food. As I expected Bear demanded to come. I had to use the stern voice which sounded harsh to silence him. Erik the Navigator had learned to use it when he became a father, but he hated using it and the first mile of the journey was in silence for Bear's tears had upset me.

Chapter 2

I had seen the land through which we passed but I was more familiar with it from the sea, and then we headed inland and passed through forests that had only game trails. I knew that the camp would be close to the Peace River and the place where my brother and so many of our warriors had died at the fight on the falls. The size of this new land constantly amazed me. Our home, to the south of the Land of the Wolf and north of Mercia, had been, in comparison, crowded. Here, we walked for a whole day and saw no sign of humans. If this had been the home my father had tried to build to escape the greedy King of Norway, we would have seen many dwellings, farms and paths. You could have hidden every Saxon from Mercia and Wessex not to mention Danelaw, in this single forest through which we passed. Perhaps my people had been meant to come here. Would others follow? If my brother had returned home safely, as I believed they had, then would he have told others who might seek to follow? That thought cheered me. I might not be alone.

"You are quiet, my friend. You are not afraid, are you?"

We had made camp in a clearing by a stream. Runs Far and Long Walking were catching fish for our meal and Black Bird looked concerned. "No, but I am troubled. I thought the death of Wolf's Tooth and his warband brought an end to this blood feud. It seems to me that I have merely set the Penobscot on the vengeance trail."

"Vengeance trail?"

I nodded, "Back in the land from whence I came, warriors take the vengeance trail when they wish to avenge a wrong."

"This is not the same, Erik. You were the one wronged. The archers they sent to slay you with poisoned arrows were in the wrong and the gods punished them by drowning them."

"But not all and that shows me that the sisters are spinning still." I had explained to Black Bird and the others about the weird sisters and they understood the concept. "I do not mind them playing with me but there is now Laughing Deer, Bear and Cub, not to mention the clan." The others came back with eight river fish. We would eat well. "Perhaps I will divine an answer on this quest."

The Clan of the Otter lived not far from the land where we had first encountered the Penobscot. It took many days to reach it. I saw now why the Penobscot chose the Clan of the Otter to begin this conversation. Laughing Wolf's clan lived within a day or two of them. I recognised the river. When I realised that we had seen no signs of them when we had sailed up the river it confirmed that not only a man but people could be lost in this land. Had Arne chosen we could have found somewhere none would have discovered us and we could have done what we came west for, we could have made a new home. Mighty Water was the chief of the Clan of the Otter and he was an old man. He would not go to war again and that was probably another reason why he had wished to avoid war. I knew from Snorri Long Fingers that old men, especially warriors might wish to die in battle, but they would not wish others to die too.

We sat with the elders of the tribe. On the walk, we had come to know Long Walking and I regarded him as a friend. We let him do the speaking for us and he was eloquent for he was sympathetic to us. Mighty Waters nodded when he had heard the story. He examined me with rheumy old eyes, "Your tale would be unbelievable if another had told me of it, but I see you here and unless I am in the dream world then it is true. I think it is wrong for the Penobscot to seek vengeance for something which they began."

That was not strictly true, but I did not correct the chief.

He continued as he explained, "The Penobscot are ready for war. They have begun to raid our fish and animal traps. It is as though they are trying to provoke a war. We do not wish that."

I nodded and spoke, "I do not wish war and I do not wish to fight but I can see that I need to speak with the Penobscot to try to end this blood feud." The relief on the faces of the elders was clear for all to see. None wished for war. Glancing up I saw that some of the young men were unhappy about that. "If you will give us a guide then we will visit this tribe and use words instead of weapons."

Long Walking stood, "I will go with you, Erik, Shaman of the Bear, but I do not trust the Penobscot. It would be better if he had a small escort so that they do not try treachery." The use of the poisoned arrows had angered the Clan of the Otter too.

Mighty Water nodded, "I agree, it would be wrong to simply let these brave warriors go alone for they do not need to do this. The Penobscot would not have found him otherwise."

That thought had struck me. They only knew where our summer camp lay and not our winter home. Had this been some sort of scouting expedition to find me? Now they would know where our summer home lay. The question came into my mind, how did they know of us if all their warriors had been killed in the storm? If I survived, then I had decisions to make.

13

The ten men who would come with us were chosen and we were fed and housed comfortably. We left the next morning. Only four of the warriors who came with us were young men. Long Walking knew the danger of hotheads who might try to provoke a war. This time we had just a two-day walk to reach their camp and I saw it was the camp where I had first seen Laughing Deer not far from Fox Water, the bjorr beck and our camp. We had hunted and fished in this area. I wore my bearskin over my head for Long Walking said that would ensure that they knew who we were. I did not wear my byrnie. We were seen long before we saw their camp, but Long Walking had wapapyaki with him. The sign of peace ensured that when we were found we were not attacked although the glares and aggressive stance of the warriors did not bode well.

The camp was huge. It would have swamped ours ten times over. It looked to be a gathering of clans and that worried me. I saw that the men of the Clan of the Otter were nervous too and fingered their weapons. The air of threat was all around us and there were fewer women in sight than men. That was unusual in such a camp. The women were there but they were out of sight. The fact that it was more than one clan became obvious when six men, all obviously chiefs for they wore the same signs as Laughing Wolf, walked towards us but one looked to be senior for it was he who spoke.

He nodded to Long Walking, "We thank the Clan of the Otter for bringing this demon to us. Your people will not suffer."

Long Walking shook his head, "I am Long Walking and I have not brought Erik, Shaman of the Bear to suffer harm at your hands, we have escorted our friend here to visit and we shall escort him back when this is done."

Some of the chiefs reacted angrily but the high chief waved a hand to silence them, "I am Black Eagle and I command this gathering. Long Walking is quite right, and he has not heard what we have to say. Peace Long Walking. Your honour and that of your clan are intact. It is this demon with the pale skin who must answer to this council for his crimes." Beneath my bearskin, I wore just a hide loincloth and mockasins. He turned, "Bring forth Aroughcun."

A wreck of a man was brought from one of the dwellings. He had to be carried for one of his legs was wasted. He spied me and when he saw the bearskin he began to scream and tried to flee. He became so distressed that Black Eagle ordered he be taken from my sight. The chief nodded, "That is what you have done to this warrior. He was the only one who survived a raid by the men of Laughing Wolf's clan. It took many months before he could speak and when he did, he spoke of

14

a shaman dressed like a bear who could not be hurt by any weapons. That was some seasons ago and it took time for us to understand what had happened to the warriors of the wolf. We knew, from the women and the children, that the warriors had sought an enemy who had hurt them but we knew not where. Once we discovered the story, we sought the enemy who had killed a whole clan! We have been seeking you since that time."

I nodded for everything made sense now. Now I could see why it had taken years for them to act. The warrior must have, somehow, survived the storm and whatever instincts he had saved his life and took him home. I could see that the women of the Wolf Clan would not have known of our attack for we did not attack their camp but their warriors. How else would they have described us but as demons? The bodies they would have recovered after the last battle would have shown them that we were different with pale skin and lighter hair. We had beards and different clothes. I was just glad that the metal weapons and mail would sink beneath the waters of the falls and the river where the slaughter took place. If the Penobscot had recovered those weapons then they would have been unbeatable!

I stood and I saw some of the chiefs recoil a little. I contemplated taking the bearskin from me, but something told me that would be a mistake. "I am Erik the Shaman of the Bear." The word navigator was not one in the Mi'kmaq language and I did not use my real name for fear of causing even more confusion. I spoke as I thought Snorri Long Fingers might speak, in a calm and reasonable manner. "You are right, we did destroy the warband which raided us. We did not invite the attack but defended ourselves as all men will. The clan which attacked us asked me to fight their champion, Wolf's Tooth. I defeated him and men with poisoned bows sought to end my life. They failed and they ran back to the sea. My god, Njörðr, then conjured a storm and they were all destroyed. I see now that he sent one back so his people would know what happened. That is what happened and is the truth." I sat.

One of the other chiefs jabbed an accusing finger at me, "You must have used magic for Wolf's Tooth was the greatest Penobscot warrior and he had slain more than ten men in single combat."

Black Bird could not contain himself and he stood and he also pointed a finger at me, "And Erik, Shaman of the Bear has killed more than thirty warriors. Your tribe is treacherous and without honour!"

All my good work had been undone and I saw anger amongst the enemy. Our Otter friends' hands went to their weapons and I stood once more, "Let us have no anger. I am not proud of the men I killed in battle. I would rather have killed no one. We came this day not to make

15

the fire of feuding greater but to douse it. What is done is done. It is in the past and we cannot change that. Laughing Wolf and his warriors killed my brother and many of my friends. I have put that behind me and now I try to live in peace." I sat and gave a warning glare to Black Bird who nodded. I could see that he regretted his outburst.

Black Eagle nodded, "Your words make me believe you but I still cannot see how you defeated so many men and yet there is no wound I can see."

I smiled, "Oh there are wounds, Black Eagle, but they cannot be seen."

For the first time, he did not scowl and that was a beginning, "I see no reason for the tribe to continue this feud. There is no dispute that Laughing Wolf raided the Mi'kmaq and has paid the price. Do any of the clans wish to continue the feud?"

I saw immediately that most did not for they nodded but two obviously did and one stood and pointed a finger at me, "This feud is personal. I am Grey Hawk, and my clan is the Clan of the Hawk. Laughing Wolf was the brother of my wife. Had I not lived far to the south then I would have joined Laughing Wolf on this raid to slay the demon with the pale skin! I will continue the feud!"

As he sat the other rose and pointed his finger at me, "I am Red Knife of the Clan of the Moos and I just do not like you. The feud will continue."

I had no idea what would happen now. Black Eagle stood, "Then Grey Hawk and Red Knife, you have a choice, you either make war on this clan or fight their champion, Erik, Shaman of the Bear."

Red Knife stood, "I need no champion to fight for me. Let us end this now. I will fight this demon and then the feud is over. When he dies there will be no retribution."

Runs Far stood and said, reasonably, "And when Erik wins, what then?"

"That will not happen but if I die then my clan will choose another chief and there will be no retribution."

I stood and readied myself. I would don my byrnie and prepare for combat. Black Eagle ended any chance of that. "If this is to be done then we do it now. Have you weapons with you, Erik of the Shaman?"

I patted my sword and my seax, "Aye, Chief Black Eagle but I would prepare for battle."

He shook his head, "You are a shaman and cannot use magic. You stay here where we can see you so that we know you do not fight treacherously. Make a fighting circle!"

16

Runs Far and Black Bird knew that I needed my mail shirt, but they were powerless. Long Walking did not know. I still had my helmet beneath my bearskin. I think they allowed me my bearskin as they thought it would encumber me.

Red Knife was not bare-chested. He had a vest made of some sort of animal quill. I could see how it would be effective against a stone knife but both my seax and sword would slide through it easily. I saw in his belt a stone club and a knife. Grey Hawk handed him a small hide shield and a stone-headed spear. He was grinning until I took out my sword and my seax. The sunlight glinted off them and Red Knife looked less confident.

Black Eagle also looked worried and he came over to me, "What are these?"

"They are my weapons." I looked at Red Knife, "I am not from this land. I sailed from a land far to the east where men all have such weapons."

Black Eagle said, "From beyond the Great Sea?"

"Aye, it took many moons to sail over the water."

He looked at Red Knife, "Do you still wish to fight this man from across the seas?"

He nodded, "Having a shiny stick will not save him. We will fight!"

Black Eagle stepped back and said, "Then fight."

I had learned much about the way Skræling fought. They liked to use speed and sudden action. They knew that their weapons were most effective when used rapidly and a sudden stab with a spear might draw blood. I also knew that if I could defeat him quickly it might deter others from seeking a confrontation. Those were my thoughts and my plans but I had forgotten the three sisters. He lunged at me with his spear. I held my seax before me to block the strike as I brought down my sword and hacked off the end of the spear. He now had a stick with a jagged end for a weapon and he hurled it at me. I lowered my head and it hit the bearskin covered helmet. He drew his club and began to advance. This time it was a more cautious approach, and he kept his eye on the sword. As he swung his club at me, I jabbed with my seax. The point was small, but the curve of the blade made it a good ripping weapon and the edge sliced across his hand, severing a finger which fell at his feet and blood poured from the cut. At the same time, I lunged with my sword at his shield. His shield would have stopped a stone weapon but the sword slid through and whilst it must have missed his arm it sliced open his side and I saw the bone of his ribs.

17

He looked down at the severed finger and the long wound along his side. I said, "I do not wish to kill you. I have drawn first blood. Let us end this now."

All the chiefs, except for Grey Hawk could see the outcome and were willing the warrior to agree but pride was at stake and as is often the case pride can kill a man! He ran at me and I could see his intention. He would punch me with his shield while hitting my skull with the club. He was fast for the loss of blood had not yet slowed him. I blocked the shield with my sword which I held horizontally and stabbed at him. The blade enlarged the hole I had made with my first thrust and cut his left arm. He swung the club at my head and my seax only slowed it. The bearskin and my helmet, with my bjorr hat beneath, softened the blow. He looked at me with shock on his face for he saw no reaction to his blow. Our faces were close together and I said, "You cannot kill me!"

"Then I will die trying!"

He was a brave man, and I knew he might get lucky. I owed it to my wife and children to live. My seax was close to his hand and when I pushed with my sword his natural reaction was to move his club to block the blow. My seax slid across his throat. The blood spurted and the light left his eyes. He slid to the ground. Black Bird and Runs Far wisely remained silent. The Penobscot looked at me with a mixture of shock and terror on their faces. The combat had lasted moments. I had struck a handful of blows and there were serious wounds on the chief and none on me.

Black Eagle stood and pointed to me, "Red Knife said that if he lost his clan would not seek retribution. If they do, they risk being outlawed from the tribe."

The warriors from the Moos Clan all nodded.

Grey Hawk stood, "I made no such promise! This is not over, Shaman of the bear! You have no honour and you cheat."

My heart sank. Had he tried to fight me there and then that would have been one thing, but he did not and that meant another, he would use treachery.

Black Eagle shook his head and turned to me, "Erik, Shaman of the Bear, as far as the tribe is concerned this is over." He looked at Long Walking, "There will be no war with the Mi'kmaq. Grey Hawk, take your men and leave this camp. These warriors are under our protection and any who try to harm them will be punished."

Grey Hawk spat at me, "This is not over, monster!" He turned with his warriors and left the camp.

Chief Black Eagle shook his head, "You will stay this night and tomorrow, when you leave, we will give you an escort. Grey Hawk has now lost a brother-in-law and his best friend. He is not the warrior they were, and he will seek to kill you treacherously. I am sorry, Erik, Shaman of the Bear, you tried to avoid bloodshed. You must come from a strange people who can endure such insults and still try to tread the path of peace."

I thought of Arne and knew that there were many of my clan who would not have been so kind. "I have lost family to war and I try to avoid it if I can."

Chief Black Eagle said, "Grey Hawk is an angry warrior but his lands are far to the south of us, on the Muhheakantuck River. He may find it hard to seek you out." He shrugged, "But he is ambitious and would lead the tribe if he could!"

We were given our own lodge and we went within while the body was removed, the blood-covered with earth and food prepared. Once inside Long Walking said, "The blow to your head, you did not feel it?" I took off the bearskin and showed him the helmet. He nodded, "Now I see, not magic but just a warrior watching out for himself. I am happy now to share a lodge with you for I feared that you were a demon. I have never seen a man killed so easily. May I touch the shiny stick?"

I nodded and handed it to him hilt first, "Be careful, it is sharp enough to shave the hair from your head." He handled it as though it was from the gods.

Considering that I had slain one of their chiefs the meal we enjoyed was remarkably free from tension and acrimony. I left the bearskin and helmet in the lodge and most of the discussion and questions were about my hair colour, facial hair, and skin. I had endured the same with the Mi'kmaq and found it easy to answer them. They could not grasp the concept of a ship that could hold more than forty people. Had Black Bird and Runs Far not confirmed it they might not have believed and thought I had made up the story.

The next day, as we left, escorted by ten of Black Eagle's own warriors, the feeling I had was that whilst the Penobscot as a tribe would no longer be a problem, the Clan of the Hawk and, possibly, the Moos would and that made me silent for the week or more it took us to return to the clan's summer camp. I had gone south in the hope of ending this feud. The last few days of our journey when there were just three of us, Black Bird asked me about my silence, and I told him.

"I do not wish to bring harm to your people. I do not want the clan put in danger. The longer I stay here the more enemies I will draw to you."

"You saved the clan!"

I shook my head, "I rescued Stands Alone and Laughing Deer and brought the Penobscot to your door."

Runs Far laughed, "And you returned two of our tribe. There is no debt, and we accept the danger."

I shook my head, "I am not sure I can accept that responsibility."

There was a great celebration when we returned and the feast we enjoyed appeared to fill the clan with joy. Laughing Deer, my children and her sister were especially happy. I made sure that Wandering Moos knew of the potential danger from Grey Hawk and his clan but he appeared to be stoical about it. "Such things are out of our hands. From what Black Bird said, you gave the dead Penobscot every chance to end it peacefully. If Grey Hawk comes then we will fight. Our clan is stronger since you came, and we will not turn you away."

That appeared to be an end to the matter. I spent the summer looking over my shoulder but, as Black Bird pointed out, Grey Hawk would have to find our home first and Aroughcun would not be of much help to them. "Much can happen, Erik, in a year. Let us enjoy the moment and let the future take care of itself."

He knew them not, but I knew that he was angering the three sisters. There would be a price to pay.

I now had Bear to help me sail my snekke, '*Ada*'. The boy had learned to swim almost before he could walk. The patches of water close to our winter home and the proximity of the sea had ensured that. We rarely sailed beyond the sight of land, in fact, at first rarely beyond Bear Island, but my skill with the sail meant I could get further out to sea and we could catch larger fish. Thanks to the parallel, smaller hull attached to the boat we were much more stable and, as long as the fishes we caught were not too large, the two of us could land them. At first, Bear just wanted to sail to catch the fish so that when we landed, he could proudly point to the fish and hear the admiring comments of the other boys. When Cub was old enough and could swim then we might risk the sea. As Cub grew and pestered to come to fish with us Bear began to urge me to sail further from shore. When we would reach Bear Island, he would look at the ocean and ask what it was like out there.

He had the blood of a navigator and I felt proud, "This snekke is not large enough to sail much further out to sea. When Cub is older and can help us then we will make a proper snekke and who knows how far we can sail."

He was satisfied with that answer, but I wondered if the spirits were guiding the direction we would take. Was the thought that the only way to truly escape the Penobscot was to sail further away? I knew not but the seed was planted, and I began to look for wood we might use and tools I could find. The tools were the problem. The only edged tools I had were the axe, hatchet, sword and seax. They would have to replace the specially designed tools we had used when, all those years ago, the three of us, my father, Arne and myself, had built our first boat. For some reason, the piece of wood I had found and which had led me here came to mind.

If I did build a boat where would this one take me? Long Walking had told me of the seas to the north of us. They were not a great ocean, but he told me that a man would sail for a month or more from east to west along the water. This was not the open sea and each night a man could pull into the shore to sleep or take shelter from storms. He had heard that some tribes said that they could sail for many months along the waters which connected these seas. He was sceptical and as he had never seen such waters he did not believe the stories completely. I, on the other hand, when I heard, was intrigued. A birch bark boat could not travel far in a day but a snekke, a real snekke could. If I found this water and sailed it would I be able to find another great sea? Was this the Østersøen? From there, it was said, men could sail down the might rivers of the Rus to Miklagård. Were all these waters and seas connected in some way? The seeds were planted in my mind.

It was close to the end of summer when we caught the great fish. It was the largest fish I had ever landed. We had caught smaller sharks, but that day Bear and I caught, just off Bear Island, a fish which was as long as a birch bark boat. The line we were using was a strong one and the carved bone barb was the strongest one I had made. Added to that the wind helped us. Had all those factors not been in place then I do not think we would have brought the beast ashore. As soon as it took the bait, I knew we had a big one. It was trying to take us out to sea but the wind was heading for shore and so I secured the line to the wood joining the two hulls and used the sail to weaken the fish which thrashed around wildly. If I did not have two hulls then we would have been swamped. No birch bark boat could have landed it. By the time we slid onto the sand, it was dead and all those gathering shellfish from the rocks as well as the other fishermen helped us to drag it ashore.

Black Otter and his son Smiling Deer were the best fishermen in the clan apart from me and they helped us pull it ashore, "It is not a shark, but it looks like one."

I nodded, "When we sailed from the east, we saw fish like this in the ocean, but they were never alone. Perhaps this one was lost. The clan will eat well this night."

Indeed we feasted for two days on the beast. On the second day, the bones and the remains of the first feast were mixed with fresh fish to make a second meal, a stew. I gave the skin of the shark to those who asked for it. I did not need it. Our fishing expeditions meant that we had sharkskin to spare. I did not sail the next day for Laughing Deer reminded me that I had neglected Cub. I had and so I spent the day with my two sons around the camp and I enjoyed it.

It was late afternoon when the men came for me. "Erik, Shaman of the Bear, Black Otter and his son are in trouble!" The warrior who spoke was Stone Bird. He was Black Otter's brother and also a fisherman. He pointed out to sea. "We were fishing by your island home and he went beyond it. He said he wished to catch a fish like yours. We tried to dissuade him, but he said that as he could still see the island he would be safe. The currents and the wind took him from the island. We dared not risk following him and we saw that the waves were getting bigger. We came for you."

The sisters were indeed spinning. I must have made the catching of the fish seem so easy that others were copying me.

I nodded, "Come for I shall need someone to help me."

"Can I come, father?"

I shook my head, "No, Bear, for if we find them then the boat will be already overloaded. You stay here and watch your mother and brother."

Black Bird and the other men had followed Stone Bird. "We will light fires on the beach to guide you back. It may well be dark by the time you return."

I nodded for I was trying to work out what I would need. I grabbed my sealskin cape, bearskin and bjorr hat. It would be cold at sea. I also took my compass. As we ran to the beach I said, "You will have to follow my instructions, Stone Bird, or there will be three families who will lose a father!"

"Aye, Erik, Shaman of the Bear and if this was not my brother then I would not venture into the sea at night!"

There was just enough light for us to get to Bear Island before darkness enveloped us. Although the ocean was vast the man and his son had been in a birch bark boat and that would be subject to the winds and currents. I put my hand in the water and worked out the current and I adjusted the sheets so that the wind came from directly astern. That way I hoped we would be following the course the two men had taken. I estimated that at least four hours had passed since they had been lost.

22

They would be well out to sea. If the boat capsized it would still float and that was my hope. The waves were higher than was safe for a birch bark boat, but I knew they would be much higher soon. If we did not find them before dawn, then they would be lost. Even now the son who was not yet a man might have succumbed to the cold. I constantly checked that we were sailing with the wind and then I turned to Stone Bird who was in the other hull, "Begin to call for your brother. Shout twice and then listen. Count to sixty and repeat it. Remember to listen."

He had turned to look at me, "How can we find them in this darkness?"

"Look for the boat and look for lighter patches of the sea. If you see anything then tell me."

So began what must have been an hour of shouts followed by silence. When I had sailed from the Land of Ice and Fire and used the hourglass it had given me a good sense of the passage of time. The seas were getting rougher and I knew that if we did not find them soon then we never would. When we crested one particularly high wave I thought we might swamp but, as we descended, I saw, to the steerboard something both natural and unnatural. It was a piece of wood. It disappeared again but I took a chance.

"Hold on Stone Bird, I intend to turn." Although I risked being broached, turning to steerboard actually made us go faster and the next wave came from larboard and soaked us. "Shout!"

He shouted and, apart from the sound of crashing waves there was silence. I estimated that the wood had been four hundred paces from us. On the third shout, we heard a reply or some noise which sounded like a cry. The waves and the darkness made it hard to pin down where it was but when a shout later, we heard the cry louder we knew that we were heading in the right direction. I had stood enough watches at night to know how to make sense of things seen in the dark and I saw the man and his son to our left. They were clinging to the remains of the boat.

"There they are, Stone Bird, come across to this hull. Grab them and get them aboard. Put the boy between us and your brother on the fish platform." I would have the tricky job of holding my snekke *'Ada'* steady. If we capsized, then we would all drown!

The boy, Smiling Deer, looked to be in a bad way and I wondered if he was dead already. It was hard to keep my boat close to them and steady. The boy was placed in between us and then a shivering Black Otter was hauled on to the wood platform which joined the two hulls.

"You will need to hang on. Stone Bird, put Smiling Deer face down and cover him with my bearskin and then hold on. This will be a tricky manoeuvre."

"Aye, Erik, we are in your hands now. Perhaps the magic of your cloak will save my nephew for he does not move!"

We would have to sail a course which was parallel to the coast and then I would have to tack back and forth, against the wind to reach land once more. I had no idea how far we had come but I had endured worse when I had sailed the drekar and I would have to rely on my natural instincts. Stone Bird placed his own cloak over his brother who had not spoken since he had been landed. My bearskin would warm the boy and I hoped that it would revive him. There was little else we could do! It was a long time since I had been forced to rely on skills and senses I did not understand. There was no moon, but I knew that wind had taken us due east so to sail due west I had to keep tacking and moving like a crab across the ocean and I had to pray that I would see lights before dawn came as I was unsure if the two passengers would survive. Stone Bird forced some water down the throats of his brother and his nephew, but Smiling Deer had yet to respond. Black Otter's cough told us that he was at least, alive.

"Erik, there is water coming in."

I nodded to the leather bucket attached by a rope. It was one of the few items I had salvaged from the longhouse, "Use that and pour the water over the side. We are heavily laden and the seas are high."

He began to bail out the boat. I didn't like to tell him that he would have to do this until we reached land. He spoke to me as he bailed. I knew his muscles would soon burn with the effort. "How do you know where we are going? I am lost already there are no trees and no moss. The sea is flat, and you cannot see the stars. Is this magic?"

"No, or if it is then it is a magic I was born with. I do not know exactly where we are, but I know the direction to sail. I head towards the wind."

Black Otter must have heard his brother's voice for he said in a croaky voice we could barely hear above the wind, "How is Smiling Deer?"

"We know not. I have given him water and he has the shaman's bearskin on his body."

"You truly are a shaman, Erik. How did you find us?"

"I sailed the way I thought the wind and current would take you but, in truth, I know not. Rest and keep still. Any movement can capsize us, and I do not think that your son would survive another dousing."

My arms burned with the effort of adjusting the sail and turning the steering board. I was the only one who could do this. Just as on the voyage west the weight of others lay on my shoulders. My little boat had not been made for this sort of punishment and I knew that if we

24

survived then I would have to repair it. I wondered if the idea of building a real snekke might be the best answer. It is strange but allowing my mind to wander and to work out a solution to the problem seemed to make sailing my boat easier.

It was Stone Bird whose back must have been burning from the effort of bailing who said, "I am seeing things now, Erik. I can see fireflies dancing in the distance, but they do not live in the sea do they?"

I looked and saw what looked like fireflies. It took me some moments to process the fact and then I realised what it was, it was the fires on the beach. The clan had kept the fires burning to show us the way to our home. They were to our steerboard.

"It is the beach, but we are now in dangerous waters for there are islands and rocks. Black Otter, can you see the lights?"

He croaked, "Aye."

"Then watch when they disappear for it may be an island or a rock which lies between us and safety. If it is, then shout."

I headed south away from the lights just so that I could turn and use the wind from the south and west to take us north. I did not want to have to tack again.

"Island to the right!"

Black Otter's voice sounded strangled as he forced the words from salt-encrusted lips. I put the steerboard over and we almost stopped as I headed into the wind. I saw the dark shape loom up and adjusted the steering board so that we had way once more and we passed the surf covered rocks. There was some shelter now and the waves were smaller meaning that it was unlikely that we would be swamped. Our passage became easier. The bay was familiar to me, but I had never sailed it in the dark, yet I started to recognise things and knowing where the clan would have lit the fires helped. The last hour or so was easier when I could make out the fires and even the two men who appeared to be feeding them. I knew that it would be Black Bird and Runs Far. I spied the two men and saw that they were not looking south and east, the direction from which we were coming, but north and east. It was understandable. They were not sailors and had no concept of the effect of wind on a sail.

I raised the sail so that the tide took us in and when we slid up onto the sand they almost jumped with fright, "Aieee! Are you ghosts, Shaman?"

Stone Bird turned to me and smiled, "No, but he is a magician! I sailed with him and we rescued my brother and nephew, yet I know not how he did it!"

25

Black Bird and Runs Far pulled us up the sandy beach and Black Bird said, "He has done what he said he would do. Be grateful for that, Stone Bird!"

Chapter 3

Smiling Deer was alive, but he needed healers and Black Bird scooped him up, still wrapped in the bearskin, and hurried up to the camp. Runs Far and Stone Bird helped Black Otter ashore. He was very unsteady, and it took the two of them to almost carry him to the path. I was left alone with the boat. The light from the fires illuminated the beach and I made the boat safe. I took my compass and other gear from the boat and then pulled it above the high-water mark. The boat had saved two of the clan and was now, probably, the most valuable of my treasures. I had to ensure it was secure and I tied the bow rope to a large rock. By the time I reached the camp the sun was rising in the east and I was weary beyond words. The clan had been roused and as I entered the encampment and was illuminated by the rising sun behind me the whole clan cheered and roared. Bear ran to me and threw himself into my arms.

"One day I shall be like you and I shall sail beyond the land."

I laughed, "Aye, you shall but not for many years."

Wandering Moos approached me and gave a bow, "The boy lives as does his foolish father. We owe you two lives once more, Erik, Shaman of the Bear."

I shook my head, "I am of this clan, Wandering Moos, you owe me nothing!"

Laughing Deer with a sleepy Cub in her arms came to link me and take me to our lodge, "I prayed for you, but it is strange, husband, a voice in my head told me that you were safe and would return. Is that not remarkable?"

"Was the voice a woman's and with a voice like mine?"

She suddenly stopped, "How...?"

I nodded, "It was Gytha, she was the witch and shaman of our clan and her spirit lives here in this land. It is good that she watches over us still."

"You shall sleep now and when you rise, I will ready the steam hut for you. What you did was a good thing for Smiling Deer's mother thought her son lost but I wish that it was not you who always has to take such risks."

We had reached the lodge and stepped into the warm darkness, "It was my fault that Black Otter tried to sail beyond land. I will need to speak to the men of the clan. They need to be warned that while I can sail beyond the islands, they cannot."

"I think after this night none shall need the warning."

"Nonetheless they shall be told. Had those two died then it would have been on my mind and would have festered in the darkness there. I will tell them."

Black Bird came with my bear cloak, "Here is your magic skin, Erik, Black Otter thanks you."

I laid the bearskin down and after kissing my family lay down upon it. I was exhausted and as soon as I closed my eyes then darkness enveloped me. I dreamed.

It was the roaring water I had seen before I came to this land. I looked up at the water and held my family tighter. I tried to climb the water but failed and each time I attempted the ascent I lost one of my family until I was alone. It turned and began to head east with the sun setting behind me.

When I awoke the sun was shining and I could hear giggles and laughter from beyond the lodge. My wife entered and frowned, "You were restless while you slept and I held your hand, but it did not calm you."

I lied, "It was just a dream!" I knew it was more.

She nodded, accepting the explanation, "The whole clan speaks of your great deed. If you were not already respected this would guarantee that you were held in the highest regard. Wandering Moos is growing old and already the clan speaks of you as the next chief."

"I would not want that. I am happy being the husband of Laughing Deer and the father of Bear and Cub."

She smiled and took my hand to help me up. She embraced me and said, "In six moons there will be another child."

I kissed her and my bad dream evaporated like the morning mist, "Six moons?"

She nodded, "I wanted to be sure. We will be in the winter camp and our new child will be born when the new grass begins to appear."

I was elated and terrified at the same time. If I planned on leaving the clan then it would now have to wait until the baby could, at least, toddle. Would the Penobscot give me that length of time? Once again, the Norns were spinning. While I had been sailing back from the rescue, I had devised a plan to build a larger boat with strakes and a keel. It would take the whole of next summer. Then I had planned on sailing north, the reverse of the course which had brought us here and find this river which led to inland seas. My dream which had brought back to mind the roaring waters seemed to point me in that direction. Now those plans would have to wait.

Unlike the steam huts Gytha had used, the ones used by the Mi'kmaq were just a way of cleansing the body and, to some extent, the mind. Gytha's had involved potions and rituals resulting in dreams which could give an insight into the future. I yearned for such prescience. When I emerged from Laughing Deer's steam hut I did feel better. The salt from the sea was gone and while there were no potions, the fragrant herbs she had used somehow made me feel more relaxed, and I put my fears and worries to one side as I returned to the life of the clan at the summer camp.

Summer was almost over, and we reaped as much bounty from the sea and shore as we could. I took the axe and hewed trees which I left to season. One appeared to be perfect for the keel and would determine the length of the vessel. When next I came the trees could be split, some into planks. I did not waste the branches and the smaller ones were tied into bundles to make kindling. The work was interrupted as people came to speak to me about the rescue. Black Otter was a fool, but he was a popular fool, and all were happy that the two of them had been saved. Each family in the clan gave us gifts that they had either made or hunted. Laughing Deer said that it was the way of the clan. If I stayed, then I would live with a loving and generous people but I would also bring death to them. I knew that the winter would be one where I would reflect on my position, I would make a decision.

The trek back to our winter camp was, perforce, a slow one. We had others like Laughing Deer who were with child. There were the old ones who could not walk as fast and there was all that we had gathered at the shore. When all the materials we used each day and our clothes were added we had much to take. I had tried to make a wheel but although I knew what one looked like I was unable to replicate it and so I used what all the others used; two saplings joined by smaller branches and dragged by me. The Mi'kmaq called them a sledge and used them in winter when there was snow on the ground. The mail byrnie made mine much heavier than the others, but I knew that it had saved my life and the extra effort would just make me stronger.

After many days of travel, we reached our home in the north, by the waters. Animals and the weather meant that we had much work to repair and renovate our lodges. We were lucky, the rains did not begin until we had finished, and the clan gave thanks to the gods for their kindness. We set the traps for the bjorr. One of the patches of water teemed with them. My metal headed spear meant that some could be easily hunted rather than trapped and the first couple of weeks was

29

spent gathering as many as we could. The meat was good and the fur invaluable for winter. We also went hunting. This was the season of the rut and we helped nature by hunting the stags which had been hurt in the rut. It kept the herds healthy and also gave us meat, bones, gut and antlers. Nothing was wasted. I thought back to our time in the Land of Ice and Fire. Often people would become so thin as to be close to death because of the lack of food. There was plenty in this land.

The tribe often had gatherings at this time of year where the chief and his senior warriors would join with other Mi'kmaq and speak of the past year. This time there was no such meeting as a messenger arrived to say that in the northern tribe lands there was conflict with other tribes. We were lucky in that we only had Penobscot to worry about. The richer lands further north were sometimes red with blood. It was not every year, so Black Bird told me, and sometimes five years might pass without conflict. In those years the tribes prospered. He shook his head as he told me that this would just further weaken the tribe. He said that the only clans of the tribe who did not endure such attacks were the ones who lived to the northeast on the large islands there. I knew which direction he meant for he pointed. They did not use a compass but knew where the sun rose and set. They knew the north for moss grew on that side of trees and they knew the south because it was warmer but north-east and north-west were not in their language. I wondered if the Skrælings who had attacked my snekke when we had first landed on the island to the north-east had been Mi'kmaq. I had given it much thought and searched my memory. I did not think they were the same tribe as the way they had looked was different.

When we had repaired the lodges, we hunted the grounds which burgeoned with game and the women and children had stripped all that there was to strip from the bushes and the shrubs. Despite my skills as a hunter I was sent by the men of the tribe to guard the women and children who gathered berries. Bears and their offspring were particularly fond of the berries and a she-bear was very protective of her cubs. Because I was called Shaman of the Bear the tribe thought I had magical skills that might protect them. I did not but I went, each day, with my bearskin over my byrnie, my spear and my sword and I stood guard. Bear was especially proud that his father had been selected for the task. We worked our way out of the village in a circle. This was the way they had always done it and it made sense for bears were less likely to forage close to the lodges of men. Perhaps my presence gave confidence to the clan for Redbreast, the wife of Hawk Eye, told me that we were working far faster than they normally did. I think that was the reason we had trouble with the brown bear and her cubs.

30

We were far from the village and at the extreme edge of the land the clan normally gathered when there was a scream from ahead. I knew it meant either humans or an animal. Both meant that I was needed, and I shouted, "Behind me!"

Laughing Deer grabbed Bear and Cub and obeyed me instantly. I held the spear before me. Some of the older boys had slings and I shouted to them, "Do not use your slings until I give the command!" I knew that the stones were more likely to anger an animal rather than deter it. The women and children ran towards me and I could hear the roar of the bear as the beast hurtled after the threat to its young. From what I knew bears gave birth in summer and the mother would be ensuring that her young were healthy enough to hibernate. We were a threat, and she would do all that she could for her young. The one who charged towards me was at least the length of an arm taller than I was but when she saw and smelled the bearskin I wore she paused. I did not want to kill or maim this mother but nor could I risk the clan. I roared at her. She raised herself on her hind legs and roared back at me. She looked to be even bigger when she did that.

"Move back towards the village but do not run, walk!"

"I will stay with you, father!"

"You will obey me!"

Some must have run for the bear lurched towards me. I jabbed with my spear, not to kill the beast but to make it stop. I drew blood from her shoulder, but it stopped her movement. Each moment I held her gave the women and the children more time to get to the village. The two cubs suddenly appeared behind their mother. That seemed to make her more aggressive and she came at me so quickly that I had no opportunity to use my spear effectively. I just managed to hold it before me and that meant her claws, which she used to rake me were not used with as much power. The claws hit first the bearskin and then the helmet. My head rang but the force was downwards, and I kept my feet. Her second claw came at my chest and scratched and screeched down the mail byrnie. The noise seemed to upset her and she stepped back. I used the opportunity to step back also and jab with my spear. I hit her jaw and that made her roar and move back again. I had to assume that the others had moved away, and I stepped back slowly. She roared and I roared back but continued to move backwards. My spear thrust to her mouth had made it bleed and perhaps she thought it better to leave with a minor wound than risk one which might endanger her cubs. She did not pursue. I walked backwards, glancing around to ensure I did not fall until I was beyond her sight and then I turned. I reached the village just after the women and children who all stood watching the path.

31

Laughing Deer ran to me as I emerged, and the women cried out in joy. "I think," I said, "that the clan has enough berries and nuts!"

She nodded and, as she stepped back said, "And your bearskin now looks less impressive."

I looked down at the byrnie. The claws had damaged some of the rings, "I fear that my mail shirt, while it might have saved me, may not be as effective if I have to go to war again." The men of the clan seemed to regard my byrnie as some sort of lucky charm. I looked at the damaged links. I would be able to repair it, but the repair would always be a weakness. Even the stone spears of our enemies might be able to penetrate it.

I was thanked by the men when they returned from their hunt. Wandering Moos was philosophical about the whole thing. "Thanks to you, Erik, Shaman of the Bear, we have collected more food than ever before. We now know the edge of our land and we will respect the bear for the Shaman of the Bear saved the women and children, but we will not risk angering them again."

That was their way. The clan tried to live in harmony with the land and the animals who dwelt there.

The fact that we did not have to travel again allowed Wandering Moos to hold his own conclave. That he had something important to say to us was clear for he wore his full regalia. I saw that the other warriors did too and so I wore my bearskin. We had repaired the part which had been damaged, the head. The chief gestured for me to sit on his right while Black Bird was accorded the left.

"Since my son Eyes of Fire was killed," the men of the tribe could not but help look at me, I was the cause of the death of Eyes of Fire, "I have had no son to follow me. I am old. I rise more times in the night to make water these days than I spend sleeping." Some of the older warriors smiled. "Soon there will come a time when I will forget things. I will not have a warrior death for I have no strength any longer. It is time for me to name my successor. There are two warriors I have in mind. Erik, Shaman of the Bear has shown that he has powers and knowledge which would be invaluable to the clan. Black Bird has shown that he is a brave warrior and is wise."

He paused. I did not know the rules of such a gathering. If this was a Thing, then I would have known but I just spoke anyway. If I was Wandering Moos' heir, then I would be forced to stay with the clan and I was not certain that was a good idea from anyone's point of view.

"Chief Wandering Moos, I am honoured that you would consider me as a chief, but I have to say that I would not be able to accept such a position. I am of your clan but not your people. I am Erik the Navigator and in my heart is always the need to look for new lands. I am happy here and I have a family who are also happy but I cannot predict what my heart will say. My brother, Black Bird, would make a better chief and I would happily help him in any way that I could."

I sat and was then assailed by questions from all but Wandering Moos who merely smiled and nodded. The old man understood when others did not. After the inconclusive conclave, Black Bird and Runs Far took me to one side.

"You cannot wander off Erik, Shaman of the Bear! You are part of the clan!"

I tapped my chest, "I cannot control what lies in here and I fear that the Penobscot have not done with us. So long as I am here then I will draw them as a flower draws a bee."

"We will beat them!"

"And men will die because of me. I do not say I will go but I cannot promise that the three of us will grow old together and sit around the fire like the other old men."

"I thank you for your belief that I can be chief, but I am saddened by the thought of you leaving us. I am your friend."

"And I am yours and that is why, if we are attacked again, then I must leave. Perhaps my people are not meant to be living in this land."

He looked at me with a look which suggested he had thought much about this, "And yet your blood is here. Even if you were to die Bear, Cub and your unborn child would still be here and in them would course the blood of your people. You are here and cannot undo the past, no matter how much you might wish to."

He was wise. We then spoke of the time when he would be chief. "How much power does the chief actually hold, Black Bird?"

"He is chosen by his predecessor, but the clan have to approve him. So long as they like his decisions he can do whatever he pleases."

"Do you wish to be chief?"

"No, but I must do for had Eyes of Fire become chief then the tribe would have taken the path to war more than the path to peace. I know that I can tread that line, but I do not relish the responsibility."

There was no immediate change for Wandering Moos was, for his age, in good health and his mind was sharp. The only change which happened was that Black Bird spent more time with Wandering Moos who imparted his wisdom to my friend.

When during the longer nights of winter I spoke with Laughing Deer about my dilemma, she was understanding. Her sister, Stands Alone, was her responsibility too and she did not wish her sister placed in jeopardy. "I do not wish to leave the clan but, equally, I do not wish the

Penobscot to persecute the clan because of us. I suppose, in a perfect world, we would live somewhere far from such a vengeful clan. I am your wife, and our lives are woven together so that where you go so shall I."

The winter was spent preparing for summer. I carved fishhooks from bones. As we would travel further out to sea than other boats, we could expect to find larger fish. My seax was perfect for such carving. Bear used a stone knife to roughly shape them and when I had finished then Cub, who always wished to be involved with his father and brother, would put them in a bag of river sand and rub them smooth before taking some shark skin and polishing them. When there was no ice on the water then I took Bear down to teach him to swim. That would enable him to come to sea with me. Other fathers took their sons and the boys all made a game of it. Cub would have been taught this winter but he developed a coughing sickness. Many children had to suffer it and for a month he was poorly. The result was that when he was well the other boys his age could swim and he could not. We were ready to leave for the summer camp by the shore and I could begin to build a real snekke as I had done on Orkneyjar with my father and brother.

Chapter 4

The baby, Little White Dove, was born just before we left for the summer camp. Unlike Bear and Cub who would be given names when they were older Little White Dove was named for the bird which landed on the lodge at the moment of her birth. I was outside with the other men and we saw it land just when we heard the cry from within. Such things are not to be ignored and the name suited her.

Bear had now seen more than eight summers or so and when we named Little White Dove he asked, "When do I get my real name, father?"

Black Bird had been listening and he laughed, "Your name is waiting for you, but it is not yet ready to emerge. You must be patient."

"Where did you get your name from?"

He smiled. I had not heard this story and I was intrigued. "I had run away from my father for I had hit Runs Far and was to be punished. I ran and rolled in the mud and then climbed a tree so that I would not be found. I thought that my father would worry about me and the punishment would not be as great when he found me. I was wrong for he followed my tracks and looked up into the tree. He said to me, 'Come down Black Bird and take the punishment which is due to you.' I came down and was beaten and made to go without food and I had to clean my clothes. I was doubly punished for black birds are carrion." He shrugged, "The name was waiting for me and put the idea in my head." He wagged a finger at me, "The secret is not to misbehave. My brother's name is better for he is the best runner in the clan and can outrun any man. That is a good name to have!" I had learned as much as Bear about the naming of the clan.

Out of concern for Laughing Deer and the baby, I delayed our departure to the coast and the rest of the clan went to the summer camp without us. Laughing Deer was quite happy to travel but I did not see the need to rush. We had the winter camp to ourselves for two days while the others went ahead. It was quite pleasant to travel through the verdant land with Laughing Deer and Little White Dove on the sledge while Cub and Bear tried to help me pull it. I did not mind the hard work for my sons were doing their best to help me and I needed to strengthen my body. I knew that when I began work on the snekke I would have to work harder than when I had helped my father. It was then I realised that this would be the same as it was for my father. Instead of Arne and me helping him it would be Cub and Bear helping their father. In fact, for me, it would be easier as we would not have to sail to the mainland to fetch back the timber. I looked up and said, "Sorry, father, I have it much easier than you did."

Laughing Deer said, "What?"

I smiled. "I was just apologising to the spirit of my father. I had thought I had it as tough as he but, as usual, I am wrong!"

She laughed and that marked our whole journey together. We were a happy family and we laughed. We had no reason to put on a face for others. We were complete and I was almost sad when we reached the summer camp and the smiles of the rest of the clan. We were no longer alone.

The day after we had arrived, I went with Bear and Cub to the shore. They had some of the tools. Bear proudly carried the axe while I let Cub carry the stone club I would use as a hammer. It had belonged to one of the Penobscot and as a weapon, I did not like it but as a tool it was useful. Most of the men were hunting. I would not bring any food to the clan for a few days but none of them seemed to mind. I enjoyed a privileged position. I would take the snekke, *'Ada'* out to fish once I had repaired it, but I needed to spend a few days splitting the timber I had hewn.

There is an art to splitting timber. You needed to find the grain and then split it down the middle. After that, each half was split until you had timbers of roughly the same thickness. The width and the length did not matter for they could be cut but you needed the same thickness for the strakes. I first made wooden wedges and while I made them, I let Cub and Bear use stone scrapers to strip the bark from the timber. It would not be wasted for, dried, it made good kindling. Once I had the wedges, I made the boys stand back and took a mighty swing to split the tree. I had to use four or five blows. Although the split closed up again I was able to use the wedges and the stone club to drive them in. Once I had split the first one the boys, especially Bear, saw what they had to do. When I started to split the half-timber Bear said, "Can I try to drive a wedge in while you do another? It will save time."

"You think you can?"

He nodded, seriously, "I can try!"

"Then here is a wedge, you go to the bottom end and I shall use the flat of the axe to do the other." It took him many blows, but he managed it and looked so pleased with himself that it brought a smile to my face. "Well done, Bear. We shall do this in no time!"

Poor Cub was just four summers old and looked crestfallen.

"I have a solution, Cub, I shall let you be in charge of stripping the bark from the next tree. Let us see if you can take it all before we have finished making the strakes."

That day and the four which followed were amongst the happiest of my life. My boys and I worked together, and we did so with a smile and laughter. It made me feel guilty about the way Arne and I had sometimes bickered when we had helped my father. Once the strakes were made, and I made more than we would need in case we made mistakes, we managed to make a start on the keel. Cub enjoyed stripping the bark and Bear helped him for the carving of the keel was a crucial part of the building of the snekke. I had promised myself four days of work and then I would take out the birch bark boat. I had not finished the keel by the end of the fourth day. I convinced myself that time was not an issue. We had the whole summer to work on the boat and my family was a happy one. Laughing Deer would bring food and Little White Dove at noon and we sat in the shade of a rock and ate. The boys would tell her what they had done in the morning. It was good.

'Ada' needed repairs for the rescue had caused some damage but by the end of the fifth day, all was well. Bear had pestered me about coming to fish with me and he took a keen interest in the work. Cub also asked to come and, as we headed back to the camp he asked again. He knew that I had promised Bear he could come. I said, "So, Cub, can you swim?"

He shook his head, "Why should I need to be able to swim? The boat is sound and will not sink."

I laughed, "It is good that you have such trust, but I will be going beyond Bear Island. Bear can swim. This winter I watched him as he swam in icy water. He would survive in the sea while you would soon sink unless I managed to save you."

He looked as though I had struck him. He was very young, and his eyes welled up. I knew that our time together meant he did not wish to relinquish the banter and the fun. Bear put his arm around his little brother, "How about this, Cub, I will teach you to swim here at the beach?"

Cub sniffed back the tears, "How long would that take?"

Bear grinned, "That, little brother, all depends upon you!"

I confess that when Bear and I left the shore and raised the sail, I was nervous. Although Bear had been out with me before I had not thought of him falling into the sea. I thought back to Smiling Deer when we had hauled him aboard. He had been older than Bear and had looked more dead than alive. As we headed east, I said, "Heed every word I say and watch for the ropes and the sail. If I say 'Duck!' then do so immediately."

"I will."

I knew that he would for the worst punishment would be if I left him ashore with Cub. I had given him a stone knife and the Penobscot club. When we landed a large fish, he would have to kill it and stop it thrashing about. He knew that but I do not think that he knew how hard it would be. We had fishing lines with hooks we had carved in the winter months and plenty of fishing lines but the fish we were hunting were often hunters themselves and could be hard to land. We had bait in the form of pieces of meat that had gone rotten. We had found that the ones with maggots in their carcasses were particularly good for they seemed to attract more fish. We also used limpets cut from the rocks. They were the least edible of all the shellfish and did not result in a large catch but they were all useful. I had developed the technique of trailing lines behind the boat with many hooks and small pieces of bait. As we neared Bear Island, I lowered the sail and then Bear came next to me and hauled in the lines. We discovered that we had a good catch. There were twenty shiny fish. The two of us stunned them and dropped them into the woven basket in the centre of the boat. When I built the new snekke I would make part of the deck into a hold so that we could catch more fish. Once the lines were baited once more, I lowered the sail a little to give us way and we headed out to sea. Mindful of Black Otter I kept the island to larboard. I knew from our time here, the best places to fish and we used those first. That first day of fishing we caught two small sharks and two of the fish with the red flesh. It was not a huge catch, but I knew we would have more shiny fish from our trailing lines and when we slid on to the beach the other warriors were amazed at our catch. It was easier having my son to help me.

Runs Far had been fishing and he shook his head as we unloaded the fish, "You have spent five days repairing this boat and yet in the one day you have fished, you have caught more than the rest of the fishermen did in three days!"

I smiled, "Whatever we can do for the clan, I am happy."

And that was the pattern for the summer. Bear and I went out again for the next two days and harvested from the sea. Then, with an eager Cub, we worked on the snekke. Stone tools were useful for rough work and there were enough to allow Cub and Bear to work the wood. We saved the axe and the hatchet for finer work. I think my sons were disappointed at our lack of progress. The first days had seen us produce all the strakes we would need but then the keel took another four days of hard work to even approach a finished product. I would not rush the part of the snekke which would give her strength. Cub was keen to learn to swim and Bear spent an hour each day teaching him. They were helped by the other boys in the clan. They were eager to help the Shaman of the Bear and his family.

When Bear and I went out on our second fishing foray I curtailed the day, mainly because we had managed to catch a larger than normal shark. It was landed easier than I had expected as it showed signs of having been involved in a fight. I landed the boat at the jetty on Bear Island.

"Why have we come here, father?"

"Because I am hoping that we can find treasure."

"Treasure?" His eyes widened.

"Aye, when my clan left, they left in a hurry. I have already collected all the larger items, but I hope to find nails. I can make wooden ones, but iron ones would be better." That excited my son, but I gave him a word of warning, "None come here now and there are animals which could hurt a boy like you. Stay close to the buildings."

He nodded, seriously and asked, "What do we seek?"

In answer, I went over to the place we had worked iron. The heavy tools had been taken and weeds had begun to sprout in the years since the clan had left. I ferreted around and found one. I held the discarded and forgotten nail up, "This! If you seek here I will try to find them elsewhere." I found a broken pot, "Put them in here."

I used my memory of the way we had moved about the settlement and where we had worked. We had brought plenty of nails from the west and, in the early days, had been careless with them. I found ten of the precious objects and returned to Bear. He had managed to find a further eight. Leaving him to his work I went to the longhouses. We had used nails to secure the leather hinges to the doorframe and I used the hatchet to cut away the leather. I managed to salvage a number from the longhouses. When we returned to the mainland, I would burn the leather away. I found a further sixteen by doing this. I knew that if we ventured across the island, we could find the dwellings built there and find more but I did not think it worth the risk to my son. When I saw the sun begin to lower in the western sky, we collected our bounty and headed back to *'Ada'*. We had done well, and Bear had been diligent. We had more than fifty of the precious nails and that was double the number I had hoped. Bear was unhappy that we had stopped the work and that spoke well of his character. We returned to the shore with our catch and our nails.

When Bear told Cub of our adventure, he became cross. He had what he thought was an angry face. In truth it made me smile but it was a sign that he was upset, "Bear has all the fun and I am left on the beach with the babies! When can I come with you?"

"When you can swim!"

"I can swim now!"

I looked at Bear who shook his head, "He is much better but…"

I nodded, "I promise not to go to the island again without you. The test will be that when I moor *'Ada'* one hundred paces from the shore you will be able to swim out to me."

That satisfied him and the angry face disappeared.

The next three days saw Bear and I simply fishing. He was getting better at it and I began to teach him to sail. I let him have the steerboard when we were unladen and heading out to sea. I always stopped before we reached the open sea and, although he made mistakes, they were not disastrous ones and, more importantly, he learned from them. Of course, Cub met us each afternoon when we returned, and I could see that he was not happy. What would my life be like when Little White Dove demanded as much attention?

Then we returned to the building of the snekke. I already had a name in mind, but it was bad luck to mention it and so when I spoke of it, I just said, 'snekke'. This was in many ways, the most crucial part of the whole process; if the keel was not right then the boat would never sail true. I would have preferred the adze but the hatchet and the axe, so long as they were kept sharp, sufficed. When I had chosen the tree I had picked one which suited my preferences. It had a curve at both ends. The one at the prow end was particularly pronounced. I would still have to make a join for the figurehead and the stern piece, but I had minimised my work already and the joints would be above the waterline. It took all four days simply to get the shape I needed. I used the axe and hatchet to shape it. The boys collected the shavings for kindling. Bear and Cub used sand glued to sharkskin to smooth and polish the wood. They were both disappointed that we could not begin to attach the strakes, but they were learning patience and that was never a bad thing.

When Bear and I walked down to the beach to launch *'Ada'* for her next fishing expedition, Cub was waiting for us, "I am ready for my test!"

He looked determined and I nodded, "Strip to your breechclouts. Bear, wait halfway between the shore and *'Ada'*.

Already there were others on the beach. Most of the other warriors needed to leave earlier and return later and still, they did not have the catches we did. Children and women were searching for shellfish and salt was being collected from the pans, but all stopped work to watch for it was clear that something was going on. I took the snekke and held it eighty paces from the shore. I did not use the sail but simply paddled. I dropped the anchor and watched. Bear was a confident swimmer and he trod water as he waited for his young brother to step into the sea. I nodded and Cub began to wade towards me. He waited until the water was up to his chest before he began to swim. That was clever for it meant he only had fifty more paces to swim. He was neither an elegant nor a smooth swimmer, but he was determined. Some of his friends were on the shore and they cheered him for they all knew why he did this. Bear also shouted encouragement and that pleased me. I remained silent. He was thirty paces from me when, perhaps excited by the shouts or maybe because he thought he had done it, he swallowed some seawater. Coughing and spluttering his head went beneath the water. Bear began to swim toward him.

"Hold!" As Cub's head came above the waves I shouted, "Cub, calm yourself and tread water. You are almost here. Start again when you have control." He retched and coughed up seawater and then began to swim. Amazingly his stroke was smoother and more confident. It was almost as though he had realised that he could swim. He reached the side and I hauled him up and embraced him, "Well done, my son, I am proud of you!"

Sailing *'Ada'* with the three of us meant a readjustment for Bear and me. Cub, being the lightest was placed in the centre and Bear was able to move further forward. We also ran lines from the bow and that meant that Cub and Bear could harvest the sea as we sailed to the fishing grounds. I had expected the experience to be a nervous one for me but Bear helped Cub and I felt far calmer than I had expected. I was able to put my thoughts to the new snekke. My father had designed *'Jötnar'* but this would be my design, a new world snekke. We would have a deck so that we could store fish beneath it. All that was required would be more wood and there were plenty of trees. That would enable me to have a taller mast. I had my eye on a pine tree already. There were many fine pine trees close to the shore and there would be no shortage of tar which would make my snekke watertight. Finally, the figurehead would have to be made. *'Jötnar'* had not had a figurehead but I wanted one. I would carve my wife's face although I would not name the snekke after her. I had other ideas for that. We did not land as many large fish on the first voyage with Cub and Bear but that was because we had spent time with the test and Cub had to be taught how to be a sailor, but we still brought in more than the rest of the clan. It was clear to me that we had caught enough fish for there was a limit to how much we could salt and dry. I made the decision to spend six days working on the snekke before we went back to sea.

The first task was to hew another tree and to split and season the wood. That was the work of one day for the three of us were able to strip the branches from the tree quickly and Cub and Bear knew how to strip bark better. On the second day, we finished the keel. I made the hole for the figurehead while the boys completed the smoothing. I had no chisels and so I improvised. I used pieces of sharpened stone and the flat head of the hatchet to make the rough hole and then gave the boys the task of smoothing it. I went with my axe to select the mast. I found a tree that was longer than I needed and after I had dragged it back, we prepared it for seasoning. The third day was the most exciting for Bear and Cub as we began to fit the ribs. These gave the snekke its strength and I used more than my father had. It would make the snekke heavier and therefore sit lower in the water, but I was giving it a higher freeboard. I made it wide enough for three to sit abreast. It took the whole day to fit the four ribs because I used a drill to add wooden nails as well as the iron ones. We needed a solid construction.

The boys were, again, disappointed when we did not work on the snekke the following day. Instead, we went to the stub of the pine tree I had hewn. We dug out the root and I showed them how to make an oven and we made a channel to run into the broken pot we had used to collect the nails. The last time I had done this had been on the Land of Ice and Fire. We lit the fire and left it. When we collected it the next day the pine tar was still seeping from the oven and I had to find another broken pot to collect the rest. We took the first pot and with a brush made from the tail of the horse deer, I showed them how to paint it on the joints on the snekke to make them stronger. My father had done so with me and I was preparing my sons so that they could make their own snekke when I was in the Otherworld. That done we began to cut the strakes to fit the snekke. Bear had thought we would just cut them all the same length, but I pointed out that the keel was curved, and we needed the wider ones close to the bottom of it.

It was the next day when we began to nail the strakes to the keel. It took both of them to hold one end while I nailed the other. We left the ends to stand proud for we would cut and smooth them later. I had to use the nails carefully. The fire had burned the rust on the nails from the hinges and a sack of sand had cleaned the others. Even so, I wasted not a one. I decided to use the last of this first batch of pine tar to coat the strakes and hull, I had seen a stand of four others and that would give us enough to recoat the whole snekke and make it as watertight as possible. We made a fire and reheated the tar. It was messy work and we all bathed in the sea at the end of the day. It helped to improve Cub's swimming skills.

That was as far as we got for, the next day, Long Sight, who had set off early to fish, waved to us. He was close to Bear Island. He needed to contact us and so I left the strakes, and, with Bear and Cub, we launched *'Ada'*. Since the attack by the Penobscot, we had been vigilant and other warriors took to their boats to paddle out to Long Sight and his son Beaver. The sail meant we reached him first. We hove to next to him and he pointed out beyond Bear Island.

"Erik, Shaman of the Bear, there is a man out there and he clings to a log or perhaps a wrecked boat, I cannot tell. He must have come from the south for the current is taking him north."

After the experience of Black Otter, I did not wish to risk my son. I also feared that it might be a trap. The last time any came from the south it was the Penobscot. "I will investigate. You and the others watch to the south in case it is danger for us."

I reefed the sail a little so that we could approach slowly, and I could assess the potential danger and threat. I saw that it was a warrior, but he was not a Penobscot. The tree was also an unfamiliar one. This warrior had travelled far.

The second hull bumped into the tree and he did not move. "Friend, who are you?" There was no response and I wondered if he was dead and his hands had a death grip on the tree. "Bear, come to the steering board." When Bear had it securely in his hands, I lay on the second hull. I reached over to grab the warrior's hand and, as I did so my fingers felt a beat. He was alive. I prised one hand from the tree and began to pull him up on the second hull. His second hand came free. I made sure that he was in the bottom of the second hull. The only thing we had in *'Ada'* to cover him was my sealskin cloak and I put that over him. "Bear, come and keep hold lest he slips into the sea."

I took the steering board and after loosing the sail turned to head back to the waiting birch bark boats. As I passed Long Sight I shouted, "There appears to be no danger, but he is barely alive. I will take him to the shore." We fairly flew across the water and Bear gripped the man's arm as though his life depended upon it.

Black Bird and Runs Far had not been on the beach but had been summoned by the women. They were waiting for me.

"Long Sight spotted him out to sea. He is alive but only just."

As Black Bird and Runs Far lifted the warrior Black Bird said, "He is Powhatan. They live far to the south; beyond the land of the Penobscot. This is only the second warrior from that tribe that I have met. There is a tale here. We will take him to the healers."

43

As we dragged *'Ada'* up on to the beach I felt a shiver up my spine. It was not the sea breeze, it was the Norns and they were spinning.

Chapter 5

We continued to work on the snekke, but my heart was not in it for I knew that the arrival of this stranger was ominous. We finished work early and headed back to the summer camp. The boys were excited not only because of the rescue which had been an unusual event but also because we had nailed enough strakes to make the snekke begin to take shape. When we reached the camp, I saw Black Bird and he came over to me.

"You have saved that man's life. Long Sight could not have brought him aboard his boat."

I nodded, "Has he come to yet?"

He shook his head, "The healers are keeping him warm and trying to get beer and gruel into him."

"And what brings him here?"

Black Bird laughed, "You know that better than any, Erik. It was the wind and the currents."

I shook my head, "Long Sight said that the Land of the Powhatan tribe is further south than even the River of Peace. I have sailed there in a drekar and a snekke. It takes days and that is with oars and sails. This man cannot have come from south of there for he would not have survived. He came from the land of the Penobscot."

Black Bird's smile changed to a frown as he digested the information, "You are right. What brings a Powhatan warrior who bears many battle scars, one of them very recent, from the Land of the Penobscot? You are a Shaman for you see things which are there before us, but we cannot."

"I am a navigator and what I know are the winds, the waters and the seas."

Laughing Deer had an explanation of sorts, "When I was a slave of the Penobscot, Stands Alone and I saw many other slaves and prisoners. We saw children from the Powhatan tribe. I can speak some of their words, but we never saw any warriors, not alive, at least."

"Then the tribe makes war on the Powhatans?"

Laughing Deer nodded, "On any, I saw other tribes taken too: the Catawba tribe, Cherokee, Lenni Lenape, Croatoan, Tuscarora, Tutelo and Saponi. There are two mighty rivers to the far south of the Penobscot land, the Rappahannock and the Powhatan. I have never seen them but I have been told that they are as wide as a sea. The Penobscot often raid that land for slaves and for the leaves that they burn and inhale."

The word she used was one of the few words I had not managed to get my tongue around, but I knew that the smoking of these brown leaves was used as medicine and also in certain religious ceremonies. I had yet to try it, but I had been offered some when some of the younger warriors asked me a question. I knew that it grew well further south and explained why the Penobscot might risk these mighty rivers.

The man had still to awaken the next day and so I went with the boys to the sea. Most of the fishermen were staying much closer to the shore. The sudden arrival of the man had caused concern. Laughing Deer's explanation appeared to be the one the rest of the clan accepted and although there was no evidence of real danger the suspicion was enough. Chief Wandering Moos sent sentries to watch the land from the south just in case the warrior's arrival presaged another attack.

We threw ourselves into the building of the snekke and by the end of the day, we had almost finished the fixing of the strakes to the hull. The two boys used their weight to hold the strake in place and I hammered home either an iron nail or, twice in each strake a wood one driven through a hole I drilled. It was the wooden nails that took the time. We would also need a gunwale and that would require carving and shaping. The last task before we returned to the camp was to give another coat of pine tar to the strakes. We used the last of it and we would have to make a larger quantity to complete the sealing. That would have to wait until the snekke was finished. The summer was drawing to an end and I wanted the boat sealed and protected from the elements and animals during the winter. I planned on using Bear Island and one of the longhouses as a shelter. It seemed appropriate somehow and I knew that the spirits of Snorri Long Fingers and Gytha would watch over it.

The man had not awoken and the three of us were covered in pine tar. Before we ate, we went into the steam hut. It had been used by the healers to try to revive the Powhatan warrior. Although it had not worked completely his sleep appeared easier and as he was now taking more gruel and beer then there was hope that he might live and tell us his tale. Cub and Bear did not get as much pleasure from the steam hut as I did but it got them cleaner quicker than the usual method. It felt better to eat food feeling clean. The boys were more interested in talking about the snekke than the Powhatan and as soon as they had eaten, they hurried from the lodge to speak with other children.

Laughing Deer, Stands Alone and the other women, in contrast, had done nothing but talk of the stranger all day. In the case of my wife and her sister, it brought home to them the fear of the Penobscot. That they

46

could raid such a large territory was worrying and we all knew that they had not finished with me. I tried to put Laughing Deer's mind at rest although I was not convinced myself. She would speak with her sister the next day. Stands Alone took her meals and slept in the lodge reserved for those girls who were maidens and about to become women. The old woman who watched them ensured that none had dalliances before they were wed.

I used my reasonable voice to calm Laughing Deer's fears, "True, the Penobscot might return but Wandering Moos has put sentries in place. I do not doubt that we will keep them when we return to the winter lodges. That would be my worry. They could discover where we live in winter and then they would only be deterred by the weather rather than the seas. Last winter we had little snow and if we had another such winter then they might come. However, we have more warriors than we had the last time they raided, and we know how to defeat them."

"But warriors will die."

"Of course."

"And you might be one."

"Perhaps."

She nodded and started to feed Little White Dove, "Then finish the snekke as soon as you can so that we may flee if they come."

I shook my head, "I will finish the boat, but I will not abandon the clan just because danger threatens. If we leave then we leave at a time of peace. We cannot leave in the snekke until next summer at the earliest."

The disappointment on her face told me what she thought of my words, but I had to give her the truth and, in my heart, I knew that my brother and now me, had hurt the Penobscot so much that a return was inevitable. Even the arrival of this warrior was a sign for it showed that the tribe thought they were unbeatable. We had defeated and hurt them!

The next morning I was greeted, as I left my lodge, by Long Sight. As the one who had found the warrior, he felt a responsibility and had taken on the task of watching over him. "Erik, the warrior has awoken. I have spoken to him and although he is very weak, he asked me to thank you for saving his life."

"You can speak to him?"

"I know enough of his words and others helped me. Our languages are similar enough."

"What is his story?"

"His name is Brave Eagle, and he was the chief of his clan, the Eagles. They live far to the south beyond the land of the Lenni Lenape.

47

The Penobscot raided his village when he and his warriors were hunting. They tracked the Penobscot over many days to their home and tried to rescue their families, but they were ambushed. All of his warriors were killed until only he was left alone, fighting off many of the Penobscot. His back was to the river."

My neck prickled. I had been in just such a position.

"He was hit by a stone club and he fell into the water. The next thing he knew he was at sea and, somehow, he was clinging to a log. He tried to kick the log closer to shore but the current was too great. He found himself out of sight of land and he kicked for shore again and then a storm arose, and he had to cling on to the tree for his life. That is all he remembers until he woke up in my lodge. He said it was like a dream for he would sleep and hear the cries of seabirds and then he would wake to the sound of seabirds. He says he chewed on the bark of the tree and found insects which he ate."

"Remarkable that he lived for so long."

Long Sight nodded, "Vengeance will burn into a man's heart and keep him alive when he ought to be dead. All he wants is to kill the Penobscot chief." I knew before he said it, the name of the chief who had raided the warrior's home. Long Sight gave me a sad smile when he saw the look on my face, "Aye, Erik, Shaman of the Bear, it is Grey Hawk."

I nodded. Cub and Bear grinned at him as they raced past me and headed for the beach. Life was a game for the two boys, and I hoped that it would remain so for as long as possible. They did not enjoy working the gunwale. It was painstaking work for it would give strength to the boat and had to be perfect. I cut and they smoothed. The work could not be hurried and it took two days to shape the wood and, on the third day, we fitted it. I added two rowlocks for the oars. I had made two for I did not think we would ever have enough on board to warrant more. When the rowlocks were fitted, I think they thought that we could launch the snekke there and then. I quickly disillusioned them.

"We have to trim off the strakes and clean up the rough wood. Then we need to make a great quantity of pine tar. That will take a week, at least to make the tar and then paint it all over the boat. It may be that we have to stay here after the clan returns west. The snekke will not be launched until next year but the more work we do now the sooner we shall do that."

Even Cub threw himself into the work and I knew that the three of us were embedded in the snekke and that could only be a good thing.

It was four days later when I got to speak to Brave Eagle, or at least communicate with him. We had just returned from a long day of work and the boys needed some of Laughing Deer's salve on their hands. While they went to their mother Long Sight brought Brave Eagle to speak with me. Brave Eagle looked to be a little younger than I was and he had the scars of battle upon his body. Long Sight had spent time with him and improved his skills with words but I still struggled to find the right Mi'kmaq word. There were many words that they shared in common but the conversation was relatively stilted. He thanked me for his rescue and then tried to ask me questions about the boat I used. Of course, that was hard enough in Mi'kmaq and impossible for Long Sight in Powhatan! I told him that it would be better if he could come and see it. That would answer his questions. He seemed happy to do so. I had planned on beginning to make the pine tar but a delay of a day would not hurt and the warrior seemed genuinely interested to see the vessel which had saved his life.

It was only when Brave Eagle saw *'Ada'* and the shock filled his face that I realised how different she looked. The other men in the clan were used to her but the sail was something none had ever seen. As I showed him the boat, I began to think about how I might use this. If I painted a design on it then the new, as yet unnamed snekke, might appear alive. The carved figurehead would help but if I had a winged design on the sail then it could be used as a weapon should we have to sail amongst belligerent tribes. From what I had learned it was not just the Penobscot who enjoyed war. It seemed that some tribes arranged for war and would meet each other far to the west where they would fight and kill. I could not understand that. Even a Viking warrior who loved fighting would only do so if there was something in it for him. For some tribes, it was the glory of war they wished. As I thought about the design I decided that I would use a dragon's head and two large wings.

As we sat on the beach and ate the large crab-like creatures which lived in the bay and were quickly cooked, I asked him of his plans.

He tried to tell me but it became easier for Long Sight to give me his words. "He wishes to return to his homeland. His tribe do not use summer and winter camps as we do. They keep to the same land for they farm and grow crops. There will be people there. He hopes that some of his clan remain. The ones who were left by the Penobscot were the old ones, but he knows that some of the boys would have fled into the forests and he believes that some of the prisoners will try to escape. He wishes vengeance on Grey Hawk. His family and his wife's friends are all prisoners. If he could rescue them then he would die a happy man for he believes he has failed in his duty to his family."

I knew that he had not. When he had led his men to hunt it had been so that the clan would prosper. The slave raid could not have been foreseen.

We did not return to the beach the next day, but we began to hew the pine trees and dig up the roots. It was hard, back-breaking work. Black Bird, Runs Far, Long Sight and even Brave Eagle came to help when at the end of the first day they saw how we suffered. With five men working we soon completed the digging and then I had them gather stones and rocks from the beach to make the oven. The other four were as attentive as a hawk hunting a squirrel. Their eyes watched every movement and they rattled questions when I did anything unusual.

When it was finished, I lit the fire and Brave Eagle's eyes widened when he saw how I made a fire. "You are a shaman! Can you see my family?"

I smiled and shook my head, "I can do some things which appear as though they are magic, but they are not."

He looked disappointed.

"I will have to stay by the oven for it will soon begin to produce the tar and it must be stored." When I had been on Bear Island, I had discovered a barrel. The lid was broken but I had managed to repair it. Along with the broken pots, I would have enough containers for the tar. The boys wished to spend the night with me but I forbade it and after they had brought me food I sent them back and I sat beneath my bearskin to watch.

Long Sight and Brave Eagle came to join me. Long Sight said, "Brave Eagle has made you a gift." He handed me a pipe. I had seen Wandering Moos and the other warriors use one.

"Thank you but I do not use one. I know not how."

Brave Eagle smiled and Long Sight said, "We will show you for it helps to keep away the flying insects and a man can see into his own head. There is magic in this, Erik, Shaman of the Bear."

I knew that it would be seen as rude if I did not comply and so I did as they instructed. Brave Eagle crumbled the leaves and packed the bowl. He took a twig and lit it in the oven and after placing the pipe stem in my mouth he lit the leaves. They had told me to suck in the smoke and then to blow it out. I was sceptical and after a couple of coughing fits, I wondered what the point was. Long Sight persuaded me to persevere and when I had the pipe glowing, I began to feel a little lightheaded.

Satisfied that I had some skill the two bade me good night and left a leather pouch with more of the leaves. As soon as they had gone, I put the pipe down and tended to the oven. The tar had begun to trickle down the stone channel we had built. I made sure that it went into the barrel and then took up the pipe again. I needed to watch for a little while longer before I snatched some sleep. I would need to wake in case the barrel was filled, and I needed to replace it. I managed to light the pipe and this time I was ready for the light-headedness and slight nausea. What I was not ready for was the vision. There was a slight breeze behind me but not enough to dissipate the smoke. It seemed to make it join the smoke from the oven and to make a fog before me. I stared into the smoke which seemed almost hypnotic. A face began to form in the smoke and I saw it was Gytha. Then her voice filled my head or perhaps it came from the smoke, I did not know.

Enemies are coming for you, Erik, and when they do you will have to flee. You and your family have a destiny to fulfil. Had Arne not had such a weakness of character then all the clan would still be here and the Skræling who come for vengeance would have been defeated. Wyrd. You have helped these people and while they will be sad at your leaving it is inevitable.

The smoke dissipated and I saw the sea stretching out beyond Bear Island.

When you leave, then you will be leaving me. My spirit must return to the east. There I will join with the other spirits in the Land of the Wolf and we will watch over your brother and the rest of the clan. You have left that clan and will start a new clan and a new tribe in this new world.

I tried to speak but I could not and the next thing I knew I was woken by rain on my face. The smoke was gone, and the barrel of pine tar was almost full. I put Gytha from my thoughts as I quickly changed the barrel for a large but broken pot. I would not be able to sleep again. I watched the tar trickle and thought about Gytha's words. It confirmed what I had thought. I would have to leave but I now knew when; it would be after the Penobscot attacked and, from her words, that might be soon. The clan needed to be warned and preparations made. By the time the sun came up the tar was still flowing freely and when Bear and Cub arrived with my food, I sent them back for more pots. The tar was like liquid gold. Once more I saw the shortcomings of the new world. Without iron then the tools we could use were limited. I knew that there would be clay for pots it was just that I did not know where to find it.

It took two days for us to collect all the tar and then we took it down to the beach. I felt as though I had been away from the clan for weeks rather than days. Black Bird, Long Sight and Brave Eagle all came to the beach so that Brave Eagle could see my new vessel. *'Ada'* was an adaptation and a useful boat but the new snekke looked like a real ship and was much larger than *'Ada'*. While we made a fire to heat the tar and then begin the task of coating the hull, inside and out, I told the three of them about my dream. The clan believed in the spirits and they were not surprised by my words.

Brave Eagle nodded. "Then it is good that I am here for if they come to hurt this clan, I can repay them and have my revenge!"

Black Bird had taken his new role as the next chief seriously and he said, "I will speak with Wandering Moos. We have enjoyed a good summer and we could go back to the winter village early."

I was left with the other two and they took a keen interest as I began to coat the hull with the pungent mixture. We had just the hull, gunwale, and strakes to cover. When that was done, I would begin to make the deck, mast fish and steering board. The figurehead would be the last thing I would make. I did not want to rush it and if the clan went to the winter village early, I could continue to work on the carving there. This time it was just me who was covered in pine tar and I stripped off naked and swam in the sea. I rubbed sand between my fingers while I was in the sea which helped to make my hands clean, and I would not need the steam hut.

The four of us were the last ones off the beach and as we stepped on to the path darkness was falling. The others, my sons included, were preoccupied with talk about the new snekke. My mind was elsewhere. It was seeking counsel from Gytha. Perhaps that was why, as I came along behind the others who chattered like birds that I heard a sound to my left. It was not an animal sound but a human one. It sounded like a grunt or perhaps an exhalation, a sigh of surprise. I stopped and the others carried on walking. I slipped into the forest. This was not the thick forest close to our winter home, here sand and wind made it thinner and I saw a movement ahead. It was a man and not an animal. I drew my seax and began to run. The sound of my footsteps was deadened by the sandy soil and I made little sound. I did not know who I was chasing but as they did not stop made me think it was not one of our clan. Behind me, I heard shouts as the others noticed my absence. It was their cries which made the man I was chasing turn, allowing me to see him but, unfortunately, allowing him to see me. He had a bow and in one movement he loosed an arrow and as I took cover, he vanished once more.

Long Sight and Brave Eagle appeared behind me, "We sent the boys back to camp and..." He noticed the arrow embedded in the tree and whatever else he was going to say was forgotten. He pulled it out and examined it.

Brave Eagle said, drawing the stone knife which was the only weapon he had on him when he had been rescued, "Penobscot!"

I pointed to the south, "He was running that way." I hurried to the bush where he had loosed the arrow and saw the broken branches he had damaged when he had run. Long Sight knelt to examine the ground. In the time it had taken me to get this far darkness had fallen. Long Sight shook his head, "It is too dark to see more. We must return in the morning."

I shook my head, "And by then he will be gone!"

As we headed back to the trail Brave Eagle said, "You have good ears, Shaman, if you heard him for I did not."

"It was Gytha, the spirit, she has made my senses keener. I like this not, Long Sight. Had we not seen that the arrow was Penobscot I might have thought it was just a wandering warrior who was afraid when he heard the noises. This is more worrying."

The boys' arrival alone had made the warriors gather in the middle of the lodges. Long Sight held the arrow for all to see, "Erik found a Penobscot. We will need to track him tomorrow."

Runs Far said, "He will be long gone."

I nodded, "Aye, he will but was he alone? A single scout is one thing but a scout from a warband is something else."

Black Bird looked at Wandering Moos who nodded, "I have spoken of your dream, Erik. Tonight we keep sentries to watch for enemies and tomorrow we take half of the warriors to hunt them."

That I would be going was obvious for there was a connection to me. Bear hoped I would let him come but he was going to be disappointed. I shook my head, "Tomorrow you gather pebbles for your sling. I should have made you a bow before now! We will remedy that as soon as I return. I have allowed the snekke to take up too much time for all of us."

When we had eaten and the boys had gone to sleep I told Laughing Deer the complete vision I had seen. "Then we will be leaving?"

"I fear so and Gytha's spirit will not be coming with us. What about Stands Alone?"

"I have spoken to her about the possibility of our departing and she wishes to stay. She has friends now and she is becoming a woman. It is one thing to take three children to, who knows where, but quite another to take a young woman. She suffered at the hands of the Penobscot but

53

she was not rewarded with the love of her life. I am happy to make this perilous journey for I have you and my children. Stands Alone will stay. It will be a sad parting but…"

I nodded and cuddled her. I knew that I was a lucky man.

I wore just my breechclout and hide vest and my best mockasins for we did not know how long we would have to run. I left my sword in the lodge but took my hatchet, bow and arrows. Long Sight led and we went first to the place the Penobscot had tried to hit me with an arrow. There had been no rain overnight and Long Sight was a good tracker. He and Runs Far led as we followed the trail south and west. The warrior had not been on a trail and he had damaged enough of the shrubs and trees so that even I could see which way he went. I was glad we had not tried to follow him the night before for we could have been heading into a trap. Brave Eagle was evidence that the Penobscot were cunning. We passed the Chickawaukie Water and saw where he had stopped to drink. So far he was alone and that was comforting. Then he changed direction and headed due south.

Runs Far said, "He is heading to the Chickawaukie River."

The river was just ten miles from our summer camp and the idea that an enemy warrior had been so close was most disconcerting. There was still no trail and this was a thicker forest than the one close to our camp. There was game but there were easier places to hunt it. This was a vast and empty country. If we were back at Larswick then we would have seen farms and houses by now. We saw no one. When the trees stopped Runs Far opened his legs and took off. We could all see him and there was no chance of ambush. He ran along the river. I was tiring when I saw him stop. By the time we all reached him, he had explored the ground.

He pointed to the fire, "There were three of them and they had a boat. You can see where they placed it." The undergrowth showed where the boat had covered the vegetation, changing its colour. It told us that they had been there for many days. "I think we can assume that they were Penobscot. The bones of the fish and animals they ate are clear to see. They were here for some time."

Black Otter asked, "But what were they doing? It is late in the season. If they were scouts, then by the time they reach their home we will have left our summer camp."

Black Bird shook his head, "Aroughcun was the only survivor of the attack. It might have taken them until now to find our home. We are just lucky that they did not sail further north for they would have found our camp far quicker that way. They know where we are now. Erik heard their scout when he was close to the village. They will know our numbers and also the layout of the village. Perhaps we should use a different camp next summer."

Long Sight asked, "Have they gone?"

Runs Far pointed down the wide river, "Had they not been disturbed they might have stayed but one of them sent an arrow at Erik. Only a fool would stay."

We headed back but there was a real air of depression as we trudged home. I for one had hoped we might have another year, at least, before they discovered where we lived. Grey Hawk's clan came from far to the south and so Black Bird was right; there would be no attack this year as they could not yet know where we had our winter camp. I would have to ensure that the new snekke was well hidden or I risked losing the boat and all the hard work we had put into it. Gytha's appearance now made more sense. She had been warning me of the danger.

The sentries placed around the summer camp were reassuring but I knew we would not be able to relax our vigilance for the rest of the summer. When we returned, if we returned, then we would have to keep guards to watch for our enemies and that meant we would not be able to gather as much. This was a web that threatened to strangle the clan and we could do nothing about it.

Chapter 6

The debate about moving out of summer camp would have to wait for the tribe were keen to harvest as much as they could from the camp and move a week or so earlier. For me, that created a problem for I would not have the snekke ready. As we stood by the hull, I told the boys my decision. "We will make the steering board and the mast fish. The mast can be prepared but we will take her to Bear Island without her mast and deck fitted. That will have to wait. We will coat her hull again and when she has dried, we will fit the steering board and the mast fish. That way we can give the inside another coat and we will tow her to the island."

The boys looked crestfallen. All their work appeared to have been wasted.

I shook my head, "Do not be downhearted. The snekke will be even better for she will have the winter to dry out, but we must work harder than ever. We need every moment of daylight that we can find."

Mi'kmaq boys rarely have time for play, but poor Cub had even less than most. My decision also gave more work to Laughing Deer. She had a baby and all the preparations to make for the migration to the winter camp. We had little time to speak for when we had eaten, we were all ready just to sleep. Of course, Little White Dove had other ideas and that meant Laughing Deer had less sleep than any of us.

I did not use nails for the mast fish. The ones we had left were too valuable and I saved those for the steering board. It meant drilling holes for the wooden nails. It was lucky that we had so much bone to use for the drills. The steering board was the most vital part of the snekke, and I worked as hard on that as I had on anything before. While I worked on it the boys finished the mast but, despite all our efforts, we were a day behind the rest of the clan.

Black Bird came to speak with me, "We must leave tomorrow Erik."

I shook my head, "I cannot. At least I cannot leave in the morning. I might be able to start the journey in the late afternoon, but I must take the new snekke to Bear Island. I will not leave her on the beach in case of storms, or mischief."

"I understand but we have much work to do on our winter camp. Suppose the Penobscot come there?"

I spoke quietly, "Black Bird, this may well be my last winter camp with the clan. I bring danger to all. Grey Hawk will seek us out and I draw enemies to the clan. This will be good practice for us. Next year, when the snekke is finished then Erik the Navigator and his family will sail away!"

He looked genuinely distraught, "You cannot do that! You are part of the clan and we will fight to defend you!"

"Black Bird, if I was not here would the Penobscot come?"

He had been with us when we had met with Black Eagle and he knew the truth of my words. None had sought to end the lives of him or his brother.

"We have the winter to speak of this. I will ask Brave Eagle to stay with you. He is eager to begin to repay you for his life."

I was relieved. I had not relished the prospect of trying to carry the snekke with my sons. Even with another warrior, it would be hard, but we now had a chance.

The next morning the clan began to pack up their belongings. I left Cub to help Laughing Deer. He was unhappy but he did as he was asked. He was growing. Brave Eagle and Bear came with me and we put the steering board on the snekke. I knew her name but until she was finished, and the prow attached it would be bad luck to name her. Once the steering board was attached and I was happy it would not fall off we tied the mast to the mast fish. Leaving Brave Eagle to stand in the shallows holding the prow of the snekke, Bear and I launched *'Ada'*.

"You know, my son, that I must steer the snekke and you must sail *'Ada'*?" He nodded, "Brave Eagle will obey you, but you must make the right decisions."

"It is my test father. It will mark my change from a child to a youth. I will not let you down."

I looked up at the skies. They were cloudless, "It promises to be kind weather but if it blows up then I will cast off the tow. I know how to sail."

He climbed aboard and I took the rope, "Brave Eagle, sit in the front of *'Ada'*. My son will give you instructions. He is young but he has sailed beyond the island!"

"I will."

I held the bow and tied the rope to the wood which stood in the joint which we would use to attach the figurehead. I climbed aboard and sat on the thwarts at the stern. It was lower than it would be eventually for we had a deck to fit. I tested the steering board and then shouted, "Set sail, Bear!"

'Ada' struggled to move, and I wondered if this was a mistake but then the tide caught us, and the wind made her sail billow. She moved and the new snekke followed but I still had to use all my skill to keep a course which would follow *'Ada'* and not put stress upon the birch bark

snekke. I looked at the sky. It could take all morning to reach the island and that meant we would not get far at night when we followed the clan. It could not be helped. Bear did a fine job and he managed to bring *'Ada'* to a gentle halt next to the jetty. I knew that the winter storms would weaken the jetty further but that could not be helped. He tied her off and then untied the rope to the snekke. I used the current, wind and the steering board to ground the snekke on the beach. There were logs on the beach already. We had made a corduroy road to help bring the drekar on to the beach so that we could work on her. Now, after unshipping the steering board I stepped into the water and then pulled the rope so that the snekke floated towards the logs.

"Now we work together."

The three of us hauled on the rope and I confess that the snekke moved easier than I had expected. It was as we neared the longhouse that I realised we would not be able to put it inside. There was no longer a door but the entrance was not wide enough. I looked around and saw the weaponsmith's workshop. There was a roof that still had three walls and with the anvil and tools removed there was a perfect space for it.

"Take the mast off her and let us drag her in here."

Getting the mast off was easy but without the rollers manhandling it into the space was hard and then I made it even harder by asking Brave Eagle and Bear to help me turn over the snekke. We managed it and then I set to covering the hull with anything I could find to protect it from the elements. The cart we had used until its wheel broke was useful as were some of the tables and chairs from Gytha's. It was not perfect, but it would have to do. While I was doing this Bear took Brave Eagle around the settlement. When I had finished, I said, "Come we have much to do back at the camp."

As we headed for *'Ada'* Brave Eagle asked, "Your people, do they always build like this?"

"Normally but they also build in stone."

"And they travelled here in one boat?"

"There were three at one point but one was lost and we built a second drekar here at Bear Island when the clan returned east."

"You are a people unlike any I have ever seen before." He was right and it was only when you saw the evidence of what we had done in such a short space of time that you realised that.

I put Brave Eagle at the fore and Bear in the middle. We made the journey back in a much shorter time. I sent Brave Eagle and Bear back to help Laughing Deer while I took the sail from *'Ada'*, unshipped the mast, removed the steering board, and then dragged the boat up past the high-water mark. I filled the bottom of the two hulls with rocks to weigh them down and then used my seax to cut bushes as extra protection. I carried the mast, steering board and sail back with me. By the time I reached the almost deserted camp Brave Eagle, Cub and Bear had loaded the sledge and Laughing Deer was giving Little White Dove a last feed. I put my treasures in the lodge and then strapped on my sword, donned my helmet, and put on the bearskin over my mail. It was not that I expected trouble, but it would be less for us to pull. It was much easier pulling with two warriors and two sons who had grown stronger over the year. We had to camp alone that first night and Brave Eagle and I shared the watch but the next day we had caught up with the clan by noon. The whole journey took four days.

I had become used to the routine of the winter camp. Now, however, I had Bear and Cub to help me and that made a difference. It meant that by the second day we were able to go to the waters which lay close by and lay fish traps. A day later we were also the first to hunt the bjorr. As soon as the rest of the warriors joined in it would be harder.

I had helped the boys to make stone spears. Cub's was shorter and, in all honesty, more for show but if an animal came at him then he could protect himself. Now that Cub could swim, we were able to get closer to their lodges by the water knowing that if he fell in, he would not immediately drown! The first hunt with my two sons reminded me of going with my father and Arne. Then I had just had a fire-hardened spear. My boys were better equipped for the flint we used was very sharp. One or two other warriors were also out hunting but I had brought the boys to a bjorr lodge which was further around the small cove and we had it to ourselves. Bjorr were just the start. The boys would join with the other boys and warriors to hunt deer and, if we were lucky, the Moos. The lessons they learned that first day would stay with them for life.

I took my time for they were both new to this. I taught them how to determine the direction of the wind and then how to walk so as to make no noise at all. This was a good age for both of them as they regarded it as a game. It was when we closed with the bjorr that it became less of a game for a bjorr has sharp teeth and is quick. Once below the water, it is lost to a hunter. I also taught them hand signals and I used them to point to the two bjorr busy chewing at a tree trunk. Cub and Bear approached their prey silently and I was proud that they were able to concentrate so well. I focussed on the male bjorr I hunted. I thrust hard with my metal spear and skewered it in one blow. Bear struck almost a heartbeat later and Cub a moment after. The first spear mortally wounded the bjorr, but it was not dead. Cub's strike, less well struck, pinned the tail of the second bjorr to a branch and Bear was able to retract his spear and kill

59

the animal. Had I planned it that way it could not have gone better. Both learned lessons and the joint kill bound them closer together. I thought back to my first knife and the blood on the blade which had bound brothers and a cousin. I hoped their bond would not end as bloodily.

We gutted the two animals and threw the guts into the water to feed the fish. We headed back towards our home passing other warriors as we did so. We checked the fish traps and found four good-sized fish and three others we threw back. We gutted them too and headed up the trail where I saw ducks and decided that we would hunt those for it would improve the skills of Bear and Cub. They were not yet ready for war but when the Penobscot came then everyone in the clan would have to fight and the boys' slingshots would be invaluable. I saw Long Sight and Brave Eagle who were hunting muskrat and so I took us further from the water. It was there I spied treasure and we stopped. The waxwings and thrushes which took to the skies as we approached identified the tree.

"What is it, father? We have these animals to take home and skin."

I nodded and pointed to the conifer, "It is time you both had a bow like mine, and these make the best ones. It is yew. The berries are poisonous, but the branches are strong. Let us cut four or five of the branches."

"Why so many?"

"Because, Cub, we might make mistakes and who knows how quickly you might grow." I took my hatchet and cut branches that were the same length as my sons. I used a leather thong to fasten them together and took our bounty home. It was early afternoon when we reached the camp, and it was filled with the clan busily making lodges habitable and preparing food. For the boys, this would be a lesson preparing what they had hunted, and I sat with Bear and Cub to show them how to use the stone knife and skin the bjorr. That was their only lesson that day for butchery would be the work of another day. Little White Dove was asleep and so Laughing Deer began to joint the bjorr.

She nodded towards Wandering Moos' lodge. He no longer hunted, and he was seated outside smoking. "Doe Eyes could use some of this and we do not need all of it, husband. We have the fish as well as the bjorr. This will last them a week."

I nodded, "A kind thought. Bear, Cub, gut the fish and put them on twigs. We will cook and eat them while your mother makes the stew." Thanks to the metal pots I had salvaged from Bear Island we were able to make stews which made even the toughest meat tender. They nodded and I took one of the skinned and gutted bjorr to Wandering Moos and his wife. "We managed to hunt two of these. We thought you might like it, Doe Eyes."

Her only son was dead and all that she had left was her husband. I know that she looked at my children and saw the grandchildren she would never have. She took it and nodded, "Your boys are kind, Erik, Shaman of the Bear and are a credit to you and Laughing Deer."

She took it away and Wandering Moos said, "Sit and talk. You are always a busy man and I would like to speak with you."

I sat and he offered me his pipe, "No, thank you. I find that smoking takes away my appetite."

"Aye, but I do not need to eat much, and the smoke helps me to remember." He said nothing for a moment or two and blew out smoke. "When you and your people came, I thought it was the end of the clan but I was wrong. I know that you are sad that your people have gone but I have had much time to reflect on that." He held up his pipe. "This helps me to see clearer. I know that you have spoken of leaving us. Black Bird spoke of this. He will be a good chief for he is close to the heart of the clan. The clan will be sad to see you go but I know that it is necessary, not for the clan, but you. I see you always looking to the horizon. We call you shaman, but I know that you see yourself as the navigator." He smiled. "If I was young then I would like to come with you when you explore. I know the lands between the bjorr water and the summer camp at the sea as well as I know the back of my hand but that is all. The Penobscot lands you visited might as well be on the other side of the ocean. There are places I should like to have seen. The roaring waters in the land of the Iroquois, Mohawk and the Huron must be a wondrous place. The rivers which are as wide as the seas would be a marvel and I have heard of distant mountains filled with caves where people can live, sheltered from the weather. No, Erik, I will be sad when you leave but I know that you must."

I saw him wince. "Are you unwell, Wandering Moos?"

He gave a wry smile, "I am the oldest man in the clan and if I wake up without an ache then it is a good day. I have to rise four or five times a night to make water and I have a cough that keeps me awake. If I survive the winter, then that will be a miracle. I am content. Had Eyes of Fire been a different sort of man then I might have grandchildren and be blessed and comforted by their laughter." He nodded towards Bear and Cub. "Your boys seem to have their feet on the right path. I made the mistake of neglecting Eyes of Fire for then I was a new chief, and I gave too much time to the clan and not enough to my son. There is a balance, Erik, and you seem to have it. Never lose sight of the power of the family. Strong families make for a strong clan." He laid the pipe down. "And now if you would help an old man to his feet, I need to make water again!"

The next day we did not hunt for we had food enough for two more days. Instead, we began to make the bows for the boys. I handed each of them a yew stave and gave them their stone knives. "First you strip the bark and then shape them like mine." My bow was also yew but mine came from the land close to Larswick across the Great Ocean. It was also longer than theirs, but it was a model. As was my practice I only strung it when I needed to use it. That way it retained its strength. If they thought they had a quick job ahead of them they were wrong and when Cub rushed and made the notch for the bowstring too deep and ruined his bow it was the most valuable lesson of the day. He held back his tears and Bear showed that he was a good big brother. He laid down his own bow and selected another yew stave.

"Come, little brother, we can learn from the first one and I will help you with this."

I left them to it and joined Laughing Deer who was adding greens to the stew on the pot. Little White Dove began to mewl, and my wife said, "Pick her up and talk to her. You give all your attention to the boys and she now notices more. She needs more of your time."

It was as close to criticism as my wife ever came. I picked up Little White Dove. As usual, I always felt clumsy and awkward when I did this. The boys had seemed more robust while Little White Dove always felt as though she would break in my clumsy hands. I smiled and she smiled back. Her little fingers reached out for my beard. I was the only man in the clan with a beard. My seax kept it trimmed but she could still grab it and pull. I feigned pain and she giggled. I played a game with her and managed to have her laughing. I caught sight of Laughing Deer and saw that she was smiling. My wife was right. I owed it to my daughter to give her as much attention as the boys.

Black Bird had asked each warrior to be on watch for one night each week. It meant we had six sentries guarding the camp at night. The main task was to make sure that we were not being observed. During the day it was not necessary as the waters and the forests were filled with the clan as we foraged and hunted. It was no different to what we had done each year but since the discovery of the scout, the clan was more observant. That night was my first watch and along with the other five warriors, I went to the edge of the forest with my sword and my hatchet. I leaned against a tree and I watched and listened. This was not only my first watch but also the first time I had been in the forest at night. Long watches sailing to the new world had enabled me to stay awake, but I was more used to the creak of ropes, sails and masts rather than the animal noises. In Larswick we might have heard an owl in the night or a lark or thrush at dawn but here many birds were calling at night and animals were hunting too. In the east, we had foxes and rats but here they had many such nocturnal hunters and foragers. It took some time for me to be able to blank them from my mind and listen for human sounds. Over the winter months, I had endured many watches at sea and they prepared me for life in the forest. Even in the depths of winter when the snow lay on the ground and I wore squirrel lined mockasins with my bearskin over my head, I was learning much about my new land and my new home. In many ways, the threat from the Penobscot was welcome for had I not stood those watches I would not have come to know my new home as well as I did.

The next day, after that first watch, I refreshed myself with a bath in the icy stream which lay close to the settlement. I went downstream so as not to damage the drinking and cooking water. Refreshed I came back to our fire and I prepared our food for my family were not yet up. After they had risen we worked on the bows for an hour or so and then I took the boys and their slings to search for wood to make the arrows and to hunt duck. Other warriors used dogs to retrieve the animals they killed but we had none. We would have to kill them where we could fetch them. Not only would they be good eating, but they would also provide feathers for the arrows. A duck is a good target for a boy with a slingshot. They are large enough to make a bigger target and, generally, fly slower than most birds. They also swim slowly but they are harder to gather. I let the boys have the first hour of hunting. It took time but eventually Bear killed two birds. Cub was becoming downhearted and so Bear coached him and when he killed a brightly coloured male duck then he was delighted. After that, I used my bow to hunt larger, more elusive birds and I hit two. The five we had would be enough both for eating and for their feathers.

We then set off to find wood for the arrows. These were not the trees from home, and I did not know their qualities. "We seek branches which are as wide as my little finger and as long as my forearm. If they are not straight, then we do not need them."

It was not as easy as they expected. Some of the branches bent or snapped easily and they learned to choose the harder less pliable ones. In the end, we found thirty which I knew was a good start and I was helped when I recognised leaves which were like the oaks at home and although they were not exactly alike, they seemed to me to be similar. Our next task would be the heads of the arrows; we would need to find and shape stone arrowheads. I contemplated melting down my byrnie to make metal ones, but something stopped me.

63

Our life in the winter village followed this pattern for day after day and week after week. We made the bows and the arrows and I gave the boys lessons before we actually fitted the heads. They were both disappointed that both bows and arrows had been finished for a month before they were allowed to hunt with them and they hit nothing for the first two weeks. Even worse, unlike the stones they used, they had to retrieve their arrows. They learned to be patient and to use their missiles wisely.

In the long nights of winter, I carved the figurehead of the snekke. It would be much smaller than that of a drekar, but I wanted it to have as much detail as I could. I found that the hatchet and the seax made good tools to carve and by the time the days became longer I was able to begin to stain the wood before painting it. Pine tar would hold whatever colour I used. I would be limited in the colours I could use but as it was going to be Laughing Deer's face I concentrated on making red and white. The black was easy for there was always plenty of charcoal. While I left it to dry, I began work on the sail. I intended to use the skin of young deer. It was strong and yet supple to work. More importantly, the light colour meant I could use charcoal to make a black design so that the sail would look like a pair of wings. I knew from the Mi'kmaq that our drekar and its sail had been as terrifying as the warband!

That winter was the harshest the clan could remember. The snow made our watching easier as we could identify strange tracks a lot easier. The icy weather also took its toll on the old and more than eight of the older members of the clan succumbed. We almost lost Wandering Moos. His cough became worse and we thought he would die. Black Bird and Doe Eyes came to me with a request.

"Erik, Shaman of the Bear, Wandering Moos may be dying. The clan is not ready for him to go. Would you allow him to be covered with your bearskin and for you and Black Bird to smoke pipes while you watch him?"

Doe Eyes looked at me with such desperation as she asked me that I could not refuse but I was unsure of what effect it would have. The whole clan gathered that evening as the two of us and my bearskin entered Wandering Moos' lodge. His wife stayed with Black Bird's family so as not to dissipate the magic. Gytha would not have approved! I used the pipe which Brave Eagle had made for me and Black Bird filled it. "This is a special mix. There are leaves and plants which if eaten would kill you but when smoked they have a healing effect. Smoke until the pipe is empty and then we watch."

I nodded and laid the skin over the chief. He seemed to be barely breathing. Black Bird lit the pipes from the fire, and I sucked in the smoke. The smell was incredibly strong and, once again I felt lightheaded. I did not dream this time and I had no vision but even though he did not move I heard Wandering Moos' voice in my head as he told me of his family, his time as a young warrior, his courtship of Doe Eyes and the birth of his son. His lips never moved but I heard the words in my head. When the pipe died so the words stopped. Wandering Moos appeared to be breathing more easily. Black Bird was still smoking and so I just sat and watched. That night I realised that there was a skill in the smoking of the leaves for even though our pipes had been identical and filled the same, Black Bird was able to smoke for an hour longer than I did.

When his pipe went out, he laid it down. I turned to him, "Did you hear Wandering Moos' voice?"

He shook his head, "You are the shaman, and it was your skin which healed him."

"Healed him?"

"The skin and the smoke have done their work; see he breathes easier and he has not coughed since before your pipe went out. He lives and the clan has another reason to be grateful for your presence."

I felt like a fraud for I had done nothing and yet I was pleased when, as dawn broke, he awoke and smiled, "I hope, Erik, that my rambling tale did not disappoint you."

"You spoke to me!"

"Aye, I was in the dream world and our minds were one. I shall not die before we return to the summer camp and that is good for I should like to see the sea again and watch you sail your new boat!"

The experience had a profound effect on me. Gytha had been a volva and a witch. I knew she had powers. Wandering Moos, by his own admission, was just a warrior with no supernatural powers. Was I the one who now had powers?

Chapter 7

We had a decision to make, as the new grass appeared. We could not stay much longer at the water for the flies and the summer sun would make it unbearable, yet we knew not if we should return to a camp that the Penobscot had scouted. Wandering Moos had recovered sufficiently to be able to join in the discussion. Indeed he felt that he had been saved by the bearskin just so that he could take part! He said little but, since his illness, I had spent time with him, and I think I knew him. He was much like Snorri Long Fingers and reflected carefully about his words. He also listened and watched men. He was as different from his dead son as it was possible for a man to be.

There appeared to be no resolution for the arguments on both sides were balanced and then Wandering Moos put his hands up and Black Bird and Runs Far helped him to his feet. "I have listened to the clan and all the arguments are persuasive. However, there is one unalterable fact which we must consider; we have to return to the coast for that is what we do." He looked around until men nodded. "That means we either return to the place we know, or we find another site which is just as good." Again men nodded. Wandering Moos smiled, "And where is that? Have all the other Mi'kmaq clans overlooked it? Is there some beach which is as perfect as the one we use?" I saw those who had been in favour of finding a new summer home have their hopes dashed by the simple argument of the chief. "The fact is there is nowhere else which we can find. Our clan has used it since the time of my grandfather and longer. We chose it because it is ideal for us." He pointed to me, "Even Erik and the clan who came across an ocean saw that. We were willing to fight for it and they were fierce warriors. Should we do any less against the weasels that are the Penobscot? We defeated them once and we learned from Erik how to fight them. Let us show them again." Men turned to talk to their neighbour. "I am old, but I will fight alongside my clan if we choose to do that which we have always done."

I do not think that it was bravado or an attempt to gain sympathy, but it was a convincing argument, and we chose to return to our home. The difference would be that a band of warriors, myself included, would leave a day before the main body to ensure that all was well and there was no ambush waiting for us. As others would have to pull my sledge, I wore my byrnie, helmet and carried my shield, spear, and sword. I was laden. Runs Far and Long Sight ran ahead of the main body of warriors which was led by Black Bird. All of us were dressed

66

and armed for war. Some warriors reminded me of those I had met at Bear Island, the ones who had attacked us. They too painted part of their face and wore animal bones in their hair. Others, like Black Bird, simply had a few black feathers tied to the back of their hair. None had the shaven or half-shaven heads of the Penobscot.

Travelling, as we did, without anything to encumber us we were able to run and we needed just one night of sleep before we reached the camp. Runs Far and Long Sight returned to say that they had seen no sign of an enemy and that the lodges looked to be intact. They had just suffered winter wear. Even so, we formed a long line and with bared weapons headed into the village. We carried on towards the beach for the track I had seen the scout lay in that direction. While the majority of us headed to the shore Runs Far led five warriors to get as far down the track as they could. We approached the headland cautiously but when Long Sight crawled to the edge, peered over, and gave us the safe sign we knew that our enemies were not here.

I took off the bearskin, helmet, shield, and byrnie at the top of the cliff and followed the path down to *'Ada'*. I saw that my precautions had been wise for four of the birch bark boats had been wrecked by winter storms while another six had some damage. Their owners would probably build new ones. *'Ada'* had weathered the winter well and there was no damage. However, when I found the pine tar, I saw that a rockfall had destroyed two of the pots and the pine tar had seeped into the sand. Only the barrel remained intact and that would not be enough to finish the job. If that was the only problem we encountered then I would be happy. I left the boat without removing its protection. I would need Bear, Cub and Brave Eagle to retrieve the snekke.

Picking up my weapons I lugged them back to the camp where a fire had been lit and soon we would start to cook our food. It would take some days for the rest of the clan to catch up with us and that gave us the chance not only to put the lodges in order but to make changes to the defences of the village. Wandering Moos and Black Bird were not fools. If the Penobscot had scouted out the village over a period of time, and the fire and food suggested that they had, then they would devise a plan of attack based upon that information. We had to disrupt it as much as we could.

We had time before dark for some of us to wander the edge of the settlement. Long Sight, Black Bird, Runs Far and Brave Eagle joined me. Brave Eagle pointed to the trees, "They are too close to the lodges. When they attacked my village one of the survivors told me that they sprang their attack from the trees and caught people unawares."

I nodded, "We can use trees for I will need some wood for my snekke but if we cut and sharpen some branches then we can line a ditch with them."

"A ditch?"

"Yes, Black Bird. The way the Penobscot fight is to use speed and to run. I saw that when they fought us. They will probably outnumber us, and our strength lies in a solid line."

Runs Far added, "We can use some of the trees we hew to make shields. They stopped the Penobscot arrows last time."

I turned to walk back to the centre of the village. "We will not have a ditch all the way around. For a start, it might be a danger to our people, and we want to channel them on to our shields and our spears. Do you remember the stones on the ropes?" All but Brave Eagle nodded. "If they are concentrated in large numbers then the women and boys can hurl them over us."

We headed back to the centre of the lodges for the others were ladling out food into wooden bowls. "How can you be sure that they will come in the direction you want?"

"We can't, Brave Eagle, that is why we dig a ditch and embed stakes to make it easier for them to come the way we want. If you wish me to be truthful then I would say we should take the time to build a palisade behind the ditch so that they cannot easily cross it."

Black Bird nodded, "But that would take time and if we have guards to watch for them then we needed every remaining warrior hunting and gathering food."

We sat and began to eat. It allowed me time to think. "They came to scout by boat." Black Bird nodded. "All of the rivers and fjords that I have seen on this coast run from south-east to north-west. They will either have to cross many rivers and watersheds or come by boat. When my snekke is finished I can sail fifty miles in a day. I would be able to see them. Once we know that they are coming then we can have all the men work on the defences."

Stone Blade was a warrior who had killed six Penobscot in the last battle, "Is this honourable, Black Bird? We are giving their warriors no chance. We are warriors who can beat them without tricks." He gave me a shrug, "I am sorry, Erik, Shaman of the Bear. I can see that you mean well but these are just tricks that you ask us to use."

It was Brave Eagle who answered, "Tricks, Stone Blade? Do not speak of tricks to me! Grey Hawk waited until old men were guarding our lodges and they were all slain. They left a clear trail so that they could ambush us and slaughter almost every warrior. This clan has no honour! This tribe has no honour! Erik and Black Bird are right, we do everything that we can to kill and hurt them before they even get close!" He nodded to me, "When you sail this magic boat of yours, I would come with you for I will know of ways to hurt them before they even get here!"

Stone Blade was in the minority and the rest were of the same mind as Black Eagle and me.

I did not have my axe with me and so, the next day, I used a stone axe to hew down the trees. It was hard work, but the axe worked better than I might have expected. The difference was that sharpening it merely made it smaller and, to my mind, slightly weaker. However, they did the job, and, by the end of the day, we had eight trees we had felled. I had the thicker parts to split into planks for my deck while the narrower tops were perfect for sharpening and using as a palisade. The ones not felling trees dug the ditch. As Long Sight pointed out as the men started to dig in the damp soil, it would also keep the camp drier in the wet season.

That night we began as we would go on. Five of us watched. The next night would be a different five and we continue until the rest of the clan arrived. As well as felling trees I also had to repair our lodge and the next night, when I was not on watch, I had to take the sail and steering board down to 'Ada' for as soon as my family arrived, I would sail out to Bear Island. When the clan reached the camp, I was already exhausted, but we had begun to dig a ditch and there were wooden stakes to afford some protection. We had yet to complete the defences but now that we had more men, we would be able to accomplish that. However, we only had enough food for a week and that meant when we were not working or watching, we would be fishing or hunting!

As soon as the clan arrived, Long Sight and Runs Far set off for the river where we had seen the Penobscot camp. There was some debate about taking more men just in case our enemies were there already, but Long Sight pointed out that we had too few warriors to risk losing a large number and two men would be able to hide. I had managed to repair the lodge and so I took my sons to 'Ada'. Although it took Brave Eagle from the work on the defences, I needed someone to help me float the snekke. I had fitted the sail and steering board to 'Ada' already and we managed to head for Bear Island when there was still two hours of daylight left. I left Cub on the shore so that he could help me with the rope when we returned. He was unhappy about the task but knew that he could not sail either boat while Brave Eagle had the strength that I would need. Sailing across, Brave Eagle seemed calmer than on the first voyage. This time Bear rather than me leapt on to the jetty which I noticed had suffered more damage during the winter storms. Soon it would disappear and eventually so would the wooden houses. With *'Ada'* tied up, we hurried to the weaponsmith's to see how the new snekke had fared. There was no damage, and I thanked the spirits for watching over it. We hauled the new snekke into the water, and I fitted the steering board. I just tied the mast to the mast fish and with a rope attached to the framework on *'Ada'* we set off. It was a choppier trip back and I was glad that, as the sun set ahead of us, Cub grabbed the rope thrown by Brave Eagle and the two snekke were hauled ashore. We pulled them both above the high-water mark and then trudged up to the camp.

As we walked Brave Eagle asked, "When you sail south to scout for the Penobscot I would like to come with you."

I was wary, "Why?"

He smiled and that made me mistrust him. "I am interested in sailing on the new boat. You will need a crew will you not?"

"Let us be realistic, Brave Eagle, my sons may be boys, but they have more sailing skills than you do. Be honest with me?"

"You are right, my friend but it is not a complete lie. However, I am anxious to see the Penobscot and discover their plans."

We had reached the top of the cliff and I shook my head, "We will just be watching. I will not get close enough to identify who they are just that they are Penobscot."

"I know but I beg you, give me the chance!"

"I will sleep on it and speak with Black Bird."

Bear said, "You will not leave me behind, will you?"

I said, "I will make my decision when I am ready. No one will hurry me into making one."

As I had sailed the snekke across I had seen flaws in the design that needed to be remedied and work that had to be completed. I had hoped to launch her in a few days but the loss of the pine tar and the flaws I had seen meant we would have a week of hard work before we could try her out in the bay. The two scouts had come back from the deserted campfire by the river. The good news was that there was no sign of fresh tracks, but Long Sight wished to visit the place every three days or so to ensure that they had not returned.

Black Bird turned to me, "Erik, your plan to use your boat to give us an earlier warning of an attack is a good one but when will it be ready?"

"A week, perhaps less."

He nodded, "You work on the boat and we will fetch food for your family."

The next day we split the trees to make the deck. There would be no nails in this part of the snekke. I wanted to be able to use the whole of

70

the hold for cargo and that meant it all had to be removable. Once we had split the wood and roughly cut it into manageable lengths, we carried it to the beach. Here I missed the saws we had used. We used the axe and hatchet to shape the wood and then Bear and Cub smoothed the edges. There was a rhythm to our work that reminded me of the way the warriors had rowed our drekar across the ocean. As I trimmed each piece, I passed it to the boys who worked quickly and efficiently so that when the next piece was ready, they were too. By the second day, we had the tricky job of making the three pieces of deck. We shaped the wood to fit the snekke and then used wooden nails to make a framework. This would give the deck strength and enable us to make compartments. By the end of the day, we had three pieces that could be lifted to give access to the bottom of the snekke. The only part which was not removable was a section at the stern for I had plans to build a chest there which would remain fixed to the boat. The last thing we did before we returned to the camp was to fill the bottom with large rocks for on our first voyage, we would have little to carry.

As we wearily headed back to the lodge, I nodded at the barrel of pine tar. "Tomorrow we coat the deck and the hull with the pine tar. We will have no time to make more before I leave on the journey south. That will have to wait until I return. The day after tomorrow we fit the mast and figurehead and the day after that we launch her and sail her to Bear Island and back."

I do not think I had ever seen the boys so excited and both were up before dawn. It was not the painting of the hull and deck which excited them but the fact it brought them a day closer to the finishing of the ship. I knew how they felt. It had been the same when we had finished *'Jötnar'*. While the drekar we had built had been an achievement, so few had been involved in the snekke that my brother and I had felt part of the boat which we had made from the keel up. It was the same with Bear and Cub. The new snekke would be part of their life too.

I took the figurehead with me to the beach and we lit the fire to warm the pine tar. We laid the deck on rocks and, when the tar was hot enough, coated the inside of the hull. We were more careful this time for we had a limited amount. I used some on the figurehead and prow and then, with the help of some of the other fishermen, we inverted the snekke and used the last on the hull. We started on the keel and worked our way up. We could always coat above the waterline at a later date but below was the most crucial part. We left the wood to dry. We had laid traps in the shallow sea close to the beach for the large shellfish which inhabited the waters and I dived down to retrieve them. It helped to clean me. We had caught six and that would give us a good meal and

71

then, using dried fish and meat, we would make a soup for the next day. Other warriors had given us some of their catch but for two days we would feed ourselves.

The succulent white flesh we sucked from the shells seemed tastier after such a hard day of work. We discarded the shells back into the pot. We had already dropped in root vegetables and the fire would continue to cook the soup all night. The salt seawater we used to cook when at the summer camp always made the food tastier. I knew that if we stayed with the clan, I would ask to live at the summer camp all year round. I knew why the clan chose a winter camp, it was better hunting and protected from violent storms but I had always lived within sight of the sea and I felt an affinity to Njörðr and Ran. Even as the thought crept into my mind, I dismissed it. If we stayed with the clan then enemies would come. If I was to keep the clan and my family safe, then I knew we had to disappear, and the rivers further south. which Brave Eagle had told me about, seemed the best place. The Penobscot lived by the coast; if we could travel deep into the heart of this new world along rivers that were like seas then we would have a chance of living peacefully. I would have to become the shaman they all thought me to be. I would make five people and a snekke vanish!

The last thing I did was to go to the trap I had left in the trees and retrieve the squirrel. It was a large male and that was good. I placed it in the chest I used to keep my mail byrnie. The byrnie would be needed.

The warriors in the clan knew what we had planned and there were more warriors at the beach than normal. I carried my chest, byrnie, shield and helmet. Laughing Deer brought Little White Dove. My daughter was now toddling, and the beach was safer for her than a crowded village with a stake filled ditch surrounding it. There was great interest as we inverted the snekke and dragged her along the soft sand to the sea. We had drilled a hole in the gunwale, and we passed a rope through it to tether the snekke to the shore. I did not allow Bear and Cub's eagerness to make me hurry. I did everything carefully. We fitted the mast to the mast fish and I carefully hammered home the wooden pegs which secured it. We hauled the crosspiece and sail into position, and I stood on the mast fish to hammer that peg into place too. The snekke did not need a ship's boy to scramble to the crosstree and reef the sail. The mast fish was big enough to act as a step and I could do so. This snekke had been designed with great and careful thought. I attached the steering board and placed the spare one in the hold. I hoped we would not need it for a long time but I had decided to make a spare. The spare crosstree and the sail from *'Ada'* were also placed in the hold along with my byrnie, helmet, shield and spear and then we fitted the deck. The pine tar had made the boards expand a little and they had to be hammered in place. The handles I had fitted would help us to remove them, but the tight fit meant that the hold would be almost watertight.

The only one who understood the significance of the fitting of the figurehead was me. A drekar was only fitted with the figurehead when she was ready to sail. It was bad luck to keep a figurehead on a drekar when she was not at sea or moored in a port. I slid the carved wood into the slot and carefully hammered home the peg. That done I turned and saw a sea of faces watching me. I had an audience. I went to the chest and reached in to grab the squirrel. It bit me and drew blood which dripped on the steering board. I smiled for that was a good thing as part of me was now mixed with the snekke. The animal was not going meekly to its death and that too was a good thing. I walked to the prow of the ship and held the squirrel in the air. Drawing my seax I said, "Njörðr, I make this blót to you so that you will watch over this snekke which I name *'Gytha'* in honour of the spirit who watches over my family and the drekar my clan built here! I pray to the Allfather that it carried them safely to the east." I rammed my seax into the squirrel and its blood burst over the prow. That some of my blood from the bite was mixed there was no bad thing either. I hurled the squirrel's carcass high into the air and it fell into the sea. There it would be consumed by Njörðr's creatures and the sea would smile upon my snekke.

The clan all cheered the sacrifice. It was not a custom they used but they understood its significance. I climbed aboard and said, "Cub, board your snekke." He half swam and half walked. This was not *'Ada'* and the higher gunwale meant he struggled to climb aboard. With one arm around the steering board to keep the snekke in position, I used my other to haul him aboard. "Bear, untie the rope and bring it out to us. You may board your snekke."

It all sounded formal but this was a significant event in the boys' lives and the rest of the family. I had not told them, but we now had the means to sail, if not east to Larswick, at least north to the Land of Ice and Fire or south to the land of the Powhatan. I had done so in *'Jötnar'* and if I had to then I could sail there once more. Bear was bigger and he managed to clamber aboard unaided. After coiling the rope he and Cub sat by the mast. I had been checking the wind as I had waited and now I said, "Loose the sail!" This was a bigger sail and would give us more power but it also had a design painted upon it and as it fell, flapped and then filled I heard the gasp of awe from all but Laughing Deer who had helped me to paint it. The black wings made the sail and the snekke seem alive. The blót had been a good one for Njörðr gave us a good wind and we raced away south and east. The looks of joy on my sons' faces made me laugh with happiness. They were sailors. This was *wyrd*.

We were larger than *'Jötnar'* had been but not by much. It was the larger sail that made the difference and we fairly flew. The boys had only sailed in *'Ada'* and there was no comparison. "I should hold on to something until you are used to the snekke. Feel her and her mood. Today she is a newborn and wishes to show you what she can do. There is no shame in hanging on to the mastfish." I saw them hesitate and said, "I am going to come about and head for the channel close to Bear Island. Hang on!" My serious voice convinced them and as I put the steering board over the snekke heeled so much that I feared we might capsize but she did not and I saw that my sons were white-knuckled. It was time to begin their training. "Tighten the forestays and backstays. That is your job from now on. If the sail flaps we are losing wind. You keep it taut. I steer and you two work the sail! Keep your feet as far apart as you can. It will help." 'Ada' had been too narrow to allow such a stance.

They both grinned for we were skimming the wave tops and, as we were straight, they had more balance, "Aye, Captain!" They chorused together and I knew that the four of us were one.

"Thank you, Gytha, for watching over us!"

Chapter 8

I had only intended to sail to Bear Island but the joy of the snekke meant I sailed around the island and out to sea. I wanted to see how the snekke coped with the larger waves. She was wider than *'Jötnar'* and more stable. She coped well and once I had passed the northernmost point of Bear Island I said, "Prepare to come about!" I took us due west and passed Horse Deer Island before heading back to the beach,

Bear shouted, "She is more like a bird than a boat, father. She seems not to be in the water!"

I nodded, "She is unladen and faster, but you are right, and you can be proud of your work."

Cub saw the beach approaching rapidly and said, "We are not returning, are we?"

I nodded, "We have done that which I wished. I have work to do for the clan. There will be time to see what *'Gytha'* can do later."

I had the difficult problem now of choosing who would sail with me south and whoever I chose the ones I did not would be unhappy!

Black Bird walked up the path with me, "The new boat will be ready to sail soon?"

I nodded, "I could sail now but I need a crew and supplies. I will leave in the morning."

We walked in silence and I could almost hear the thoughts in his head. "How long will you be away? I only ask for the clan will be waiting for your return. You bring good fortune and each day you are away they will worry."

"I know. I do not think I will be away for more than half a moon. It could be within two days but then that would mean I had spotted the enemy. The longer I am absent the better the news. I will have to deal with tides as well as wind and weather. This is a good snekke my family has made but she is not tested. If the needs of the clan were not so great, I would spend another month on her. I would make more pine tar and coat her all over. I would take her beyond sight of land. There are many things I would do but I cannot."

We had reached the village.

"And who will you take?"

I saw Bear and Cub looking up at me and I shook my head. "I will speak with Laughing Deer, but I will speak to those I will take before the sun has set."

"The clan will be grateful. I will speak to Wandering Moos."

When we reached the lodge I said, "You two make the most of today. No matter if you come with me or stay here the next fifteen or so days will see you working hard. This is the last afternoon you will have to enjoy yourselves."

Bear said, "We enjoy being on the snekke!"

I laughed, "Away with you. You will learn nothing until the sun starts to set. Now go I must speak to your mother and I would like some time with my daughter."

Little White Dove, naked as were all the babes under two summers, was crawling in and out of the lodge while my wife prepared the evening meal. I knew that Laughing Deer had her eye on the toddler. I scooped up the babe and swung her around my head so that she squealed. "She has just eaten. If she is sick over you then you are to blame."

"I care not! You are my little bird are you not?" She squealed again and I brought her down to snuggle my face into her tummy which made her squeal even more. As I lowered her, she grabbed my beard and began to pull at it."

"You have decided who to take, then?"

I nodded and opened my mouth to roar at Little White Dove who squealed and laughed again. I had seen Bear and Cub take their bows and enter the forest and knew that it was safe to speak, "It will be Bear and Brave Eagle. I would take Cub, but he is too young. He will be disappointed, but it must be."

"I know. I will keep him occupied and give him more attention. I can teach him how to prepare food. He will enjoy that."

"And he can hunt. It will make him feel more useful if he brings food for the pot."

"And Brave Eagle?"

"He is not of this clan and I know it sounds harsh but if anything were to happen to him then the clan would not suffer. He also has knowledge of the waters further south. My fear is that he might choose to do something reckless." I shrugged. "If he does then I can do nothing about it except leave him and return home."

"You will not take risks."

"With Bear on board? Of course not."

"Good. I have prepared some dried deer meat and pickled some of the fish you like. There are two skins of ale ready. I will brew more while you are away."

"We have fishing lines and fresh fish eaten raw is a treat."

She shook her head, "I will take your word for that!"

76

I kissed her and took Little White Dove into the lodge, "Now you sit and play with this." I took my amulet from around my neck and she began to play with it. While she did that, I collected my treasures to take with me. I took the compass. Bear would begin his navigation lessons on this voyage. My shield, spear, byrnie and helmet were in the hold and I did not think I would need them but if I did, they were to hand. I would leave the axe at home, but I would take my sword, seax and hatchet. The bearskin and seal skin cape were necessary as were the sealskin boots. I took the bjorr hat as I knew that at this time of year it could get cold. There was also a cloak made of bjorr skin and I took that for Bear. I used the cloak to make a sack and tied it all inside. I picked up Little White Dove, leaving the amulet in her hands and slung the sack over my shoulder.

"I will go to the snekke. I will take Little White Dove with me."

My wife nodded and went back to the preparation of our meal. My long legs and the ground gave me an uneven gait which had Little White Dove squealing again and I began to sing the nonsense songs Ada had sung to Lars. My people had been singing them for as long as I could remember and they were a comfort to me.

Down the fjord comes a man
Comes each day with the new sun
Goes back home when the day is done
Up down up down following the day
Comes back soon the very same way
Comes each day with the new sun
Goes back home when the day is done
Up down up down following the day
Comes back soon the very same way

It was nonsense and as it was in Norse, she understood not a word, but the rhythm seemed to amuse her and she tried to make the sounds. I wondered if one day I would forget my old language. The silly song was the first I had spoken since Fótr and the others had sailed. It was still there. When Gytha spoke to me it was in Norse. When I dreamed words, they were in Norse but lately, the words of the Mi'kmaq had been creeping into my dreams and I wondered if I was changing. Was I becoming a Skræling?

The beach was almost empty. Most of the foragers and fishermen had taken their bounty back to the camp. I saw half a dozen boats still out fishing. Once we reached the boat, I put her on the sand and headed for the snekke. I slung the sack on board and then hauled myself up. I opened the chest and carefully placed the items inside. When that was done, I covered the chest with the bjorr cloak and then looked to the beach. Little White Dove had disappeared. I leapt over the side and then I heard a squeal. She was crawling in the shallows and the waves were splashing her. Even as I watched I saw a bigger wave pick her up and begin to pull her out to sea. She was just ten paces from me but it might as well have been ten miles for I had to wade through water. Then her head popped up. I saw that she was still clutching the amulet and although her eyes were wide with shock she was not crying. I scooped her up and she laughed.

"Thank you, Njörðr, for returning my daughter to me!" Little White Dove put her hands around my neck and squeezed tightly. "Let us not tell your mother of this, eh little one?" I kissed her on the cheek and headed back up to the camp.

By the time we reached the camp, she was almost dry although her hair was a little damp. I handed her to Laughing Deer who gave me a questioning look. I took the amulet back and said, innocently, "She enjoyed playing in the sand!" Before I could be questioned, I hurried off to Long Sight's lodge. He and Brave Eagle were seated outside each smoking a pipe.

"Welcome Erik, Shaman of the Bear, would you like to smoke a pipe with us?"

I shook my head, "I am here to speak of my voyage tomorrow."

Long Sight nodded and gestured for me to sit. I did so.

"Black Bird said you might come."

"Brave Eagle, I would have you as part of my crew."

He nodded as though he had expected it and Long Sight said, "Why not one of the clan?"

"Njörðr is our god of the sea and he must like Brave Eagle. He could have taken his life many times on the way north, but he did not. There may be others favoured by Njörðr, but I do not know them. I know that Brave Eagle will bring luck and he knows the lands to which we travel better than any of the clan."

Long Sight nodded, "You have thought this through well. I hope you both return safely for while neither is of this clan both of you are important to the safety of all of us."

"What will I need, Erik, Shaman of the Bear?"

"It will be cold at night and you will need a cloak, a skin with water and dried food. We can catch food from the sea, but it is good to have some dried food in case the fish choose not to bite."

"Weapons?"

"You can take them, but you should not need them. We go, Brave Eagle, to scout and not to fight. If we have to fight, then we have lost."

"Nevertheless, I am a warrior, and I will take them with me." He gave me a shrewd look, "You will have your magic weapons will you not?"

I kept my face straight, "Aye, but I am the Captain and I do as I wish!"

"Captain?"

"The master of the snekke and I command all who are aboard her. If you cannot take orders, then do not come."

"I can obey. I will be at the beach in the morning."

Leaving them I saw that Cub and Bear were at the fire, but they were looking, expectantly, at me. They knew that I had chosen one and so I headed towards them. I could not keep them in the dark any longer.

"Bear, you shall come with me tomorrow, go and prepare what you will take. You will need your cloak, sling and bow, as well as your knife." Cub's eyes began to fill with tears and I picked him up. He was getting too big to do so. I put my mouth close to his ear. "The next voyage you shall be with me, but I need someone who can steer the snekke while I sleep. You cannot do that. I need Brave Eagle for he is a warrior and can fight if we have to. If you were the elder, then this would be you." I kissed his cheek and held him a little away from me so that I could see his face. Salty tears streamed down his face, but he held my gaze. "Do you understand?"

He nodded, "But I am not happy. One day will I be your favourite?"

"What makes you say he is my favourite?"

"He is your firstborn and you take him with you."

"He is not my firstborn. I have another son, Lars, who lives, I hope, far across the eastern sea. He will now be almost twelve summers old. I have a daughter too, Ýrr. All of my children are equal."

"What is Lars like?"

I shook my head, "I know not for he left this land with his mother when he was just a little older than Little White Dove."

His tears stopped and he asked me about my first family. It seemed to help him accept my decision.

We went to bed early. I snuggled into Laughing Deer and we cuddled. Little White Dove slept between us. I knew that when I was away Cub would take my place. "Watch our son, husband."

"You have sailed this voyage with me and know that while we are away it is higher forces which are in control, but I will do all in my power to return safely with Bear."

It was dark but I knew she was weeping.

79

It took some time for me to fall asleep. I dreamed of great seas and monstrous winds. I was woken by a movement and when I opened my eyes Laughing Deer was bolt upright.

"What is it?"

She smiled and kissed me before lying down, "A dream, it is nothing. I am content."

I woke before dawn and went outside to make water. It was still dark, but I could hear the night guards moving around and already some of the women were rekindling fires. When I had finished, I went to the fire and blew on the embers. When flames began to lick, I added small twigs. I added more branches until I was satisfied it was going. Laughing Deer ghosted up behind me and put her arms around my waist.

"You have a spirit watching over you, husband." I turned to look at her and I saw that she was smiling. "Last night I dreamed, and a woman entered my mind. She was one of your people. She did not speak but she planted words in my head and like summer corn they grew. You will be watched while you are away, and the spirits will guard you. I saw you, Bear and the snekke return."

I nodded, "It was Gytha."

"You have often spoken of her. She felt... warm?" She shook her head, "I know not what that means except although I did not see her or hear her, I felt that she was kind and warm. How can that be?"

"You have been in the spirit world. Just accept it. I am content."

And I was for I knew that Gytha was still close and had yet to depart for the Land of the Wolf.

Bear, of course, was awake before I was but he had wisely waited until I went outside to rise. Laughing Deer smiled when she saw that he had everything hanging from his neck and back. She affected a frown, "And where do you think you are going?"

"To the beach!"

"Not without food inside of you! Your father will be eating and so will you."

I found myself smiling as Bear ate the food faster than anyone I had ever seen. "You know this will be the last hot food until we return? I for one am savouring this. You will be eating raw fish in a day or so!"

He grinned, "I care not for I will be sailing with Erik the Navigator!" He was irrepressible.

Most of the warriors, except those on sentry duty came to the beach to see us off. Brave Eagle was seated cross-legged on a rock. He looked like he was part of the landscape. His eyes were closed but as we approached, he said, "I am ready, Erik, Shaman of the Bear!" He opened his eyes. I saw he had a bow, shield and spear. The last two items he must have made for he had come with nothing. Around his back hung his cloak and two leather skins. I guessed one had his food and one his water or ale.

"Bear, climb aboard and store your gear. You will be in the middle close to the mastfish. I leave the stays, sheets, and ropes to you. When I need to attend to the sail then you shall steer." He was aboard in a flash. There was enough room in the chest for his gear. He then went to examine every rope. "Climb aboard, Brave Eagle. Your place is by the bow. If you use your cloak you can make a shelter from the spray."

He nodded and climbed aboard. I could tell that the warrior was nervous.

I turned and hugged Laughing Deer. There were no more words needed. I waved a hand at Little White Dove, "I will see you soon, little one!" I made the face that always made her giggle and she duly obliged.

I climbed aboard and took out the compass and tied it to the peg I had placed in the gunwale. I licked my finger and held it aloft to confirm the wind direction. Black Bird and Runs Far held the rope which tethered us to the land and as I said, "Loose the sail," I nodded to them and they threw the rope to Brave Eagle who caught it and began to coil it. I put the steering board over and the tide and wind, as Bear let loose the sail, made us almost spin and head south. The clan cheered and I saw, standing on the cliff, Wandering Moos and Doe Eyes. He waved.

Chapter 9

As we would not be out of sight of the coast, I need not have bothered with the compass, but I wanted Bear to learn how to be a navigator. I waited until Bear Island was a dot on the horizon before I waved him to me, and I showed him how to use it. There was a piece of charcoal and he marked the position of the sun. I do not think he understood what he was doing but that did not matter. I could explain it later. It also gave him something to do and to learn how to be disciplined.

I called to Brave Eagle, "Soon we will be passing the mouth of the river they used last time. Yesterday there was no sign of them. We will sail up to their camp and see if there are scouts. As soon as you see anything then shout a warning and we will turn."

"Aye!"

"Bear, reef the sail!" As soon as the sail was reefed, we slowed but I tacked and turned so that it did not affect us too much. I headed into the estuary and caught the tide as it was turning. It made for a bumpy passage until we reached the river proper. With a reefed sail I had a partial view of the river and land ahead, but it was not a clear one, and I was reliant on Brave Eagle. That was another reason why I had wanted a warrior and not Cub. We reached the burned-out fire. Although the fire was long gone, I recognised the spot. I turned the snekke and we raced down the river. "Loose the sail!" The snekke loved river water for there were no waves and we made rapid progress. Getting back into the main channel at the sea was bumpy again and I saw Brave Eagle clinging on to the figurehead as he peered ahead.

I saw that the sun was beginning to set and we needed somewhere to anchor. I would not risk the mainland and I called Bear to join me, "Go and sit with Brave Eagle. We seek an island for I intend to camp." He would have a better idea of the sort of place we could land.

He nodded and I was left alone at the steering board. A navigator is always learning and in the six hours or so that we had been sailing I had learned a great deal about the snekke. It was as though *'Gytha'* was speaking to me. Everything I learned made me a better sailor. I made tiny adjustments to see how she sailed. I tightened or loosened the sail and saw the effect that had. We were now some forty miles from our camp and there was no sign of any people either at sea or on the shore. This part of the land did not have beaches and that was another reason for us to stay at the summer camp we had. It was perfect.

"Three islands lie directly ahead!" Bear pointed slightly to steerboard and I saw the dark smudges. The sun was already much lower in the sky and the islands were perfect. We would be hidden from the mainland and that meant from the prying eyes of any Penobscot scout. I did not think that they would travel at night and so we had the chance to start early to seek them. After Bear had reefed the sail I headed for the middle island and we ground up onto a sandy beach. There were no trees on the island and no water. I suspected we were the first men ever to set foot on it. Bear tied off the snekke fore and aft and we landed.

"No fires. We have cold food tonight."

The trailing fishing lines had caught just four fish and we ate those along with the dried food. I used my seal skin cape to make a shelter for Bear and me and we wrapped ourselves in our furs and slept relatively well. When I awoke it was not far off dawn and I saw that Brave Eagle was not there. I stood and saw him on the highest part of the island. He was sniffing.

"You are trying to smell the Penobscot?"

He shrugged, "The wind is from the north and west, why not?"

"Today, we have more chance of seeing them. We will have to sail up every river that we find." I pointed north and west, "I suspect that there is a river up there and that means a slow passage for we will either have to row or tack back and forth." When we had sailed back from Bear Island, I had explained tacking. "Of course if we see them and turn, we will easily outrun them but, if we can, I would avoid letting them know that we are on to them."

I woke Bear and we left the island and headed up what was clearly a river. It took quite a while to sail less than half a mile. It took all day to sail up the river and we saw no sign of either boats or the Penobscot. The river narrowed and I took a chance that they had not used this river. What we did see was a couple of places where stones had been made into a circle and the earth was blackened. They were old and could only have been used by one or two warriors.

We turned around and sailed south, reaching the island we had used to camp just after dark. All of us were downhearted that night. The Penobscot could be anywhere and if the wind continued to be against us then we would struggle. That night I relented and allowed Bear to use my flint to light a fire. We had seen no Penobscot and a mist had spread from the land which would hide us. We would be warmer and hot food would cheer us up.

Bear looked disconsolate and I smiled as I stirred the small pot in which we had food bubbling, "You thought we would find them quickly?"

He nodded, "It is not just that, but this land is so big that they could be within a short distance of us and we would not know."

Brave Eagle nodded, "There would be signs of a large number, but you are right, and they may not even come. Your clan, Bear son of Erik, is being careful. I wish that my clan had been as careful and that way I would not have lost three sons."

The sadness in his voice affected me and I decided to be positive, "At the end of a few more days when we have looked along the next two rivers, we will sail back and it will be with good news. If we have not seen a large number of boats, then that means they are either not coming or have not set off and that would give us a month at least. Long Sight and Runs Far will be looking closer to home for signs of their scouts. This is pleasant is it not? We sail without having to use any effort. We can eat and drink when we like. For the Penobscot, if they are coming, they will have to paddle for most of the day and carry their food in a birch bark boat which can barely carry enough warriors. We have an easy life."

Brave Eagle nodded, "Aye, this is easy. I have paddled a boat up these rivers and it is hard work. Your gods smiled on you, Erik when they showed your tribe how to make such boats."

The food was soon ready and I began to ladle it into the wooden bowls, "I do not think that they will travel the whole way by water, Brave Eagle. The scouts we saw would have taken more than a moon to reach the camp we saw which means they must have left their camp soon after we did. If you were Grey Hawk would you risk the fate of Laughing Wolf and the wrath of the sea? I think they will only use their boats for part of the journey. The fires we saw today might have been scouts they sent last year. Who knows, tomorrow when we sail up the next river, we may find more fires?"

Brave Eagle looked up, "More scouts?"

I ate some of the stew and nodded, "One boat up each river would be sufficient. The warriors could scout and return. When Grey Hawk pools the information then he will have a picture of the land."

"A picture?"

I put my bowl down and went to my chest on *'Gytha'*. I retrieved the maps I had made. "We call these maps." I pointed. "This one is part of an island of ice and fire far to the north and this one is the bay where we live and the land to the north."

"This is magic!"

"No, Brave Eagle. After we have finished the meal, I will use a black stick and add the details we saw today. If there is magic, then it is the skill I have in knowing how far we have travelled. At the moment only I can read these maps, but I will teach Bear and Cub how to do so. I will pass on my skills."

The mist had disappeared by the middle of the night. I knew for I got up to make water. I heard the sound of the night birds from the mainland. Sound travels at night and there were no warriors close by.

It took until noon to reach the next river. I ignored the small streams for many reasons. They might be too shallow for the snekke and would not be of much use to a large number of boats. We passed many islands but none looked to have people on them. I knew this was Penobscot territory and there should have been people gathering food on the shore but there were not. It was then I realised that this was the river we had used on that fateful voyage which had seen my brother killed, the misnamed River of Peace. We were in the valley which led to the Penobscot camp where we had met with the tribe. This was not the land of the Clan of the Hawk; that lay many days to the south but the other Penobscot whose village we had visited was ahead.

"I know this river, it is the River of Peace. It widens to almost a sea at a place we named Fox Water and then narrows. A day or so up ahead lies the village of Laughing Wolf. I do not know if any live there still. I know that the tribe still use it. Would the Clan of the Hawk use it?"

Brave Eagle turned and shivered. The wind had changed since we had set sail from our bay and over the last days had veered to come from the north and east. That brought cold and, as we headed up the channel, keeping to the centre to avoid rocks and islands, a mist like the one the previous night descended. If we had been in Larswick we would have called it a sea fret.

Brave Eagle said, "I sense the presence of an enemy. Let us sail further upstream. What have we to lose?"

I contemplated stopping at an island for I feared that Brave Eagle was so desperate for vengeance that he might like us to run into Penobscot, but something made me push on. I would trust his feelings and Gytha would warn me of danger. I reefed the sail and we tacked back and forth. Brave Eagle was now used to the motion and more confident about his role as a lookout. With the mist, he needed every one of his senses and when he held up his hand, I turned the snekke into the wind and we stopped. I saw him lean over and reach down to the water.

He returned to me with his find. In his hand, he held a feather. "We have found them!"

85

"It is a feather!"

He smiled, "It is the feather of a hawk and it did not fall from a bird for you can see it has been worked and there is a thread bound around it by a blue bead. This is the sign of the Hawk clan of the Penobscot and came from a warrior. The land of Grey Hawk and his clan must be at least three days south of here. This is beyond the range of their hunters. They are here, Erik, Shaman of the Bear. I can feel them. We need to travel up this river and find them."

I looked at Bear. He was eager but Brave Eagle's plan, while it made sense would put him in danger. Then I remembered Laughing Deer's dream. Gytha watched over us and I nodded, "We will stay as close to the steerboard bank as we can. If you are right Brave Eagle, then they would try to cross this river."

We edged through the murk and mist for another three hours and I thought to land and wait for the fret to disappear when Brave Eagle pointed and I saw, to steerboard, the holed birch bark boat, it was Penobscot. It did not tell us that Grey Hawk and his clan were there, but it confirmed that there were Penobscot about. That in itself was not a surprise. After all, I knew that there was a village ahead. The mist hid not only the enemy and us but also hid the banks of the river. I tried to think back to the last time I had sailed here when Laughing Deer and I had fled the Penobscot. It was no use, I had been so afraid that she and her sister would be recaptured that I had barely noticed the banks of the river. It was then that I remembered the island which Bear Tooth, Ebbe, Stig and I had used. As I recalled it was not far up the river and when a large shadow loomed up and Brave Eagle held up his hand I realised we had found it and said, "Bear, reef the sail!"

"Brave Eagle, tie us to the nearest tree." He jumped ashore and while Bear pulled on the ropes to secure the sail I jumped to my feet and, standing on the mastfish tied the cords around the sail. "Bear, sit at the steering board. If there is a danger then you can head back downstream."

I drew my sword and walked down the snekke to step on to the land. It looked vaguely familiar but there was a simple test.

"Brave Eagle, nock an arrow and watch my back. I will see if this is the place, I think it is."

I headed north and then turned sharply right to the east. I found water. I retraced my steps and then kept going. I found the river again. To confirm what I already knew I walked to the end of the island. I smiled at Brave Eagle, "It is the island I remember. We can camp here tonight. I now know what to expect tomorrow. If you are right, then before the end of the day we should see the Penobscot. All I want is a glimpse and we will race back to our village. They can reach the clan within ten days from here and do not need boats."

Events were not turning out the way I hoped. If Brave Eagle was right, then the Clan of the Hawk were already here!

I looked at the Powhatan warrior, "No fire tonight and you and I will take it in turns to watch. We will not have a full night's sleep, but we will have some."

The fur I had brought for Bear kept him warm for the fret which had now disappeared had kept the warmth from the vegetation and it felt icily cold. Neither Brave Eagle nor I saw anything but when it was my turn to sleep, I found it difficult to do so and that, I think, was Gytha, nagging at my mind.

We set off before the sun had fully risen. Often a fret such as the one we had suffered the day before was followed by a sunny and hot day. The wind had turned and was now a little warmer and from the west and that was a good thing as it meant we did not have to tack as much. We sailed with a half-reefed sail and I had both Bear and Brave Eagle at the prow, one watching each bank. We ate as we sailed for I wanted to waste not a moment. My poor sleep had been as a premonition. Having found the island the river was more familiar. I had made this voyage twice before and when I had been with Bear Tooth, he had pointed out memorable places. I estimated, at noon, that we had travelled more than eight miles and I suspected that the River of Peace would soon widen as it came to the large open stretch of water we had named Fox Water. When I saw the river ahead suddenly narrow, I edged closer to the steerboard bank and said, "Reef the sail. We will land." As Bear, aided by Brave Eagle who had seen over the last days what he needed to do, reefed the sail, I made a complete circle so that we were pointing downstream. We tied the snekke to the shore and we cut shrubs to disguise her. To be seen a warrior had to be within four paces of her.

I grabbed some dried meat, my bow and a handful of arrows. I donned my bearskin. "Brave Eagle, we will scout out Fox Water. Bear, you will watch the boat and keep an eye out for any Penobscot. If you think any are near, then cast off and anchor in the middle of the river."

He nodded and I saw fear replace the excitement. On the voyage here it had been an adventure but now he saw the danger we were in. I turned and began to climb through the trees. I saw no signs of humans but there were animal droppings all the way along the game trail we followed. After a mile or so we reached the top of the small ridge and I peered through them. There was Fox Water ahead, I saw the sun reflecting off the ripples made by the wind but I could not see it all and we would need to get closer. As we descended then the insects began to bite. That told me that there was a slow-moving patch of water close and so it was. We found a small river which we would have to cross to climb the ridge ahead of us. We walked upstream until I found a jumble of logs that had formed a barrier and we used them to cross. The next ridge we climbed was not as high and this one afforded us a good view of Fox Water. We both squatted behind a stand of trees to survey the patch of water.

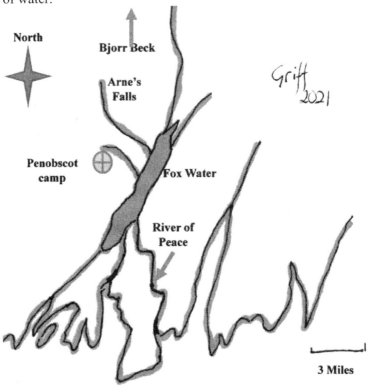

As I stared it all came back to me. We were about six or seven miles from Bjorr Beck and that meant the Penobscot camp where I had found Laughing Deer and Stands Alone was less than ten miles away. The falls, where Arne and the rest had died, were even closer. I saw the mouth of the river which marked the way to them. The water looked to be empty, but we waited, and we watched. Brave Eagle said not a word. I was in command and he would continue to study the land and water before us. Standing long watches at sea had taught me patience and given me the ability to use my eyes well. I spied movement on the far shore. A party of warriors paddled two birch bark boats out of the small river to the water. Had we been seen? I dismissed the idea for we had not moved and it had only been their movement that had alerted me. However, they paddled out into the middle of the water and looked to be heading towards the river close to where Bear was waiting for us. That they were Penobscot was obvious for the far shore was their land but what I could not tell was what was their clan. We had a good place to watch and we did not move as the warriors paddled across Fox Water. It soon became clear, for the sun had already dropped lower in the sky, that they were not going to paddle down the river, at least not yet. They used a net to catch fish which they hauled aboard their boats. They had no suspicion that they were being watched. This was confirmed when they turned around and sailed back across Fox Water to the river they had used to come to the Water.

As they neared the far shore I asked, "Brave Eagle, are they Hawk Clan?"

He shook his head, "I cannot tell but whoever they are they have a camp not far from the far shore of this water. Could we sail to that shore? I could scout it out."

I looked at him, trying to read his thoughts and intentions, "We could but is it worth it?"

He stood and I did so too, "Erik, Shaman of the Bear, you and your clan assumed that the Penobscot would come to raid you by sea." I nodded. "The journey we have taken has told me that they will not do that. Your story of Laughing Wolf is the reason they will not. It is too far and there are too many risks. They might use their boats to cross this water. You have a picture in your head of this land. How far is it, would you say, from where we stand now to your village?"

My map was in the chest but by closing my eyes I saw it. I pictured the rivers which would necessitate either boats or fords and then the unknown forests. They would have to avoid the camp of Chief Mighty Water and the Clan of the Otter. Long Walking and the other warriors had made it clear that they would fight Grey Hawk and the Penobscot could not afford to lose warriors before they reached my village. "More than fifty miles."

He nodded, "If they land here then, by boat they can be at your village in two days. It will take us at least that long to return will it not?" I nodded. "Then we need to see if they are ready to come. You need not come with me."

"Let us get back to the snekke and I will consider your words."

The sun had set by the time we reached *'Gytha'* and the grin from Bear showed his relief. Everything that Brave Eagle had said made sense and yet I was risking Bear. I now regretted bringing him, but Brave Eagle was right, we had to know.

"We will sail across the water and up the small river."

We turned the snekke around and by the time we entered Fox Water the sun had set but, in my mind, I had a picture of the river and we sailed silently across the water. The night birds could be heard but that was a good sign for it meant that the Penobscot warriors were not moving through the forest. I waved Bear to the steering board when we neared the other shore, and I reefed the sail. I needed to be able to see and we did not need much way on us. The river was just twenty paces wide and began to narrow almost as soon as we had progressed less than five hundred paces. Brave Eagle was leaning so far out to the larboard side that I feared he might fall into the river and make a splash which would alert the Penobscot. We managed a mile before he held up his hand and I turned the snekke into the wind to effectively stop her. The river was just ten paces wide and I had contemplated stopping in any case. He smiled and pointed ahead. I could see many birch bark boats drawn up on an open area that had been cleared of trees. He cupped his ear and sniffed. I listened. In the distance, I could hear noises but more importantly, I could smell woodsmoke. We had found their camp and their boats. I turned the snekke around and bumped her gently into the bank downstream from the birch bark boats. Brave Eagle leapt silently ashore while I pointed to an overhanging branch and Bear jumped over the side to tie us to it while I fully reefed the sail. I then secured the stern to a branch. I pointed to Bear and then the snekke. He nodded.

Brave Eagle was waiting for me. I did not take my bow, just my bearskin, sword, hatchet and seax. I followed the Powhatan into the forest. There was a trail and that worried me for it mean we might meet a Penobscot. Brave Eagle had his stone club and knife with him, but it would not guarantee to silence a sentry. The warrior seemed to know what he was doing but I still worried about his state of mind. At least his clan would not be held here. This was far to the north of his land. Perhaps he would be patient in his quest for vengeance.

The noises grew and I saw lights from fires. Brave Eagle stopped and pointed to a tree. I nodded and stepped behind it. He disappeared from view as he ghosted into the forest. He seemed to be away for an age and I had begun to fear for him when I heard noises ahead. He was returning and then I remembered how silent he had been. Whoever was coming it was not Brave Eagle and I drew my sword and hatchet. When I heard voices then I knew it was at least two Penobscot. I contemplated heading back to the river but if I did so then I risked leading them to my snekke. There was only one solution. I had to kill, silently, whoever came down the path. My advantage was that I was hidden, and they

90

would not be expecting trouble. If they suspected anything then they would be silent. I could not risk peering around the tree although my bearskin hid my features. I would have to wait until they passed me. I smelled them as well as heard them and I gauged their progress. I would use my hatchet on whoever was on my left and bring my sword up into the ribs of the one on my right. It would not guarantee silence, but it would guarantee that they died and then I would run back to the snekke.

I heard the two men and they seemed to be almost next to me. They stepped before me and I saw that there were just two of them. I acted swiftly and my sword was already driving into the flesh of one as I cracked the blade of the hatchet into the skull of the second. The sound of the blade smashing into the skull of the Penobscot seemed like a crack of thunder while there was just the soft hiss of death from the other as he died. Suddenly a third Penobscot's body fell at my feet and I saw Brave Eagle with a bloody stone club. He pointed to the river and I ran. There had been no noise but three Penobscot warriors would be missed. I sheathed my sword and put the hatchet back into my belt.

I reached the snekke first and, after throwing my bearskin to cover the chest, I untied the stern rope. Bear acted swiftly and untied the other. I loosed the sail but as we were pointing into the bank we had no wind and it hung limply. As soon as I turned the steering board and Bear pushed us off, we would catch both the current and the wind and move. Brave Eagle was nowhere in sight and I began to fear that he had been caught. Bear pointed upstream and I saw him. He was using his stone knife to damage as many of the boats as he could. It was a good idea, but we had no time for it. I dared not shout and so I waited impatiently for him to turn so that I could wave him aboard. He eventually looked up and I gestured for him to board. He began to wade towards me, and I did not wait for him but turned the steering board. I nodded to the oar and Bear pushed us off. Brave Eagle made the side and as the sail filled with wind, he pulled himself aboard. He was grinning as he made his way to the prow and I saw him nock an arrow.

The silence behind me told me that they had not discovered the bodies yet and the longer that it was silent the better were our chances of escape. In the distance, I saw a sudden flash of light and knew that the moon had emerged from behind a cloud and shone on Fox Water. It was then that I heard the cries from upstream. The bodies had been discovered. And then we were out of the claustrophobic river and burst onto Fox Water. I could use the snekke's sailing skills better on the open water and I put the steering board over to take advantage of the wind. We fairly flew and I made as much progress as I could. While the moonlight helped us see the Peace River it also illuminated us and we had not quite reached the river when I heard a cry from behind and saw, as I turned, birch bark boats as the Penobscot followed us. The Norns had been spinning and the Penobscot would know who had killed their warriors and damaged their boats!

Chapter 10

There was no longer any need for silence and after we had passed through the narrow channel to the river I said, "What did you discover?"

"It is the Clan of the Hawk and another, the markings on the other clan make me think they are the Clan of the Snake. I counted more than thirty lodges and there were no women. This is a warband."

"How many warriors?" While I was asking questions I was trying to make as much speed as I could without risking holing the snekke. The Peace River was wide and, as I recalled, rock free. Bear and Brave Eagle would have to give me advanced warning of any danger.

"More than a hundred and twenty. That is why I wanted to damage as many boats as I could. It will slow them down. They have enough to cross the river but not quickly."

Although the river was wide enough it had too many turns for my liking and each time we had to adjust the sail to make a turn I knew that the nimbler birch bark boats would gain on us. The current and the wind would be helping them, and I remembered how fast they could go. I was just grateful that, this time, they were not ahead of us to ambush us with arrows! We were just two miles or so from the mouth of the river and the sky was becoming lighter when Bear, who kept glancing behind to ensure that I was still there pointed and when I looked, I saw the first birch bark boat. They were still more than a hundred paces or so behind us, but they were gaining, and I knew there was another sharp turn ahead of us.

"Brave Eagle, bring your bow, we may need it!"

He came back to the stern and peered behind. Shaking his head he said, "It would be a wasted arrow. This boat is moving too much, and the light is not good enough. Are they catching us?"

Without taking my eyes off the river ahead I nodded, "Little by little. If we reach the sea and they are behind us we shall lose them but..."

He said, "Aye. The sun will rise soon. I have something in mind. You keep sailing this magical boat and I will deal with the Penobscot."

"Bear, you are the eyes of the snekke, we are in your hands!"

I saw him nod and grab hold of the figurehead to raise himself up. That was good for the spirit of Gytha was in the snekke as was my blood. The spirits would help us.

Ahead of us I saw the mouth of the river and said, "Another half a mile or so and we shall be safe!"

I felt him nock an arrow, "Then I will waste an arrow for they are close!"

I risked a glance astern and saw that they were just sixty paces from us. If I had my Saami bow and was not required to steer, then I knew that I could have sent an arrow to kill one of the paddlers. I shook my head; I might as well wish for a drekar full of warriors.

Before he loosed his arrow he taunted them, "I am Brave Eagle, and I am the chief of the Clan of the Eagles, the Powhatan tribe! Know this, warriors of the Hawk, I was the one slew your warriors and wrecked your boats, and I will come at night to wreak vengeance on those who took my family!" I heard the thrum of the bowstring as he loosed an arrow. There was a cry and I looked around. He had hit a paddler in the shoulder. The paddle had fallen into the river and the boat was veering to one side. I could see another three boats and they were close behind, but a mixture of his words and his arrow meant that they would not catch us. Brave Eagle had been clever. His clan lived to the south and they did not know he had survived. His words would confuse them. I decided to head south when we found the sea. There were enough islands for me to hide behind and when I was sure we had lost them we could head north. This way they might not know that our clan knew of their impending attack. For the second time in a few hours, Brave Eagle had saved me!

The sun filled the eastern sky with bright beams as it rose above the sea. I was already turning to steerboard to head for one of the many islands which lay there. The wind filled the sail and we began to extend our lead. As the larger waves struck us, I turned to look at the effect on the birch bark boats behind. The one which Brave Eagle had hit began to take on water as the warriors tried to adjust to three paddlers. It slowed them and unless they could get rid of the water then they would sink. I concentrated on using the wind to get as far from them as I could. Brave Eagle's words would suggest that we were heading for the land beyond that of the Lenni Lenape. As soon as we reached the first island, I put the steering board over and the hump of the island made us disappear. I gradually readjusted the steering board until we were heading east and then when the islands and rocks completely hid us from the mainland, I turned us to sail north and east. We would not be travelling as fast, but we would put distance between us and the River of Peace. I was sure we had lost them for the waves were lapping water up to the gunwale and that would easily swamp a birch bark boat.

It took as long to return home as it had taken us to sail south and to explore the rivers when we had sought the Penobscot. The main reason was the winds which did not cooperate. The wrecking of their boats would delay the Penobscot but even now they could be heading north and east through the forests. Our sail made us easy to spot and we were seen by our fishermen before we saw them. The result was that Black Bird, Runs Far and Long Sight were on the beach waiting eagerly for our news. Laughing Deer and Cub were not there but I did not expect that. Word would have been sent that I was safe and that would be enough for my wife.

My first priority was the snekke. Black Bird and the others recognised that and they helped us to drag the snekke up above the high water mark. Over the next days, I would if I was allowed, finish the pine tar.

"Well?"

"They are coming and there are two clans but they will not come by sea." I pointed to the forest and the south-west, "They will come by land and they could be here in the next two days!"

Long Sight nodded, "We have Black Otter and two others camped at the river where the Penobscot scouts made their camp. I decided that their scouts would have examined the land between there and where you saw them. We will be ready."

I shook my head, "Brave Eagle counted more than one hundred and twenty warriors. Even using the older boys we cannot muster more than sixty. We will be outnumbered more than two to one!"

Black Bird shrugged, "We can do little else, Erik. We cannot flee so we fight and if we die then so be it."

I looked around the village with new eyes. It now looked nothing like the camp I had first visited all those years ago. The ditch ran around two sides of the camp. At the fore, where we expected the attack to start, was a wide opening for the enemy warriors to charge. At the opposite end was a narrow exit that would allow the women and children to flee if we lost. The ditch had stakes in it. Warriors could cross the ditch and avoid the stakes but they could not do so either swiftly or in numbers. However, they could cross and it would then be down to our warriors to fight them.

Black Bird saw my look and put his arm around me, "I know you are anxious to speak with Laughing Deer but let me show you what we have done since you left." He led me behind one of the lodges where there were shields. These were not the hide ones the warriors of this land used but solid shields based on mine. "There are enough for all the warriors." He took me to the next lodge where there were large rocks tied with a rope. "The women all know how to use these, and they will rain down rocks on the Penobscot." I saw that close by were piles of pebbles and knew that the boys would be able to do the same with their

95

slings. Black Bird pointed up to the trees. I saw that something was different about the ones closest to the lodges. "There are ten boys who have volunteered to hide in those trees. We have removed some of the lower branches to allow them to see more. They will have bows and slings."

"Will they not be in danger? They will be isolated from the rest of us."

"They know the danger and besides they can climb higher into the trees and be like the squirrels. If we lose then they can escape. All the clan is ready to fight. They hope not to die but know that that might be the outcome."

I nodded and told them of Brave Eagle's attempt to throw them off the scent. "If it works then it might make them delay for a day. Brave Eagle seems to think that they might choose to punish him and his tribe rather than us."

Black Bird gave me a shrewd look, "But you do not think so."

I shook my head, "The ones who pursued us down the River of Peace will have taken a day to get back to Fox Water and by then I believe they would have begun to move their warriors. Brave Eagle's destruction of their boats will have hurt them and slowed them. I confess that I was angry when he did so for it put us in danger, but I can see now that it was the right thing to do."

He nodded, "Go to your family. We know what we need to do now."

Bear had raced off to see his mother when I had gone to speak to Black Bird. She looked up as I strode across. Little White Dove squealed when she saw me and I knew that she would try to grab my beard. I hugged them both and as Little White Dove grabbed two handfuls of facial hair my wife kissed me. "Gytha was right. She did protect you."

I nodded and said, quietly, "We found them close to where Arne died, and I found you."

Her eyes widened, "You are right, husband. If we stay here, then the past will return to haunt us. I love this clan and all the people but our presence seems to attract our enemies. I would not have Little White Dove growing up with that fear."

"But if we leave then we go without friends. We seek places where we do not know who is dangerous and who is not."

She put Little White Dove on the ground and said, "Cub and Bear, watch your sister and the pot."

"Yes, mother."

She linked my arm and led me towards the forest. I said nothing for I was curious. She did not take the path but went through the rough ground between the trees. When we stopped, we were so far from the lodges that we could barely hear them. "You have travelled this land, Erik, and you are a navigator. You know better than any that most of it is like this. We travel until we find somewhere which is empty and far from the Penobscot. When the children are older then we might return here or, perhaps, find another tribe. I have spoken with Long Sight's wife, Red Bird, and she says that Brave Eagle has spoken of his clan and they seem a peaceful one like us. There may be others like that." She turned, "Come, let us return. I just wanted you to know that I have thought about your words and I am content. I have spoken with Stands Alone and she will stay with the clan if we leave. White Arrow's son, Grey Squirrel, has shown an interest in her. He is a good boy and will make a good husband. She is not ready yet for she still has nightmares about the Penobscot, but he is gentle and kind. He will be good for her."

I knew that Laughing Deer and I were lucky. We had found each other despite obstacles strewn before us. The Norns who had spun this web were still spinning and that gave me hope. They could still trap us in their spell, but I did not think it would be for a while.

I rose early the next day for the Penobscot could come at any time. I sharpened my weapons and oiled my byrnie. I had used the flat of the axe to repair some of the damage I had suffered but I knew that it would not last many more battles. I still had some arrows with metal arrowheads, and I sharpened those too. I laid my weapons, mail, and helmet before the lodge. Our scouts would give us warning of an enemy's approach, but I wanted to dress for war quickly.

Bear and Cub saw what I was doing and joined me. "You two will need your bows. Your job will be to guard the sides of the warriors. Use your bows and when your arrows have gone you use your slings. If the Penobscot get close, then you run. You do not stand and fight for if I fall then you two must protect your mother and sister. Do you understand?"

Bear had grown on the voyage and he put a protective arm around Cub's shoulders, "I know what we must do, and I will watch Cub in this battle."

It was at that moment that it began to rain. Had the threat of the Penobscot not been imminent I might have noticed the black clouds rolling in. As a navigator, I was keenly aware of the weather. A summer storm was not unusual but when they came, they were normally violent and the drops which fell were heavy! "Get my war gear into the lodge! The flash of lightning and crack of thunder told me that this would be a powerful storm. I had witnessed enough such storms at sea. "Laughing Deer, get into the lodge!"

Despite my urgent words, we were all soaked by the time we were safe in our lodge. Those who had been foraging were even worse off. As we listened to the rain pounding on the roof of the lodge Bear asked, "Will this hurt the Penobscot, father?"

"It depends on where they are. If this continues then it will make the ground slippery and slick. As for here, it will fill the ditch with water." I shrugged, "Perhaps the storm is sent by gods to help us." He nodded but, in my heart, I knew that this was the work of the Norns. The rainstorm lasted far longer than any of us expected and when it did stop and we emerged, it was into a sodden world. I had thought the bone hard ground would have shed the water, but it had soaked in.

Laughing Deer said, "Cub and Bear see if you can find some dry kindling. We will have to relight the fire."

"I will help them." As I passed the ditch, I saw that it was half-filled with water. It would gradually drain away over the next days, but the bottom would still be sticky and muddy. On the other hand, if the Penobscot pulled at the stakes they would come out easily.

By late afternoon the debris from the storm had been cleared and we had fires going. Long Stride, one of the scouts with Black Otter, ran in just before dark and hurried to speak with Wandering Moos and Black Bird. I wandered over to listen, "The Penobscot clans are coming. Their scouts are on the other side of the river. Black Otter and Blue Stone watch them."

Wandering Moos looked at Black Bird who asked, "Have they begun to cross yet?"

Long Stride shook his head. "They were looking for a place to cross when Black Otter sent me. He said not to return and when the Penobscot had crossed he would return."

Wandering Moos said, "When did you see them?"

"When the heart of the storm had passed over."

It was a good question and showed that the mind of Wandering Moos was still as sharp as ever. "Then we have time. They may come this night, but I doubt it. We should eat while we can and repair the damage done by the storm."

Black Bird raised his hands and shouted, "Warriors keep your weapons close to hand!"

I returned to the lodge and donned my padded tunic. I had not worn it for some time. Laughing Deer had repaired it. Bear and Cub helped me to slip the byrnie over my head. For the first time in a long time, it felt heavy. I fastened my belt around my waist and slipped the hatchet into it. I called over Runs Far and handed him the wood axe, "Here is a good weapon for you!"

98

He grinned, "The Penobscot will have a shock when I use this!"

I did not put on my helmet nor my bearskin. They could wait and I put them by my shield, spear, bow and arrow. Neither Black Otter nor Blue Stone had returned by the time we ate, and darkness fell. Black Bird had six warriors in the trees. They were five hundred paces from the village and spread out. We watched the forest and listened for the sound of the birds. We heard them and were relieved. It was getting on for the middle of the night and most of the women and children were asleep when the birds stopped, and I drew my sword. There had to be movement in the trees. To my relief, it was Blue Stone and he was accompanied by two of the sentries.

"They have camped on this side of the river. It was swollen by the rains and it took some time. Black Otter watches them. As soon as they break camp he will come."

Brave Eagle and Long Sight joined me as Black Bird said, "One man in three watches. The others sleep."

"We will be a watch of three. Will you watch first, Erik Shaman of the Bear?"

That was the easiest watch, and I shook my head, "I will take the last one."

Long Sight said, "I will wake you." I held out my arms and the two of them pulled my byrnie from me.

My family were asleep as I slipped inside the cosy lodge. I did not snuggle next to Laughing Deer and Little White Dove for I knew I would wake them for I was cold. I slept across the door so that when I was wakened, I would not disturb them.

I dreamed and it was not unexpected.

I was at the falls and the Penobscot were throwing themselves at Arne, Siggi and the others. I was in the water and struggling to get to their side but I could not and then I was falling, falling and I could not stop myself.

"Erik!" Long Sight's whispered words and his hand woke me.

I slipped out of the lodge and stood. I waited until we were close to the trees before we spoke. "The birds and animals still make their noise and there is no sign of Black Otter." I nodded and he slipped off to his own lodge. I donned my bearskin. It was for warmth. The storm had taken away the clouds and it had made for a cold night. Until I had stepped out of the lodge I had not realised. As my eyes adjusted to the dark, I saw the other sentries. They were still as was I. It was movement that alerted an enemy. Black Otter might come when they broke camp but the Penobscot could have sent scouts out without him knowing.

The sun rose quickly and filled the camp with light. All the warriors, who woke with the sun, emerged and looked at the sentries. By the time Wandering Moos had risen, I had donned my byrnie and relit the fire. It was a couple of hours later that Black Otter and the sentries all ran in.

"The Penobscot have broken camp. They are not far behind us!"

Chapter 11

Although we knew this was coming it was gut-wrenching. I donned first my bjorr hat then my helmet and bearskin. I strung my bow and hefted my shield. Black Bird had assigned us our positions. He and I would stand before Wandering Moos and the best warriors would flank us. Runs Far, Long Sight and Black Otter were the closest ones to us. Red Bird organised the boys into two groups and they stood on the flanks. I saw Bear with his hand on Cub's shoulder. I doubted that Cub's arrows would have enough power to penetrate flesh but an arrow coming towards you could be disconcerting and he might get lucky. No boy would be a bystander this day. I watched the brave young archers as they climbed up into the trees. I was nervous for them until I saw that they simply disappeared in the foliage. The only way they would be seen was if a warrior looked up and if he did that then he would be a dead man. I looked along the line of warriors. My shield was the only wooden one that was decorated. I knew that it would attract the attention of their warriors. My spear was embedded in the ground and I would rest my shield against my legs when I used my bow. We waited in silence. Our assumption was that as the enemy had not, we hoped, seen any of our scouts they would assume that we were unprepared. Their scouts had observed our daily life when they had come the previous year and I had surprised one waiting along a path. They would know that at least half of the warriors would be at the beach. They might be surprised that none were foraging in the trees but that could not be helped. Black Bird predicted that they would move as quickly as they could and simply charge us. When they saw the waiting line of warriors it might give them pause for thought but if they halted and waited then they risked our arrows and losing men early.

It was the birds taking to the air which told us they were close. Then the other woodland creatures fled from the mass of men who swept silently through the trees. We remained still and made not a sound. When the first Penobscot was seen it was they who gave their war cry and we stood firm and resolute. This was not the way warriors fought in this new world. They usually screamed, shouted and generally tried to scare their enemies. Black Bird had told the warriors to remain silent in an effort to unnerve them. I did not see Grey Hawk but the feathers which hung from many of the warriors were clearly hawk feathers. I lowered my shield and picked up my bow. I had just nocked an arrow when the enemy screamed as one and they hurtled from the trees. They came in long lines, the fiercer warriors at the fore. This was the way that they fought, a sudden violent attack that was usually met by a similar charge. We were breaking the rules. Wandering Moos apart, every warrior held his bow. My handful of metal tipped arrows would be reserved for their leaders and any shaman they had brought. Brave Eagle thought that it was likely they would bring their own shaman to counter my alleged power.

Their long lines soon saw the ditch and the stakes. The boys and the bows on the side of our line made life hard for them and when they tried to negotiate the ditch it effectively broke up their flank attack. Despite the fact that my sons were in danger, I forced myself to aim at the chief who ran towards me leading his warriors. It was not Grey Hawk and from the snake skins hanging from his belt and hair, I guessed that this was the Clan of the Snake. He had a bone chest protector and that, too, was adorned with snake skins. The bone chest protectors were quite effective against the stone arrows the Mi'kmaq used. He was fifty paces from me when I sent my arrow directly at the target. As I expected it drove through the bone, through his flesh and his own bones and I saw that it buried itself through to the fletch. It would be sticking out of his back. The warrior looked down at the arrow and then pitched forward. It made those around him stop for a moment and the rest of the warriors around me sent their arrows at them.

I nocked a second arrow and when one of the Snake Clan raised his club and screamed, I sent my second arrow to drive through his shoulder and into his neck. The boys in the trees were also having success and some of the Snake Clan hesitated. I did not aim at those but, instead chose a shaman. He had the head of a hawk hanging from his belt and I took him for a member of the Clan of the Hawk. He was racing towards me from my left and had taken two stone-tipped arrows on his shield. He was twenty paces from me when I loosed my third arrow. It drove through the shield he held up and, from the blood, his arm, before embedding itself in his skull. Their reckless bravery had brought them to within a few paces of us and I sent my fourth into the chest of a warrior before dropping the bow. As I did so two arrows struck me. I saw as I looked up, that the two warriors thought they had killed me. They screamed and raised their bows. One arrow had stuck in my bearskin and the other had hit my byrnie and stuck in the padded undergarment I wore. When I bent to pick up my shield and my spear their faces fell and then Mi'kmaq arrows ended their lives.

I knew from Brave Eagle that the Penobscot would not be afraid to die if they could kill a great warrior. I was not just a great warrior, I was a shaman and a demon. Five of them who had survived the arrow storm and remained unscathed hurled themselves at me. I thrust my spear and took one in the chest but the others all hit me with stone spearheads and clubs. My shield bore the brunt, but one spear managed to scratch my right arm. It encouraged them for they drew blood. I pulled back and thrust again. They were so closely packed together that I could not miss and a second died. Wandering Moos was behind me and it was his stone-headed spear which killed a third while Runs Far swung the axe I had loaned him and drove through the skull of one warrior and then the neck of the last of the five.

Some of the Clan of the Snake had managed to cross the ditch, and as they had been told the boys there fell back. The women then began to hurl their stones to crash into the enemy faces and chests. The Penobscot clan had never experienced this before and they were daunted but it would only be a matter of time before they used their bows against the women.

"Long Sight! Take some men and turn the Clan of the Snake!" Black Bird had seen the danger. We had discussed this possibility before the battle and Long Sight and his men left the line and ran at the Penobscot to hit them with large wooden shields. The Penobscot shields were a defensive weapon. The heavier shields we had made were both offensive and defensive as some of the enemy discovered when their faces and skulls were smashed by the heavy wooden shields. Stunned, some fell into the stake filled ditch while others were easily slain as they lay prostrate.

The movement, however, of Long Sight and the others created a gap and a spear was thrown at me. It did not hit my mail, but my arm and I rammed my spear into the soft soil. It was too unwieldy a weapon for such close combat and I drew my sword. As luck would have it the warrior who had thrown his spear and seen me drop my spear thought to take advantage and he ran at me with his stone club. In drawing my sword I effectively brought it up to hack into his arm and then under his chin. I sliced off half of his face. I blocked a blow from another club as two arrows thudded into my shield. As we had expected, I was the focus of the attack. It allowed other warriors to have greater success than they might have expected. The exception was Wandering Moos who still stood behind me. The spear which was thrust at me was easily deflected by my sword, but it drove into the leg of Wandering Moos. That angered me and I hacked so hard at the warrior that my sword half severed his head. I stepped to the side to place my body before Wandering Moos who had staggered forward.

I heard him say, "This is a good day to die!" He moved as quickly as his old and now crippled body would allow and he thrust his spear into the side of the head of a Snake warrior. Even as the Penobscot fell two others had rammed their spears at him. I managed to slice one spear in two but the other was enough to drive into Wandering Moos' chest. I punched one in the face with my shield. The metal boss shattered his nose and I thrust my sword into the side of the other. As the one with the broken nose fell, I smashed the edge of my shield into his skull. I found myself in the midst of Hawk and Snake warriors. I slashed and swung with my sword and I blocked with my shield but there were too many of them. I felt stone hatchets and spears ram into my bearskin and mail byrnie. They did not break flesh, but I felt a rib break. When a spear hit my knee, I felt my leg buckle. It was at that moment that Grey Hawk seized his opportunity. He wielded an antler axe fashioned from a Horse Deer and there was a large stone at the end. He hit my shield so hard that it numbed my arm and it began to droop. He had quick reactions and brought up the club again. I managed to block it with my sword and, in the process, cut deeply into his chest but other warriors had taken advantage too and a club smacked into my head. If I had not worn the bearskin and helmet, I would have been dead but, as it was, I was stunned. I managed to stab the one who had hit my head, but I saw Grey Hawk take his club in two hands and begin a long wide swing at my head.

Brave Eagle saved me, again. He was already blood-spattered from all the Penobscot he had killed but he rammed his broken spear up under the right arm of the war chief. I saw the stone head emerge at the shoulder but, remarkably the chief did not die. Brave Eagle reached over to my belt and in one motion took my seax and slashed across the throat of Grey Hawk. I saw the surprised expression on the Penobscot's face and then his body collapsed. Now that the two enemy chiefs were dead and their attack had been blunted, most of the warriors turned and fled. That was not surprising as the best and bravest warriors had been in the first wave and they had largely died. Brave Eagle did not relinquish my seax but led the charge after the enemy warriors. Even had I wished to I could not have moved for blood was oozing from my leg. I dropped to one knee and Wandering Moos looked up at me.

"I go to join my ancestors, Erik, Shaman of the Bear. I can hold my head up high for we defeated three times our number this day. The clan will be safe with Black Bird." Doe Eyes ran up and fell across his body. "Do not mourn, my wife. Black Bird will care for you and…" He died. I felt the same as when my father had died. It had been in battle too.

Laughing Deer, Bear and Cub ran to me, "Husband, you are hurt!"

"I am alive, and I will not die."

The only Penobscot who remained were their dead. I looked around and saw that at least fifteen of our warriors lay dead. It was too high a cost.

"Bear, take off my bearskin. Cub, remove my helmet." As soon as the helmet came off the blood began to ooze down the side of my head.

Laughing Deer shook her head, "Boys, take off his mail. He may have more wounds."

It was as they took off my mail that I saw it was ruined. The clubs and spears had managed to break some of the repairs I had made and also to create holes. I would not be able to wear it again, at least not as a mail shirt. Once the weight came off me I fell on to my back. "Bear, fetch your father some ale." I heard a cry; it was a child. My wife's voice was calm, "Cub, go and amuse your sister. I have a husband to save!" She took off my padded undershirt and I saw that not only had a rib been broken, the red and black area told me that I had suffered a more serious hurt than I had thought for there was more damage beneath the skin. I laid back as she began to tend to me. The only other men left in the village were the wounded, the rest were chasing Penobscot through the trees.

I closed my eyes and Laughing Deer shouted, "Do not sleep! Stay awake. Bear!"

"I come, mother."

"Cradle his head, speak with him and let him sip it."

Her voice told me that she was concerned and that my wounds were bad ones. Nearby I heard Doe Eyes as she wept for her dead husband. That he had welcomed death was of little comfort to me. I had liked the old man and he was one of the reasons I might have stayed in the village. Grey Hawk was dead, but would others come to seek revenge or perhaps they would come simply to test their courage? I no longer had a byrnie. My magic was gone.

My son tried to jabber encouragement at me, but he was terrified. I could hear it in his voice and when he held the skin for me to drink I saw that his hands were shaking.

"Bear, fetch a brand from the fire. The wound in your father's knee will not stop bleeding."

I could not help smiling for it was I who had taught her how to heal bleeding wounds with fire. I knew it would hurt but I also knew it might save my life. This battle had been even harder than the one against the clan of Laughing Wolf. I heard women wailing and knew that others had just died of their wounds. Wounds inflicted by stone clubs could not be healed. Bones could be crushed, and the injuries caused beneath the skin could not be tended. It was why Laughing Deer was so upset.

105

She had seen the reddened bruised flesh and she worried. I smelled the smoke from the brand. I closed my eyes for I knew that seeing the flame grow closer would make the pain worse.

"Hold his arms at his side. Your father is a brave man, but his body may jerk." I grunted as Laughing Deer knelt on my good leg.

I felt Bear's hands on my arms, "Do not fear, father. I will hold you."

"I know."

Even though the two of them were holding me the pain of the burning brand made my back arch. The stink of burning hair and flesh filled the air. "Give him more ale." As the skin was held to my lips, I heard the relief in her voice as she said, "The bleeding has stopped. Now let me look at your side." I saw her peer at the area around my ribs and then she began to look for something, "Where is your seax? I wish to release the blood."

"Brave Eagle took it. Use the hatchet. The blade is as sharp, and I did not use it."

"Bear, light another brand, I may have to seal this wound too."

When he had gone, she leaned in and whispered, "This wound looks even more serious than the knee. There is a dent in your side the size of my fist."

"It was a club. Do your best."

"I will and I would find a home without the threat of war. The family do not need this. Bear and Cub could have lost their lives too."

"But they did not, and the spirits watched over them."

"I will make the cut."

The hatchet was sharp and I felt no pain at all. The ribs ached and that was painful enough but I felt blood. "I will let the blood come forth. If it does not stop then I will seal it."

I saw Bear appear and his face told me that he was shocked by what he saw. I managed a wan smile, "It does not hurt, Bear. It just looks bad."

My wife's voice showed her relief, "It is bad, but the bleeding has stopped." She shook her head, "The ribs are broken and jagged. What should I do?"

Gytha had told me how to heal broken bones but I did not relish the cure. "You must join the broken ends of the bones. They will knit together."

"But it will hurt you!"

I nodded, "Bear, take my arms and hold them tightly. Put the handle of my hatchet in my mouth lest I bite off my tongue, Laughing Deer. Whatever you have to do then do it!"

106

Bear put the handle in my mouth and then held my hands. I looked at my wife and nodded. Her hands went down and then I felt such a pain as I had never experienced. This time my body told me it had endured enough, and all went black.

When I woke, it was to darkness. It was not like the blackness of oblivion but the darkness of our lodge. As my eyes became accustomed to the dark I recognised where I was. I almost forgot about my wounds for I tried to raise myself on my elbow. The pain which coursed through my body made me fall back and I could not help but make a small cry.

Laughing Deer's head appeared in the entrance, "You are awake! Do not move or you will undo all my work."

"What time is it?"

"It is night and the men have begun to return. They chased the Penobscot across the river and they have gone."

I closed my eyes again, "Good and let us hope that this is an end to the war."

"The men all speak of your courage, husband but I pray you do not have to prove it again to them. You will be lucky if we can walk properly when it is time to head to the winter camp."

"Perhaps we will not."

"We will have time to speak of such things now do not move and I will send Bear and Cub in. Little White Dove needs my attention now."

Black Bird came to see me, and he shook his head when he saw me, "My friend, I feel ashamed. You and Wandering Moos drew all the enemy to you, and we suffered not a scratch. Wandering Moos died and from what I saw you were close to death. The clan owes you much." He handed me the seax, "Brave Eagle thinks that this is magic. He has never killed so many warriors in so short a space of time."

"Are they gone?"

He looked at me and looked away. I knew the answer before he made up a story. "It will be many years before the Penobscot risk raiding the Mi'kmaq again."

I rolled my eyes and shook my head, "Then they will come again."

His silence filled my lodge and then he said, "We have destroyed the best warriors in three clans. They will come but not for many years."

I sighed, "Then we need to tell them that I am dead, or I have left and vanished back to the east."

"How can we do that?"

"There will be a way but if they believe I am not here then there is no reason to attack. They will have lost no honour. I cannot travel yet. Laughing Deer tells me that it will be a moon or two before I can move easily. We have time to plan."

"I do not want you to leave. None of the clan does."

"Tell that to the widows of the men who died and their children. They were part of my family and I grieve that they are dead. I do not wish to go but if I do not then this will be repeated and next time I may not be so lucky. I will stay with you until I can move and then… well I shall decide then."

Chapter 12

It took a whole moon before we left before I was able to walk.
Laughing Deer kept a close eye on me and the rest of the clan joined
her. I was a lucky charm, and they did not wish to lose me. I used a
stick at first but even then Bear and Cub had to come with me so that I
did not fall over. I spent the last month of summer finishing the snekke.
The hard part was getting down to the beach. Once there, others did the
hard work for me. Runs Far happily hewed a tree for me as I needed
more wood for the snekke. He had enjoyed using the axe in battle and
this was his way of repaying me. I made a spare mast and crosstree
which I laid on the mast fish with the others. Then I took the boys to the
pine trees which Runs Far had hewn. They dug the roots clear and
Black Bird and other warriors came to help dig them out so that we
could make the pine tar. They were fascinated by the process. Having
seen me do it before, Bear and Cub were able to help me make the oven
without too many instructions and when the tar trickled out down the
channel it was as though I had performed magic once more. The
warriors were impressed. Once we had collected all the pine tar, we
sealed the snekke inside and out. We wasted not a drop of the tar and,
after we had recoated *'Ada'* as well, added the last of it to the
figurehead. When we were ready to leave, after the warriors of the clan
had helped me to move the snekke above the high water line, I wrapped
the snekke as carefully as a mother would a newborn. Now was not the
time but come the next summer then we would leave the clan. We had
the winter to work out our destination. As we packed up the lodge I
found myself looking around it as though for the last time. Was I
doomed to never stay in any one place longer than a few years?
Orkneyjar, Larswick, the Land of Ice and Fire, Bear Island; all had been
temporary and then I had moved on. Was this my fate?

Brave Eagle was still with us. He had no way of getting home for he
would either have to take a birch bark boat and risk the ocean or face a
sea of enemies through which he would have to pass by land. He was
the one who pulled the sledge. I could walk but I still needed a stick.
Since the battle, he had spoken to me about the seax. He was both
fascinated and amazed that even a boy might own such a deadly
weapon. If I had a second, I would have given it to him. He had asked
when he visited in the evening if he could hold the sword. I knew that
he admired it. We became close, as close as he was to Long Sight and

when he returned to his tribe then I would be sad. We had spoken of his return and, as we trudged north to our winter home we did so again.

"Before we left to rescue our families, we helped the women and the other survivors to replant the fields and repair the lodges. They will be there still. When I leave your people I will return to the clan and try to find a way to rescue my family. They will be alive, and I am their chief. I made an oath that I would either rescue them or die trying."

I nodded, "It may be easier now that Grey Hawk and his best warriors are dead."

He shook his head, "Do not believe it. When I announced to the Penobscot that I was still alive, on the river as we fled, I ensured that my family would be punished. I knew it when I shouted but it had to be done or they might have caught us."

It had been a selfless gesture and I now appreciated the act even more than I had at the time.

"I will get back to them, but winter is not the time to do so. Next summer, when your clan returns to the coast, I will have prepared all that I need for the journey. I will have worked out how I will do this. There is little point in throwing my life away before I can even try to get to my family. I should like to see my wife and grandchildren again."

Long Sight was already sad that his friend was leaving. He had lost two other friends in the battle and although we had lost fewer men than might have been expected the losses were keenly felt. The young warriors in the clan had now been blooded. The heroes of the trees had all, amazingly, survived and were rightly lauded. Their arrows had killed more than twenty Penobscot and weakened their attack. They, in turn, were keen to have arrows like mine for they had seen them penetrate whole bodies and when we recovered them, they gave them the same reverence with which Runs Far had given to the axe and Brave Eagle to the seax. Had Fótr and the others left more such weapons then who knew what might have been. Perhaps we would have lost fewer men.

When we reached the winter camp and after we had repaired the damage from the summer storms, I put my mind to the byrnie. If we had been at Larswick then I might have melted more iron and made mail rings to repair it. I did not have the luxury of more iron and so I decided to adapt it. The worst of the damage was to the part below my waist. Using the hatchet I hacked away the worst of the damaged byrnie and used some of the rings to make good the other damage. It meant that if I had to fight again my body above the waist would have protection. When the winter snows came then I would make a weaponsmith workshop and melt down the wrecked metal. I would make arrowheads and, perhaps, a knife for Brave Eagle. It would not be a seax, I did not have the skill, but I thought I could make a narrow-pointed dagger. I told no one of my plan for I did not wish to disappoint any.

I went with Bear and Cub to hunt the bjorr and the deer. When the other warriors found the trail of a herd of moos then we organised a hunt. This time it was more than a hunt for food and skins. This hunt would honour our dead chief. Wandering Moos had been named for the Moos he had found and killed whilst alone. It had been a remarkable achievement. I let Brave Eagle use my bow and metal arrows while I took my spear. I did not expect to be able to move very quickly for my knee, whilst much better than it had been, was still weaker than I wished. My spear would afford protection for Bear and Cub. This would be their first clan hunt and it was important that they knew what to do. The boys who came were there to fill the gaps between the warriors. Our line of warriors would approach the Moos so that we could smell them, but they would be unaware of us. The aim was to kill as many of the beasts as we could but always trying to get the weaker ones so that the herd would be stronger. The leader, the bull, would soon be fighting other bulls for the leadership of the herd. If he was killed, then a younger one might bring new blood. The boys' task was to send their arrows into the moos hit by the arrows of the warriors. They would not kill but they would weaken.

It was a large herd and that meant we had to approach carefully. There were more than forty animals gathered in the clearing close to one of the waters. It took most of the morning for us to get into position. I stood just in front of Bear and Cub. They were eager to use their bows. In the battle with the Penobscot, they had hit the enemy warriors but not made a kill. Since then they had practised as much as they could and now had a greater range. I had promised them metal arrows once they were able to hit a target a hundred paces away. That day was not far off.

When we were in position Black Bird drew back on his bow and the others all copied him. It was inevitable that some animals would be hit by multiple arrows but, equally, more than half of the herd would be safe for they were on the far side of the animals who were closest to us. I saw one old cow hit by four arrows and even though she was a tough old animal she managed but two steps before she fell. Others managed to run a little and they were the ones the rest of the hunters loosed their arrows at. I saw that Bear and Cub had both struck an animal and that was good. The bull was hit by at least five arrows but most of them had been sent by boys and they barely penetrated its thick hide. Angered by the insect bites of the arrows and protective of his cows he turned and charged us. Some of the hunters aimed for his head and that was a mistake for there his skull was the thickest. Brave Eagle sent one of my metal tipped arrows and it struck him in the shoulder. It did not slow him and, worse, drove him towards us for Brave Eagle was standing just a few paces from me. The Powhatan warrior then compounded his mistake by searching in his arrow bag for another metal tipped arrow and he did not find one immediately.

"Get behind me!"

Bear and Cub obeyed me and I braced my spear against my good leg and held the shaft tightly. The bull had courage and, snorting and spitting, came at me. Arrows thudded into his side but they did not slow him. He struck my spear, and his speed did two things, it drove the spear deep within his own body and his antlers knocked me to the ground. I let go of my spear and, even as I was falling, held my hands out to protect my sons. His antler saved my life for although it raked my face it knocked me to the side and he thundered on for four more paces and then collapsed, dead.

Black Bird ran to me, "You are hurt?"

I used the back of my hand to wipe away the blood. My face was cut and would be scarred but it was not life-threatening. "I am good. Bear? Cub?"

The two of them pulled themselves up and they were grinning. Bear was covered in blood but from his grin, I knew that it belonged to the bull moos. Black Bird smiled, "You have your name now, Moos Blood and it is an honourable name for you and your brother stood by your father and did not flee."

Cub pouted, "Should I not have a name then, Chief Black Bird?"

"You have no blood but you have courage, the courage of a bear, Brave Cub!"

Both my sons were happy. Each thought their name was better than the other but the warriors knew that the two had earned them. Brave Eagle was most upset because of his failure. "My first arrow should have killed." He went to the bull and pointed to the arrowhead which had emerged from the animal. "I aimed badly and should have gone for the chest. I am sorry Erik."

"No matter and at least the head is not damaged."

In all, we had slain nine animals and that was enough. The herd would now move away from this place and we would not have another chance to hunt them. Warriors might hunt the deer but it would not need all the clan's hunters. We took out the guts from the animals and left them. We would take out the heart, liver, and kidneys back at the camp. Using my hatchet I cut down some saplings and using vines we made litters to carry the animals back. Even the boys were used so great was the catch. When we reached the village then the women stopped what they were doing. The moos would require everyone to help. The animals were skinned, and the hooves removed to make glue. The meat was taken from the bones and the bones put on to boil. Their goodness would be used to make soups and stews while the cleaned bones and antlers would be used as tools. The bull's head would be cleaned and when we returned to the summer camp would be placed on Wandering Moos' grave. While they worked on the carcasses Moos Blood and Brave Cub could not help but tell their mother of their naming and how I had almost been killed by a moos. She gave me an angry look and I shrugged, "I was not killed, and the boys are safe. Perhaps I should not hunt and sit here with the other old men and let warriors risk their lives for me!"

She shook her head for she knew I was right, "You take too many chances!"

"I stood there watching, Laughing Deer. The bull came for me!"

That night I was given the roast heart of the moos. It was an honour, but it was too rich for me to consume alone and I shared it with my shield brothers, Black Bird, Runs Far, Brave Eagle and Long Sight. They were honoured by my gesture and it made us closer. The winter camp, despite the weather, was a hive of activity for we had many things to do. The bjorr and moos had given us furs, skins and bone which had to be worked. Each day fish were trapped and had to be dried or cooked. However, I had a task which none other could do. I had metal to melt.

Moos Blood and Brave Cub helped me, but I had an audience for the warriors were keen to see this magic. I had made charcoal to make a hotter fire and now that we had killed the moos, I made bellows from the stomach and bladders of the bull. I had made the moulds for the arrows and the knife from wood lined with river clay. The arrowheads were my own design. They were slightly narrower than the ones I had brought from the east and that was because I had less metal to use. The barb too was not as pronounced as I was used to. I hoped that the arrow would penetrate further. I planned on giving one arrowhead to each warrior. When I left the clan it would be something to remember me by. The knife would be as long as the seax but being narrow pointed would use less metal and would have two edges to sharpen.

The hardest part was melting the mail rings. The pot I used was partly broken but still had a spout. As we made the fire as hot as we could an audience of the warriors who had not gone hunting gathered. They had never seen metal being worked. I had made a pair of mittens from bjorr skin covered with moos hide. I would have to work quickly but I hoped that they would stop my hands from being burned. It seemed to take longer to melt the metal and I feared that the pot might break. I said a silent prayer to Thor, and he must have smiled on my request for as the metal melted the pot remained whole. I worked quickly to pour the molten metal into the many moulds I had made. I had made more than I needed. The gloves worked to an extent but by the time I poured the last three the heat was beginning to burn the hide and the fur. As soon as I could I pulled my hands from the mittens and plunged my hands into river water.

The warriors gathered around the moulds, "Do not touch them they must harden."

Black Bird shook his head, "This is indeed magic. The shirt was solid enough to withstand the blow of a club and then became as water and now you say that it will become hard again?"

I nodded, "When it is then I will sharpen the arrowheads and the knife. It will take many days, but the result will be worth it."

I knew they were eager to see the results but I sent them away. I did not want my work undone.

Now that they had their names the boys needed an amulet. In Moos Blood's case, it was made of some of the bull moos' teeth. Drilling them took a long time. In Brave Cub's case, I gave him two of the bear claws from my skin. He was able to drill those faster. It kept them occupied and made them patient. It also stopped them from interfering as I sharpened and polished the arrowheads and knife. Once I had shaken them in a bag of sand to remove the rough edges I sat with my whetstone and sharpened them all. They were not identical and two of them had less metal and no barbs. It did not matter for I would give those two to Moos Blood and Brave Cub. When they were complete, I went around the camp one evening to give one to every warrior. I would only have four left to me but I knew that someday I would have to melt the rest of the byrnie and would be able to make more. Each warrior was touched by the gesture and I was given a gift in return. It was bad luck not to do so.

When I gave Brave Eagle his knife, he was almost speechless, "This gift is too much. I have nothing to give you in return!"

I smiled, "This is a repayment for my life. You have saved it twice, at least, you owe me nothing for this."

He nodded, "I will make a handle from the antler of the moos." He touched it reverently, "How do I keep it sharp?"

I took out my whetstone, "You search for this rock. I have not seen it here but there must be rocks like this. Until you find them then used my stone."

For the next days, the warriors made an arrow for the head. They chose the straightest and best wood. Hawks and eagles were hunted for their feathers and when they were completed and decorated with symbols of the clan each warrior showed them off. They would be used but selectively. All the warriors knew the power of a metal tipped arrow but also realised that when they were used there was a risk that they might be lost. Here they were special. In the land of my birth, they were taken for granted.

It was about that time that Laughing Deer discovered that she was carrying another child. Little White Dove could now toddle and was able to eat solid food. Laughing Deer was pleased that she had another child within her. "While I am young it is good that we are able to have children. Poor Doe Eyes only had one who grew to manhood and now she is alone."

It was true. Black Bird had no such problem for he had four sons and one was on the cusp of becoming a warrior. Some of the women of the clan appeared to be unlucky or perhaps their version of the Norns were spinning for there were two sisters in the clan and one had but one child and the other, although a year younger, had four. *Wyrd*!

Of course, the pregnancy caused a problem too. We would not be able to leave the clan until the baby was born. Indeed, it might delay it for another month after the birth. Laughing Deer was philosophical about it, "Whenever we leave there will be problems and if we stay then there will be problems too."

It was on the shortest day that we had something else to celebrate. Stands Alone had become a woman and she and White Arrow's son, Grey Squirrel, were married on the shortest day. It was a relief to Laughing Deer for it meant that her sister was now the responsibility of Grey Squirrel. It also provided a celebration in the depths of winter when the snow lay on the ground. We made ale and we ate some of the preserved moos meat. It was a fine feast, and we were content.

My knee had healed by then although the scar on my face still looked angry. I went in the steam hut once a week and while that helped my knee it did nothing for the scar on my face. Little White Dove was not afraid of it, rather she found it amusing to play with it as well as my beard. The boys, Moos Blood and Brave Cub, were growing. Moos Blood was almost eleven summers and Brave Cub had recently turned six. Two more summers would see my eldest become a warrior and already his body was growing into that of a young man. He was now

115

more than a head taller than Brave Cub and now came up almost to my shoulder. Within a year he would be taller than his mother.

When I had given the knife to Brave Eagle, I had seen his envious look. One day, as we returned from the bjorr lodge with three bjorr to skin and to eat I said, "You know, Moos Blood and Brave Cub, that when you become warriors, I will give you weapons." They both looked up eagerly. "Perhaps I will melt my byrnie to do so. What weapons would you have?"

Moos Blood answered so quickly that I knew he had thought about it, "A hatchet like yours!"

Brave Cub nodded, "And I would have a knife like that you gave to Brave Eagle."

"I thought, Moos Blood, that you would have wished a knife too."

"If I could have two then I would but a hatchet is a useful tool and the flat head is handy."

"Then, when you are warriors, that is what I shall give to you!"

Chapter 13

I found myself, as we prepared to leave the winter camp, looking at it with sadness. I would never return here. This would be another home I would not see again. I felt the same about it as I did Bear Island. I had been glad to leave my other three homes, but I was leaving this one reluctantly. I know that I should have been used to it for we had made this journey several times but when it was the last one you looked at everything with new eyes. Neither Laughing Deer nor myself had told anyone else, including the boys, of our decision and it was something I dreaded. It was made worse by the fact that Moos Blood noticed my melancholy and asked me about it. I did something I did not enjoy, I lied to him!

Although I was able to pull the sledge Brave Eagle helped me again. As we walked and camped together, I asked him about his plans. "It is time for me to return to my own people. My family have been prisoners for more than two years and they might think I have forgotten them."

"It is a long journey!"

"Perhaps I might ask if I can sail *'Ada'*." None had used the old snekke since I had built *'Gytha'* but she was still seaworthy and recently enjoyed a coat of pine tar.

"You are more than welcome to her, but can you sail her?"

He smiled, "I think, Erik, Shaman of the Bear that I would need lessons from you."

I did not say so but that was not as easy as he thought. Perhaps that was my fault for making it look so easy. He had seen Moos Blood sailing her too and must have thought that if a boy could sail it then so could he. He did not know that Moos Blood had been sailing since he could walk and, in his body, ran my blood, the blood of Erik the Navigator.

"I will teach you!"

As usual, the lodges at the summer camp had been damaged by winter storms and animals. Although we were leaving soon, we would have to repair ours. The difference was that Moos Blood was now able to help me and Brave Cub had become the one who watched out for Little White Dove so that she did not injure herself. It took just two days to make our home habitable again and then we descended to the beach. *'Ada'* had been neglected for almost a year apart from the belated coating of pine tar and if Brave Eagle intended to sail her she had to be the priority. Brave Eagle helped and we repaired the timber which joined the two hulls together. That had always been the weakness of the boat. We used a deerskin for the sail and although not as good as a woven one it was durable. A week after we had begun, he was ready for his first lesson. I left Moos Blood and Brave Cub to work on *'Gytha'*. We had moved her from the beach and moored her in the water, but she needed her sail to be fitted. I was confident that Moos Blood could do that and, in any case, even if he made a mistake it was easily remedied. I took us away from the shore and the other birch bark boats. Then we had the tricky task of changing places. It was good practice for Brave Eagle, and we managed it. I let him sail the snekke in a straight line first. The wind was with us and it meant he did not need to bother about the sail.

He was grinning, "This is easy, Erik!"

"Wait until you have to turn or the wind changes and then speak!"

I had him turn before Bear Island. I intended to take him past Horse Deer Island. Here we were sheltered by the island and the waves were small. He managed the first turn but when I asked him, as we neared Horse Deer Island, to make a second turn he made a move which was too extreme and I felt the snekke begin to capsize! I threw myself at the other hull and my weight made us level out. Brave Eagle looked terrified.

I tried to smile but it was hard, "Little moves are better than larger ones. Let us try that again."

By the time it was time to return he had learned to sail in a straight line and make a few gentle turns. He had even reefed the sail once, but I knew that it would be a long summer! As we hauled the snekke out of the water I said, "We will try again the day after tomorrow. I need to take *'Gytha'* and to fish."

"Could I come with you? Now I know what to look for it will help me."

"Of course." I was happy to do so for it meant we could head out to sea and catch larger fish. Moos Blood had grown but he would struggle to land a large fish.

All of us were excited as we left the shore. We were sailing the finished snekke and testing her in the seas beyond the island. Moos Blood and Brave Cub sat at the prow so that their keen eyes could spot fish and Brave Eagle sat close by the mast fish alternately watching me and searching for fish. It was a good day for all of us, the warriors, the boys and the boat were in harmony. The snekke slipped through the water as though we were one. We leapt beyond Bear Island and I saw the grey backs of the large fish. They were almost as long as we were but I did not fear them for Gytha was with us.

118

The waves were slightly larger than they had been in the sheltered bay but we still had a stable platform from which to fish. We had four stone-tipped spears with us. They had been captured after the Penobscot raid and with a rope attached could be used to spear larger fish and pull them back towards the boat. As the wind was in our favour I went after the four or five grey-backed whales that were heading north.

"Do not go for a big one, Brave Eagle. They could pull us under. Aim for the smallest one you can. Moos Blood, when the spear has been thrown then tie it to the figurehead. Brave Cub, have a second one ready."

There is an art to throwing a spear from a moving snekke and Brave Eagle did not have it at first. He threw and missed. My eldest son was quick thinking and he pulled back on the rope and retrieved it. Brave Cub handed a second spear to the Powhatan and he steadied himself. The small whales had turned, and it took some moments for me to adjust the sail and steering board so that we were on their trail again.

"This time I will try to get closer to them." I remembered when we had hunted the larger whales and we used barbed spears. The stone spears might not be able to kill quickly enough. I had seen whales dive deep!

His second throw was better for I had managed to get within three paces of the huge beast. The spear stuck in and I saw blood but I could also see part of the stone head. Brave Cub had the spear in Brave Eagle's hand before Moos Blood had wrapped the rope around the prow. The second spear appeared to have gone deeper for I could not see the spearhead. Brave Eagle wrapped the rope around the prow and the two of them held on to the rope as the whale tried to escape. I remembered the hunt when we had used the drekar. This was both easier and more frightening. It was easier for I was closer to the whales and could predict their movement easier. It was scarier for we were much smaller than the drekar and I feared we might be dragged under.

"Brave Cub, have the hatchet ready to sever the ropes if I give the command!"

"Aye, father!"

Although the stricken animal thrashed around it did not appear to wish to dive and for that I was grateful. He was, however, taking us out to sea. It was a brave beast but, gradually its thrashing became less violent until it became still. I remembered how sharks had been attracted by the smell of blood when we had hunted the whales with the drekar.

"I will turn and when I do so then pull the whale as close to the snekke as you can. Have the other spears ready, Brave Eagle, in case sharks come for the carcass."

As I turned, I saw that the islands were just dots on the horizon. The turn enabled the three of them to secure the whale to the side. It was at least as long as the snekke and I knew we would have to crab our way back. Brave Eagle's face was filled with wonder. I doubt that he had ever seen such a huge beast. It dwarfed even the bull moos we had slain. "What kind of creature is this?"

"It is a whale, but it looks to be a kind I have not seen before. My people and I hunted ones that were twice as long as this one. The bones and the flesh from this beast will give many tools and feed the clan for a week or more. We were lucky!"

Our luck continued for while our progress was slow the sharks did not come. It was late afternoon when we passed Bear Island. Black Otter and the other fishermen came next to the snekke when they saw our catch. Black Otter shook his head, "My son, see the difference in fish." He held up a long silver fish as long as his leg, "I was proud of this one until I saw the one Erik, Shaman of the Bear had caught!"

The birch bark boats landed before we did and the warriors helped us to drag the carcass ashore. "We cannot carry this to the camp. We will have to butcher it here. Brave Cub, fetch my sword."

As he raced off I used my seax to try to hack through the tough skin. Even Brave Eagle's new knife struggled. Black Otter shook his head, "Even if we caught one of these we could not get into its flesh!"

We made little headway until I used my sword. I was able to make great swings and hacked deeply into the flesh. I made squares on one side which enabled Black Otter and Brave Eagle to use their blades to remove the squares from the animal. I then moved to the other side. We found that once we had broken through the skins then the sharper stone knives could also help to remove the flesh. Warriors and women came to carry the flesh up to the camp. They had never cooked it before and I was not sure if preserving it with salt would change the taste. If nothing else we could gorge on it for a couple of days! Fires were lit so that I could continue my work on the animal. Even when the flesh was stripped the bones took every warrior to carry up to the camp.

Black Bird greeted me, "Erik, this is most unexpected. There is so much food here."

"Have you tasted it yet?"

He nodded, "My wife cut up the first square which was brought and she cooked it. It is a sweet and soft meat." He held up the square of skin. "And the skin is tough. We can use it for mockasins. Are there many such beasts out there?"

"There are but they range far into the sea. We were lucky. I doubt that we will be this lucky again for a while but we will search."

Laughing Deer had also been given one of the first pieces of flesh and when we reached my lodge she had a stew ready for us. "I was not sure how to cook this, so I put in some moos flesh."

"It is a fish, but the meat is more like that of a land animal. We will be eating it for days and you have the opportunity to try out different things."

The boys, of course, loved the taste because they had helped to hunt it. The stew Laughing Deer had made was also delicious. Even Little White Dove enjoyed it and she was a fussy eater. The next day, when the bones had been boiled and cleaned the sea's bounty was shared with the clan. Some of the larger bones could be made into axes and there were so many of them that every warrior was able to choose a good one. The tough skin was hard to cut and my metal weapons were put to constant use cutting the skin to shape. Holes were made by drilling into the flesh. The flesh was waterproof, and I made capes for my family. Because of my hacking into the flesh, they were not as good as a sealskin one and I resolved that if I was ever lucky enough to find another, I would be more cautious when it came to cutting it up! The result was that a week went by before I could give another lesson to Brave Eagle. At the end of three days, it became clear to both of us that while he could sail *'Ada'* in the sheltered bay he would not be able to do as he wanted to and sail back to his people. He retreated into himself and took to wandering deep into the forest. I think I knew his mood. He was having to make a difficult decision.

It was about the time of the longest day when Laughing Deer gave birth to our third son. He was born with a mass of yellow hair and his name was obvious to all, Golden Bear. Both my other sons liked it and it seemed appropriate. Laughing Deer had a harder time with our fourth child and unlike the first three, she was not up and about as quickly. Stands Alone came to help us. She was able to care for Little White Dove as well as helping her sister. The first two weeks of Golden Bear's life saw perfect weather for all of us and it seemed a propitious start to my son's life.

It was when Brave Eagle was returning from one of his forays into the forest that he found Long Walking and the warriors of the Clan of the Otter. They had been sent by Mighty Water. We were pleased to see our friends, but I knew that their visit was ominous. We were hospitable and served them the last of the whale meat which we discovered could be salted. The food and the new tools they saw initiated much talk as we ate.

Long Walking nodded to me, "Erik, Shaman of the Bear, you are the reason for our visit. When the Penobscot fled they passed through our lands. We did not hinder them for while we do not like them, they are our neighbours, and the tribe is a powerful one. We were rewarded by a visit from warriors sent by Black Eagle. We were told that his warriors had decided that the Mi'kmaq were now too strong a tribe for the Penobscot to attack but that there were many warriors who sought the honour of slaying the Shaman of the Bear and taking his shiny stick. They believe that your power comes from the shiny stick. You can expect warriors to come and to try to end your life. They do not believe that you are dead. They think you a demon who can only be killed by a brave warrior. These will not be warbands or clans but they will be single, probably young warriors who will travel here to kill the demon who has destroyed three clans of warriors. I am sorry."

Black Bird nodded, "Let them come and their heads will adorn our lodges."

I saw the look on the face of Long Walking and knew that he doubted our ability to keep me safe. He said nothing.

I turned to Black Bird, "Would you want us to keep men guarding the camp as we did last year? Would you want to look over your shoulder for these foolish warriors? I thank Long Walking and I will speak with my family and then Black Bird when I have had time to think about these things."

Runs Far said, incredulously, "Surely you are not afraid of these warriors! You are the mightiest warrior in this land."

I pointed first to my scarred face and then my knee, "These wounds should tell you that being a good warrior does not make a man immortal. The wounds I had after the last battle took time to heal and if it was not for the skill of Laughing Deer then I would be dead."

"They are badges of honour!"

"Which I would rather do without. I am not a warrior; I am Erik the Navigator. I thank you for your words Runs Far, but I will have to wrestle with this problem myself!"

Then began an argument between the other warriors which lasted until I rose and went to bed. Some of the clan were emboldened by our victories and some saw no problem in warriors coming to hunt me. Others like Black Bird and Long Sight understood that the burden would be too hard for me. It was a pointless argument which is why I rose and left. None of their solutions would work. The only one which stood a chance was mine. I would have to leave. If the young warriors came to the camp and did not see the demon with the fiery head then they would return home, I hoped, and tell others that I was no longer with the Mi'kmaq. That left me with the dilemma of where we would go.

I lay with Laughing Deer in my arms, for Little White Dove now slept between her protective brothers and Golden Bear, having just been fed, slept peacefully and we spoke quietly of the problem. She knew that we would have to leave, and the choices were clear. "Husband, you are a navigator and that means we use the snekke. That is good for you are skilled. We either go north to seek the river which leads to the roaring water of Onguiaahra and the great seas or we go south with Brave Eagle."

I smiled in the dark for it was as though she had read my mind. "If we go north then my dream of finding the roaring water will be fulfilled and we could keep sailing without putting down roots."

She took my hand and put it on her naked belly, "We need roots, or our family, at least, needs them. We cannot live isolated and alone. Your children and those that you will plant in here will grow and seek mates. You and I can be but not our family."

"Then you are saying we should go with Brave Eagle?"

"Perhaps."

"The problem with that answer is that Brave Eagle still wishes to rescue his family. The Penobscot hold them."

She kissed me, "And that is the other reason. I was a slave of the Penobscot. I would not have others endure what Stands Alone and I did."

I sighed, "You are a wise woman and a caring one." I closed my eyes to visualize the voyage. Thus far the seas north of Bear Island seemed more dangerous. They were colder and I remembered the lumps of ice we had seen from the drekar when we had sailed south. "The journey would be easier than heading north into the unknown and Brave Eagle tells me that, further south, there are many wide rivers that head deep inland. I will speak with him tomorrow." She said nothing but kissed me and I knew that she agreed with me.

Surprisingly, I slept better than I had for some days. I think it was that a weight had been lifted from me. I now knew that we had to leave and Laughing Deer had presented me with an answer I could live with. I rose to make water and saw that dawn was about to break. After I had made water, I walked to the cliff top and knelt. I watched the sun slowly appear above the horizon. The sea was a flat calm and that seemed a good omen. I spoke aloud for I was alone.

"Gytha, spirits of my family, we are leaving this place where we were happy. I know that your voices will be lost to me but in here," I tapped my head, "I will still remember them. Fótr, Ada, Lars, and Ýrr, I pray that you live and prosper. I shall never see you in this life but know that my thoughts reach out to you across the sea. I am content."

I waited until the sun was completely up and then I stood and walked back to the village. As I neared it, I met Brave Eagle and I smiled, "I have my answer."

He looked confused, "Your answer?"

"You were there, last night when Long Walking spoke?" He nodded. "My family and I will leave here for I do not wish harm to come to another. We thought to take you home and begin a new life there." His smile went from ear to ear. I held up a warning hand. "I will not speak of this until Long Walking and his warriors have gone. I will just tell him that I will sail away from here with my family. They will tell the Penobscot and that should ensure that the clan is safe. They may still seek me, but this land is vast. When they have gone, I will tell the others that we will take you home but nothing more."

"You can make your home with my clan."

I stared into his eyes, "My friend, you have a clan no longer. You have your families and people to rescue but you have no warriors."

His eyes told me that he knew I spoke the truth and he nodded, "I will have to seek the help of others to rescue my family and the others from my clan, but the clan will grow. It is the same as you, Erik, you have a small clan but it too will grow."

We had spent so long speaking that by the time we returned the rest of the warriors were awake and gathered outside their lodges. They looked expectantly at us. I smiled, "I have made my decision. My family and I will leave."

I saw the relief on the face of Long Walking. There would be no conflict from the Penobscot, but I saw that the Mi'kmaq warriors of the village were not happy.

"And now I must tell my sons. Farewell Long Walking. I thank you and your clan for all that you have done."

He clasped my arm, "And I thank you for you have shown me one who is a great warrior but does not wish to be. I have never yet met such a man and it will help me to understand myself."

Moos Blood and Brave Cub saw me approaching and the warriors gathered behind. Moos Blood, especially, was clever and he knew what the Clan of the Otter had told us. Brave Cub, on the other hand just looked confused.

"Come inside the lodge. I must speak with you."

124

Laughing Deer took Little White Dove's hand, "Come, you can hear this too although I doubt that it will make any sense to you."

Their eyes on me I spoke plainly, "We are leaving this clan and sailing south with Brave Eagle. We will make a new home for the Penobscot still wish to end my life. I am not afraid for me, but I would not have you hurt."

Moos Blood nodded and put his arm around Brave Cub who said, "But I like the clan. I have friends."

Laughing Deer said, "I have friends and I have a family. I will be leaving my little sister, but this needs to be done. Your father and I have spoken, and we are agreed on this."

Moos Blood said, "Think of the adventure we shall have, little brother. We will be sailing the snekke in new waters. We might find more whales or even stranger creatures."

Brave Cub looked at his brother and nodded. We had made the decision and we would leave. The question was, when? I looked at Laughing Deer who was feeding Golden Bear. "How long before he can travel?"

"He could travel now but I would prefer to wait for another week or so. It will give Stands Alone the chance to see more of him."

"Let us make it ten days and then we can be well prepared."

125

Chapter 14

When Long Walking had gone I told Black Bird of our destination. In many ways, it made it easier for him and warriors like Long Sight who had come to know and like Brave Eagle. They saw it as a noble gesture. It would not ease the pain of our departure, but the reason was one with which they could sympathise. Black Bird told me that the warriors of the clan would keep watch in the woods in case any Penobscot came before we left. It would take time for the news to reach the Penobscot and we all knew that there were wild young warriors out there.

The decision made we were faced with the problem of what to take and what to leave. Over the next days, I examined everything we owned with a view to deciding if we really needed it or not. I left all the domestic materials to Laughing Deer but, when I had made my decision about what I needed, the boys and I began to load the snekke. We took the deck off to reveal the hold. We took out half of the ballast. We would not need it and it would do no harm to let the air get to the hold. When that was done we took *'Ada'* on a last voyage with us to see if there was anything left on Bear Island which we might need. The birch bark snekke had seemed such a good vessel once but now, after *'Gytha'* I saw all her limitations. I had decided to leave her to Black Otter. He had learned his lesson and he might even be able to sail beyond the island. He was a good fisherman, and the clan would still benefit from the boat.

We had taken as much as possible already from the main settlement, but I knew that there were houses, Benni's especially, which had been left since long before the clan had departed. With my spear in hand, we trekked through the forest. The trails we had made were now almost invisible. I knew them but even the best tracker from the clan would struggle to find them. The rooves had gone from almost all the houses and my heart sank when I realised that this mark we had made would soon disappear. Nature was reclaiming the land we had held so briefly. There would be a time in the future when warriors might come to follow us and find nothing. It would have been as though we, and our homes, had simply disappeared.

We searched every decaying home and were rewarded with one small metal cooking pot. I think it might have been a helmet at one point but Eystein, whose house it was, must have converted it to a cooking pot. We went into the woods to find the outlying farms. The fields which had been cleared for crops now sprouted with saplings! We found twenty nails which were buried in the main room of Benni's house. I also found another treasure there, a seax with a broken tip. It was rusted but it could be cleaned and sharpened. We also found two pots with lids. From the smell, they had held beer. We found a good sack and put the smaller objects in it. All else was beyond salvage. We headed back to the jetty and loaded *'Ada'*. It was as I was taking a last look that I realised I had missed something. We had used good nails on the jetty. They were still there. I took my hatchet and while the boys sat in the snekke, I removed all twenty of them. Whilst they were rusted, we could clean them and still use them. I put them in the snekke and hoisted the sail. We had barely moved forty paces when I saw the first of the timbers slip into the sea. The clan would be able to land on the island, but the jetty would have disappeared in a week or so. The boys were excited about the treasure, especially the seax, but my joy was heavily tinged with sadness.

When we landed, we drew the boat well beyond the high-water mark and then emptied the treasures. "You two fill the sack with dry sand and then put the nails and the seax inside. There is a task for you. Each time you need occupation, shake it!"

The rest of the goods, along with my mail, shield, weapons, and tools we placed in the bottom of the hold. The bright morning had given way to overcast clouds and so we replaced the deck over the hold. It would not do to risk soaking the metal.

As we headed up the slope to the camp Long Sight caught up with us. He had been fishing and had seen us land, "When do you plan to leave?"

I shrugged, "The new baby has delayed us, but it will be sooner rather than later. Summer is passing quickly, and Brave Eagle is anxious to get to his lands."

"The warriors and their families wish to give you gifts. The gifts will help us all to remember each other. We do not want you to go, this is a way of parting well."

"I have a gift for the clan. I will leave *'Ada'* for them to use. I believe that Black Otter could sail her, but she will be the clan's." I smiled, "Just so long as he does not try to hunt the whale!"

"None would try that and that is a most generous gift besides which our humble offerings will seem like nothing."

Once back at my lodge we put outside the goods we would not be taking. Laughing Deer spread the word and others began to take what they wished. It was done with great care and consideration. That was the way of the clan. If one wanted something they took it but if they thought someone else would benefit then they gave it to them. There was no argument and none harboured ill feelings. I would miss the clan and their harmonious life.

Doe Eyes had not been well for some days. I had seen little of her since Wandering Moos' death the previous year and the old woman had aged. She lived in Black Bird's lodge and he fetched me. "Doe Eyes is dying. She may die while we speak with her or may last until tomorrow, but she wishes to speak with you before she goes to join Wandering Moos."

I could smell death in the lodge when I entered. It was a sour, sickly smell. I thought she was dead already, but she opened her eyes when I knelt and her thin croaky voice came to me, "Erik, Shaman of the Bear I am going to join Wandering Moos. I have something to give to you. It was something he would have wished you to have." She reached down and picked up the dead chief's pipe. Her frail, blue-veined hands gave it to me. "When you smoke the pipe think of us for we shall be together."

"He was a great chief and you a gracious lady, I take it and when I use it, I shall think of him. He was a friend, and I can give no higher praise. Farewell." She did not answer but closed her eyes. She was hovering in the space between life and death. She would choose her moment to pass over. I still had the pipe which Brave Eagle had made for me but he would understand if I used Wandering Moos' more often.

Black Bird led me from the lodge, "It is a measure of the respect in which you are held, Erik, Shaman of the Bear. I know you have thought this journey through, but you know that there will be a hole in the clan when you leave?" I nodded. "Those sisters you speak of have made your life not only interesting but complicated too." He was a wise man and a good choice for chief, "They are constantly moving you so that you do not leave roots."

He was right. It was *wyrd*.

Laughing Deer had gathered all that she needed and kept only enough for our last night with the clan. Brave Eagle had little and so the four of us went to the beach to begin the loading of the snekke. The others had never done this and thought it a simple act. Brave Cub went to put the winter furs in the hold, and I shook my head.

"All of you must do exactly as I tell you for there is an art to this. Do you see how my mail and weapons are in the centre? All of the heavy goods must be placed there. Those winter furs will be the last thing we put in the hold for they are light, but we do not want them to be at the bottom where there may be the chance of them becoming wet. The clothes, hides and spare pots can be put at the prow or the stern but I want the snekke to be packed level. We do everything with care. This

128

will be our home until we reach the land of Brave Eagle and we must care for her." It was gone noon by the time we had finished and there was still room inside the hold for more. The snekke was not riding low in the water. "You boys go for kindling. It will save us seeking it when we stop on the way south."

While they went Brave Eagle and I packed the spare crosstree, sail and ropes. We had spent many hours making ropes from the Horse Deer as well as cutting strong vines. A broken rope could mean disaster. The kindling fetched, we packed it and then placed the winter furs on the top. The last task was to fix the spare mast to the mast fish. Until we found a new home, we would have to live with the inconvenience of it.

I pointed to the empty deck, "The pots with the food we will use on the voyage will be tied to the pegs on the gunwale around the side. They will be brought tomorrow. As with the hold I need balance and they will be spread out around the snekke. Brave Eagle, your home will be at the prow. The waters into which we sail are unknown to me and while you will not have seen the land from the sea you are more likely to see features which are familiar to you. Use your cloak to make a nest. Brave Cub, your home will be with your mother, Little White Dove and Golden Bear by the mast fish. You will use the whale skin capes to make a shelter both from the wet and the sun. If it rains, we will collect the rainwater from our shelters. We waste nothing. Moos Blood, you and I will have our beds by the steering board for I must continue to teach you to be a navigator. When we are at sea we move around as little as possible. Brave Eagle and Brave Cub your task each day will be to put lines out for fish. We try to gather food every day and when we find islands on which to camp then you will forage for food. I know not how long this journey will last but as Brave Eagle was carried by the sea north and survived then I am hopeful that we will too, but it does not do to provoke the Norns. Tomorrow at dawn I will make a blót."

The last night was a celebration as well as a time of reflection and mourning for Doe Eyes had died while we had worked on the snekke. As was the custom she was laid next to her husband and the moos skull we had brought from the winter camp. Doe Eyes had been ready to depart this life and the sadness came from the thought that we would never speak to her again. As the whole clan sat and ate together the lives of Wandering Moos and Doe Eyes were spoken of and then the tales of Erik, Shaman of the Bear were retold. There were young boys there who were younger than Brave Cub and they had yet to hear of the tale of the fight with Laughing Wolf. Nor had the battle with the Hawk clan been made into a story. Now they were. I was embarrassed by the attention but knew that it was necessary. When we were gone then the stories would be retold in the winter camp to keep the memory of us alive. As the stories were told and passed on, they would change but it was comforting to know that unlike our homes on Bear Island, my story and that of the warriors from the east would not be forgotten. It would not crumble into dust. Some time, long into the future it would become a legend, something which seemed too fantastical to have happened.

Golden Bear was restless that night and I did not sleep as well as I might have done but, in the sleep I did manage, I dreamed and Gytha came to me one last time. Her face was formless, but I knew her voice which was, as ever, comforting.

'Your doom and your future are one and the same thing, Erik. You will wander this new world without putting down strong roots for you are the navigator. You did not choose the path, the Norns did. Their spell is a strong one and you cannot break it. I will not be there with you but when it is time to move on you will know. Know that Laughing Deer was also chosen. Your finding of her was a seed planted back in Orkneyjar. Your children will also wander this new land. I will go now for it is time to join the other spirits and watch over the clan.'

Her voice seemed to fade and disappear. As much as I wanted to speak to her, I knew that was not the way of the dreamworld. It was both comforting and chilling to know that I would be a wanderer. One day, when they were old enough, I would try to explain this to my children. They were part of me and bound up in a rootless future. We would be like the birds I had seen at sea who were far from land and yet still wandered the waves. I rose early and went to make my blót. Only the old men making water were up and the cliff overlooking the beach was empty. As I stood, after slaying the squirrel, I felt the wind and it was a chill wind but that meant it came from the north. We would have wind to speed us south. The blót had been received.

We ate the food left over from the feast and then, with every member of the clan escorting us we headed to the beach. I saw Black Otter looking longingly at *'Ada'*. He would sail her as soon as we were out of sight, I knew that but out of courtesy he and the others were saying their farewells.

Stands Alone and Laughing Deer wept. Stands Alone had been at the births of Little White Dove and Golden Bear. She and Little White Dove had a special bond and until Stands Alone became a mother then the absence of her niece would be painful. The parting with my wife was a long one but I would not hurry it. Instead, I was able to clasp the arm of every warrior and speak from my heart. We had been shield brothers and that made a bond which women would find hard to understand. The last two partings were especially poignant. Black Bird and Runs Far were as close to me as Fótr had been. We had not made a blood oath but we were brothers in blood for we had fought together many times. They were a hard bond to break but I knew that I had to.

Black Bear gave me a pouch with the smoking leaves within, "I know you do not smoke often but when you do, with the pipe of Wandering Moos and with these leaves then think of us for we shall never forget you."

"And I will never forget this clan. We began in war and end now as brothers."

Runs Far smiled, "Aye, I forgot Bear Tooth. He lives in the east and you in the west. The world is in balance."

I had not thought of that, "You are wise, Runs Far."

Black Bird shook his head, "We are changed, that is all. Our two people came together, and we have learned from each other."

I felt the wind on the back of my head and said, "It is time!"

The boys and Brave Eagle were eager to leave and Moos Blood was already at the steering board. Brave Cub clambered aboard and took first Little White Dove and then held Golden Bear while Brave Eagle and I helped Laughing Deer to board. I was the last to haul myself over the gunwale. Laughing Deer held our two youngest closely to her. It was a protective and comforting act. I knew that she was upset but I also knew that this was meant to be and when we camped, I would tell her of my dream.

"Loose the sail!"

My sons loosed the sail and as the sail filled and billowed the clan on the beach gave such a loud roar that sea birds took flight in fear. As I put the steering board over to take advantage of the wind, I saw that it would take us close to Bear Island and that was meant to be. The dead still lay there and would forever be part of the island. I wondered if any others would come from the east and one day finds the remains of our homes. Unless they did so soon they would find nothing. As we raced past, I said, "Farewell, Bear Island!" Laughing Deer caught my eye as I said it and nodded. She too had lived there. Then we looked south to our new future.

Golden Bear was not happy about the wind and the wetness. The fresh wind meant spray showered him. Little White Dove thought it was a game and Brave Cub was constantly having to prevent her from falling over the side.

"Moos Blood, take my bearskin and make a shelter from the spray. Perhaps the bear may calm him."

Miraculously it seemed to work for the skin made a cave-like shelter for my wife and my two youngest and they became calmer. I, who had sailed across the great sea, was learning!

This time I had a campsite in mind. The three islands we had used twice before seemed a good choice. We would reach there sooner this time for I did not need to sail up and down rivers to reach it. On my map, I had marked two other possible stopping places. One was a group of three or four islands which lay thirty miles south of Deer Island and the other was a solitary island which was forty miles south. I did not envisage any trouble, but this would be a way for me to have options and it would help to teach Moos Blood how to sail. Once I was confident that there were no issues with the snekke I allowed him to take the steering board. The blót must have worked for we passed the islands to seaward and the wind took us swiftly south. The scudding clouds suggested rain, but it held off. We caught eight good sized fish which Brave Eagle gutted with his new knife and as the afternoon wore on, I began to head for the islands I knew lay ahead. It was not long before dusk when I spied them, and I confidently landed us close to the place we had camped before. The difference this time was that we had two infants to ferry ashore and my wife. I sent Brave Eagle to the far side of the island to see if he could spy smoke. When he returned and told me that there was none then I lit a fire and we put the fish on to cook. There were pools of rainwater and we used those to wash. We would not need drinking water yet as we had one of the jugs I had found filled as well as our water skins.

After we had eaten, I made a comfortable shelter for the night. I knew from the voyage in the drekar that storms could come in from the sea with little warning and, using my bearskin as a sleeping mat, I fixed my sealskin cloak and the whale capes to provide a wind and rainproof shelter. While Laughing Deer got the children to sleep we went beyond earshot to speak.

"Your people, Brave Eagle, do they have summer and winter camps like the Mi'kmaq?"

He shook his head, "One or two do but we do not. We live on the south bank of the Patawomke River. Other clans live beyond Cohongarooton, the place of the honking geese where there is a great fall of water."

I felt a chill as he said that for I had dreamed of a falls. It had not been the falls where Arne and the others had died, and I wondered if it was the one to the north near the inland seas. Perhaps it was this one.

"And how do your people live?"

He smiled, "We are a little more civilised than the Mi'kmaq. We plant and harvest crops as well as hunting and fishing but I confess that the fish you caught, Erik, were larger by many times than any fish that we caught, even in the sea. We plant and grow the three sisters, beans, squash and the golden corn."

"And the other tribes?"

"The Penobscot are the aggressive ones and they do not farm. They are lazy robbers who steal what we grow. The Lenni Lenape are a fierce tribe but we seem to get on with them and they farm as we do. Often they fight wars with the Penobscot and I have heard of them travelling many hundreds of miles to fight the Iroquois and Hurons." He shrugged, "Perhaps we are not warlike enough for them and they see no honour in fighting us. Our only enemies, apart from the biting insects, are the Penobscot. They had to travel many miles and for many days to raid my home and they did the same with the Mi'kmaq."

Moos Blood said, "You are a good warrior, father."

It was a simple statement but I knew what had prompted the thought, "No, my son. Your uncle, Arne, was the good warrior as was my cousin Siggi. I know how to fight and I won because I had my weapons and the byrnie. The byrnie is now weaker and my sword, seax and axe could be damaged."

Brave Eagle took out his most precious possession, the knife I had made him, "How can this break?"

"It can bend and if it is bent then, as a weapon it is of no use. It would have to be melted down and recast. As you saw when we made the arrowheads, each time you melt down metal you lose some. Perhaps Thor takes it as his due. I hope I do not have to fight."

We watched the night sky in silence. The wind blowing from the north and east was icy, but I could still hear Golden Bear's moaning which told me that Laughing Deer had yet to soothe him to sleep. We could not return to the warmth of the camp yet.

"Erik, I know that it is much to ask but I would deem it an honour if you would help me to rescue my family and those who remain from my clan."

My heart sank. I had left the Mi'kmaq to avoid having to fight and now I was being asked to do just that. I shook my head, "Let us find your village first and then you can speak to your tribe. Even if I agreed then two of us could do little, could we?"

Brave Cub said, "We could fight."

My head whipped around, and I snapped, "You are too young, and it is up to you and your brother to protect the family!" My harsh words

133

stunned everyone into silence and in the silence, I realised that Golden Bear was finally asleep. "Come let us go to the shelter. We have another long day tomorrow and we know not where we shall be landing! Brave Eagle, I will give thoughts to your words but, at the moment, I fear that I could do little to help."

Moos Blood put his arm around his little brother, and I heard him say, "Father is right Brave Cub. We both have courage, but could we face a Penobscot warrior in battle? I think not."

Brave Eagle pulled on my arm, "I am sorry, Erik, I do not wish to bring conflict into your family. I am being selfish but if I cannot recover my family then I have no life at all!"

"I know, Brave Eagle, and I can hear the *wyrd* sisters as they spin and plot!"

Chapter 15

The skies were still grey as we left our island stop, but the wind had changed slightly and was now coming more from the north-west than the north. As a result, it felt warmer. I sent Moos Blood to the prow and asked Brave Eagle to join me at the steering board.

"By the end of the day, we will have passed beyond the Peace River. That is Penobscot land. I will need somewhere to land, and we are in your hands."

He nodded, "It is the Pequot people who live close to the coast. They are more like the Mi'kmaq, but they do not use winter camps. They do not welcome strangers, but they are not fierce warriors. So long as we do not try to take from them then they will leave us alone. This is the day where we might be in the greatest danger. The Penobscot fish in the sea which is close to the mouths of their rivers. The Peace River marks one boundary and the River of the Lenni Lenape, along with the Chesepiooc, the other."

"Then keep a good watch."

When Moos Blood rejoined me I had him use the compass and we took out the map to mark what we saw. This was as far as I had mapped and from now on, we would be adding to it. Brave Eagle knew of no more islands and I wondered if we might have to risk landing on the mainland. I did not wish to do so as we would have to keep a watch.

I handed the steering board to Moos Blood and said, "Stay on this course and I will go to see your mother." When I reached the mast fish I said, "Brave Cub, you can check the lines and I will watch Little White Dove." Happy to be relieved of his duty he hurried to the stern. "How are you coping?"

She shook her head, "This is nerve-wracking! I am happy to be on the snekke, but I fear for the two babes. If it were not for Brave Cub, I know not what I would do."

"We have at least two or even three days left. If there were more islands, then we could take longer for the voyage but have less time at sea."

She shook her head, "Get there as fast as you can. Such boats as yours are not for babies."

I did not say that we had sailed for many days on the drekar without sight of any land! I played with Little White Dove while Laughing Deer fed Golden Bear. Brave Eagle eventually returned with five fine fish which he had gutted. "I will leave you to Little White Dove now. I will try to land as soon as I can."

We saw a couple of islands near to the mouth of a narrow river, but it was barely noon and we had to push on while we had the weather and the wind. I spied in the distance a lump which looked like an island. Brave Eagle had not seen it for his eyes were on the shore. Our course would take us to the island, and I thought it was good fortune.

Brave Eagle turned and shouted, "Erik, there are boats!"

I looked to steerboard and saw that he was right. They were just dots but they were clearly boats and I presumed that they were fishing. "Do you know which tribe they are?"

He came back towards me, "They are too far away. Can we close with them?"

I shook my head, "There is nothing to gain from that. You said the tribes would leave us alone but what if it is the Penobscot?" He nodded. As I looked towards the shore, I saw the distinctive heads of some seal. I pointed to them, "Seals!"

He stared at them and then said, "Then I know where we are. The boats will have come down the Piscataqua River. It is rich in such animals and there are other fish too. The boats will be Pequot."

I was still unconvinced, and we kept on our course.

The boats drew closer and we were able to see them more clearly and I saw Brave Eagle become agitated. He stood and the snekke rocked alarmingly, "Brave Eagle, keep still!"

He nodded and pointed, "The Penobscot are attacking the Pequot fishermen."

"What can we do?"

He pointed to the sail, "This will scare the Penobscot!"

I was going to tell him it was not worth the trouble when it came to me that this might be a good test of our new dragon sail. Thus far we had not shown the sail to any potential enemies. The Norns were spinning and I said, "Very well, we will sail just a little closer, but I intend to land at that island ahead."

Brave Eagle looked relieved. He had a deep-seated hatred of the Penobscot and that meant that he had sympathy for all those that they preyed upon.

"Cub, watch your sister. Brave Eagle, Moos Blood, nock an arrow!"

I put the steering board over gently so as not to lose speed nor to upset the infants. I could now see that what we had taken to be men fishing was, in fact, a chase and from what Brave Eagle had said it was the Penobscot chasing the Pequot. I knew from the times that my clan had fought the Penobscot that the sight of something as strange as a dragonship was not to be underestimated. I had never been in these waters and so I knew that the tribes would never have seen anything like it. The Mi'kmaq were used to it but when I had fitted the dragon sail I had seen fear on their faces. The wind pushed us silently and swiftly towards them. We were approaching from the seaward side and the ones who were being chased looked to be heading for the island. By the time they saw us, we might be within less than a hundred paces of them.

It was the Pequot who saw us first. As one of the warriors turned to his left to see how close the Penobscot were he spied us and he pointed and shouted. The words were lost but it made every warrior in the two groups turn. All that they would see was a giant white-winged creature hurtling across the waves towards them. They had no idea what a dragon was, but it looked both terrifying and unnatural. Both groups turned and headed for the shore. I eased the steering board back to its previous course. The Pequot would be safe for the Penobscot were heading back to the river we had seen. I saw then the spirals of smoke from the shore and the lodges of the Pequot!

Brave Eagle came back with a huge grin on his face, "That was the easiest victory over a Penobscot that I have ever seen."

"It bodes well for any future encounter."

Brave Cub pointed up at the sail, "Father, if we gave the dragon red eyes and a yellow head then it would look even more fierce!"

I nodded, "Then when we reach the land of the Patawomke, you and your brother can find the beetles we will need to crush for the red and the root we will have to grind for the yellow!"

It was a good idea and I should have thought about it before. My sons were both growing.

As the island drew closer I saw that it was just a bare rock covered with some earth and bird droppings. There were grass and weeds but naught else. I took us to the seaward side so that when we took down the sail we would vanish. I was not afraid of the Pequot but neither did I want them paddling out to investigate us.

"We will have a cold camp!"

It meant we had to eat the fish raw, but we kept the heads and bones to use for bait. We had caught these fish with hooks and limpets. We could catch bigger fish with fish heads. As the boys gathered shellfish Brave Eagle and I made a shelter for us. We used my spear to drive into the ground and then used my shield and my sword to provide a framework. As we sat, Golden Bear sleeping, we ate the raw fish. Laughing Deer chewed the fish first so that Little White Dove did not risk a bone.

137

Brave Eagle spat out a bone, "There is a better island ahead, Erik. Two of them in fact. Natocke is a bare island but much bigger than this and it is out in the ocean and can barely be seen from the mainland. The other is much closer and consists of a number of islands. The largest is Noepe and there is a village on the island. It belongs to the Wampanoag tribe."

"Then we avoid that one and camp on Natocke."

"The Wampanoag are peaceful. I do not think they would harm us."

"Until we reach your river, I would avoid all contact with any!"

The grey skies had gone by dawn and the wind which had been from the north-west swung around to the west north-west. It suited me as it kept us well off from the shore. However, it also meant that any curious fishermen would have an easy passage to reach us. I noticed that the weather was also warmer. The further south we travelled then the less we noticed the cold. We saw no one for the coastline was just a thin line in the distance. This was deliberate on my part. Brave Eagle had said that the island we saw was almost out of sight of the land. I wished to remain hidden.

The baited hooks proved to be a success. We caught fish which Brave Eagle had only heard of. It was three paces long and had a sail along its back! Its long mouth had small sharp teeth and I could see that it was a hunter. I was surprised that the line we used held for the fish, when we finally landed it was as heavy as Moos Blood. As soon as we hooked it, with the hooks made from the whale, I handed the steering board to Moos Blood. "Keep on this course!"

I took my spear and Brave Eagle came to the stern with his bow.

"Brave Eagle, start to pull on the rope and I will use my spear to kill it."

The fish was a fighter, but the hook was well made and sharp. Brave Eagle hauled for all that he was worth. As we crested waves so the body of the fish I called, sail fish, came out of the water and Brave Eagle was able to pull it closer. As soon as I could I lunged with the spear and when the blood began to pour Brave Eagle pulled even harder for I saw the fins of sharks in the distance as they closed with us. We had barely pulled the dying fish aboard when the sharks began to tear at the fish heads. We lost the rest of the hooks as those savage beasts ripped the lines in two.

"Brave Eagle, gut the fish and throw the guts as far astern as you can. I do not want those sharks to keep following. Let them fight over the guts!"

It worked and as we saw the island of Natocke rise like a whale from the sea I reefed the sail. The wind on the snekke was enough to take us to the island and would hide us from the eyes on Noepe. There was the tiniest of beaches which lay on the northeast corner. There was a spit of an island to the east and that would afford some shelter. Brave Eagle and I pulled up the snekke on to the beach and drove my spear into the earth like an anchor. After helping my wife from the snekke I ran to the west. Brave Eagle came with me. I could see the island called Noepe and, as the sun began to set, I estimated that it was about five miles away. That was a long way for a birch bark boat to travel, especially at night. The island had a humped back and I decided that I would risk a fire as hot food would be better than cold, and I doubted that the Wampanoag fishermen would risk a night passage to a deserted island.

We made the shelter and then while we waited for darkness, I butchered the fish. The meat was pink and I began to salivate at the thought of the taste. The kindling we had brought and the driftwood the boys had collected meant that when it came to light the fire it did not take me long. Laughing Deer's face showed me the pleasure that the fire brought. It was a reminder of home and it was comforting. We used sharpened sticks to cook some food quickly while we continued to cut up the meat. I would use the small pot and seawater to cook the rest up and we would eat well for the next day or so. That night I cuddled in with Laughing Deer for Little White Dove was nestled between her brothers and Golden Bear was asleep on her breast. The night was warm and we had the embers of the fire so that Brave Eagle slept outside.

Laughing Deer kissed me on the cheek, "You are a great navigator, Erik. We have travelled many miles and found shelter. How do you manage it?"

"Brave Eagle's knowledge and the experience of doing something similar with the drekar. You must be having a difficult time with the two babes."

"The first days were hard, but they have adapted and Cub is like having Stands Alone with us. I hoped that the voyage would be over quickly, but I know now it will not."

"Aye, the journey Brave Eagle made with his warriors was over land. Ours is a longer one and slower. We will get there."

"And have we passed the land of the Penobscot yet?"

"I hope that we are south of the tribal lands but I do not know. The ones who saw our sail may tell others and if word gets back to the clan we fought then they may think to look south but this time they do not know the place we seek."

It was an easy day the next day for the curve of the land allowed us to take full advantage of the wind and when we stopped, not long before dark, we found yet another island. This time Brave Eagle had not heard of it, but he believed we were in Mohegan land. The mainland was more than ten miles away and there was another island, a much larger one but that appeared to be almost twenty miles away. That evening Brave Eagle thought that we were halfway there.

"I have hunted in the lands here and I passed through it with my warriors when we tried to recover our captives. If you landed me then I could be home in seven days." He smiled, "This is an easier way to journey!" He pointed to the river. "There lies the Muhheakantuck River. That marks the border between the Penobscot and the Lenni Lenape. It was there that we were ambushed. The journey we have just done was the one the water took me to reach your lands."

I shook my head, "Had I heard the story I would not have believed you, but I am even more convinced now that you were sent to me so that I could return you home. This is *wyrd*."

We had a fire once more and we had caught more fish. Sadly, none were the delicious sail fish. We had used the same bait but the ones we had seen had been too strong and the lines and hooks were taken.

When we left the next morning, I spied boats ahead and so instead of following the coast of what Brave Eagle had said was the largest island on this coast, we headed due south. The wind from the west-north-west still helped us and might save time. Brave Eagle assured me that the people there would not attack us but I thought there was little point in taking a chance. The sea stretched on forever and there appeared to be no islands ahead. I looked at the skies. There were clouds but none suggested rain and the wind was steady rather than strong.

I shouted my plans for this was not a drekar and I could both see and hear the others, "We will sail through the night. I will reef the sail but I cannot see an island on which to land."

Brave Eagle shouted back, "But who will steer while you sleep?"

"Moos Blood will steer, and I will be ready to wake in an instant. We will eat now while there is light and make water. Once darkness falls then I want everyone else, you included, Brave Eagle, secured around the mast fish."

Moos Blood looked both pleased and afraid. I had been his age when I had first steered a snekke and followed our drekar. I had done so at night. Until I had done it, I had not thought I could. I spoke quietly to him. "You maintain this course. South-west and steady. When I hand over the snekke to you I will reef the sail so that we just make progress." He nodded and I smiled, "This may well help for we will make up time and shorten our journey. Even if we just sail forty miles during the night it will be forty miles less that we have to sail tomorrow. You will sleep until I wake you and then be ready to wake me if there is anything you do not like. When I sailed from the Land of Ice and Fire, I once had to stay awake for two days and nights. You can do this."

We ate, drank and made water. I said a silent prayer to Njörðr to watch over us and then, while Moos Blood steered, made sure that my family and Brave Eagle were secure around the mast fish.

"I can watch too, Erik!"

"No, Brave Eagle, I need you sleeping here close by my family." I smiled, "You are a big man and will be a human protector for them." He nodded, "Brave Cub, keep Little White Dove close and safe." I kissed my wife and sleeping son. "Fear not, Laughing Deer, we knew we might have to do this, and the night is a quiet one."

"I am not afraid for Erik the Navigator is here."

I took the steering board and forced Moos Blood to sleep. I knew that the mainland was far to the west. There, close to where the Lenni Lenape lived there was a string of dune-backed islands just off the coast. That was my target. Brave Eagle had never been there, but he had spoken to others who had and they suggested that there were neither reefs nor rocks. In my experience dunes normally confirmed the absence of rocks. I hoped that while I steered, we would maintain the good speed we had made thus far.

Once Little White Dove stopped giggling and fell asleep, I was left with the sounds of the snekke: the snap of the sail and the whoosh from the waves as the prow cut through them. The moon's intermittent rays showed white flecked waves, but these were not the mountainous seas the drekar had endured further north. It was a gentle swell and suited the snekke perfectly. The occasional snap from the sail was a reminder to watch my course but the adjustments I made were small. When the snap was replaced by the creak from ropes and the mast, I was content. In truth, I was not tired. When I had been younger, I had needed to concentrate all the time and that was tiring. Now I felt at one with the snekke and it was almost like sleeping with my eyes open. I felt attuned to the sea and the snekke.

The night passed. I heard Golden Bear wake and watched as Laughing Deer first cleaned him and then fed him. Our eyes met and she smiled. They snuggled down when he fell asleep. Brave Eagle woke once and went to empty his bowels over the side. I watched him for it was not as easy as one might think. He waved when he had finished and went back to the mast fish. I needed no sleep, but I knew that I would have to wake Moos Blood and let him steer or he would think that I had no faith in him. When I knew that dawn was just an hour or so away I woke him. He made water and I gave him the steering board. I stood and reefed the sail so that there was just an arm of sail to push us gently south and east.

Nodding I said, "Wake me if you see anything or when the sun rises." I curled up under his bjorr fur for the bearskin was being used by my family. I was asleep almost instantly and I enjoyed a dreamless sleep.

When I woke, I kept my eyes closed and almost willed Moos Blood to wake me. I could feel the sun shining on me and I could hear the others moving around.

"Father, it is dawn."

I opened my eyes and stretched, "How was your first night watch?"

He shook his head, "You gave me a short watch."

I stood and went to the sail, "I watched until I was tired and now, I am refreshed." As soon as the sail was untied and the wind caught it, the dragon filled and billowed. I smiled as Moos Blood had to grip the steering board tightly. "I will make water, eat and then relieve you. Can you manage?"

He forced a nod. I made water and stretched and then turned to the mastfish to check on the others.

Laughing Deer stood as I approached, "Here hold your son while I make water."

He was wide awake, and his blue eyes bored into me. He had a serious look on his face, "Well, my son, you have had your first night asleep at sea. You can call yourself a sailor now." Little White Dove looked up at me. I rarely understood her words but I spoke to her as though I did. "And you, Little White Dove, you were protected by your big brother eh? This night, if the winds are right then you can run on the sand!" She giggled for I pulled a funny face.

Laughing Deer eventually returned, and I handed Golden Bear back. She asked, "How far to land?"

There was nothing in sight to steerboard and I shrugged, "I do not know but we will push on until we find this line of dunes Brave Eagle has promised us."

The Powhatan warrior shook his head, "I just heard that there was a line of sand, but I know not where it is."

"We will find it. We made time in the night, now let us use it."

Once at the steering board, I turned us a little and the wind seemed to make us travel faster. The day followed the pattern of the previous ones with the difference that there was no land in sight. The fishing lines brought us fish, but we had not had rain and we would need to fill our skins soon. Dunes did not suggest freshwater. I did not want to ration it, but I knew we might need to. We had still to broach the large jug I had found on Bear Island. If we did not find water before we started on that then I would ration the water for Brave Eagle, myself, Moos Blood and Brave Cub.

The sun began to dip in the sky before we saw the smudge on the horizon which told me that there was land. Even if this was not the sand spit we would have to land. Little White Dove needed to run. Brave Cub was having an increasingly difficult time keeping her amused. When I saw the waves breaking, as the last rays of the sun shone over the darkened dunes, I had Brave Eagle and Moos Blood reef the sail to its bare minimum and I edged her in. By turning to the north, at the last moment, I effectively stopped the snekke and Brave Eagle and Moos Blood leapt ashore to tether us to the land. Brave Cub looked at me and I nodded, "Leave your sister and help your brother."

As soon as Brave Cub had jumped over Brave Eagle took off to scout out the darkness ahead. I stood and secured the sail. We would not disembark until we knew it was safe. If we had to then I could sail along the line of sand until we found another landing place.

Brave Eagle came back and, in the darkness, his grin told me that he was relieved, "It is the spit of sand. I was told true. I can see the land to the west but there is no smell of fire nor is there a sign of habitation."

"Then we will have hot food. Boys, help Brave Eagle haul the snekke up and then take your brother and sister ashore."

I smiled as I saw Little White Dove try to run on the sand. She fell and Brave Cub laughed. My daughter was still at sea. I helped Laughing Deer from the snekke and Brave Eagle said, "We are close to the land of the Lenni Lenape. They have some villages close to the coast. We should try to make contact with them."

"Are you sure?"

"Erik, these are not Penobscot and I know that you are worried about water. We should sail down the coast and seek a village but you are the, what is the word you use? Navigator? We obey you."

That night I did not sleep as well as I expected. The sea I understood but if we approached strangers then I risked my family!

143

Chapter 16

The next day, as the sun rose, I saw how close we were to the mainland. The dunes stretched north and south. Some rose high while others were so low that a high tide would render them waterlogged. There were gaps and I knew that there was a chance that we could forage for water but as we had yet to broach the jug I opted to sail south. We saw that some of the sand spits had grass and even stubby trees covering them. It was being colonised. In the distance, we spied spirals of smoke which indicated settlements. It was noon when the last of the water from the skins was used and the morning had been a hot one. As Laughing Deer took some water from the jug, I asked Brave Eagle to look for a river. It was a couple of hours later and the wind had become gentler when he waved me to sail towards the land. I saw the gap in the dunes, and it was the widest one we had seen thus far. We reefed the sail to make navigation easier and safer; the dragon could barely be seen. We entered a large bay and I saw the river. I also saw birch bark boats fishing in the estuary.

Brave Eagle shouted, "Keep your hands from your weapons. These are the Lenni Lenape. Do not frighten them with weapons. These are fishermen."

I was not so sure. The Mi'kmaq we had first met on Bear Island had been fishermen but that had not stopped them from attacking us. I kept to the opposite side of the bay, well away from the fishermen who seemed to view us with curiosity rather than anything else. None made a move to close with us and, emboldened, I sailed towards the river mouth. The river mouth was also wide, and I saw their village. It was a large one with more than thirty lodges. I trailed my hand in the water. I had been tasting it since the bay and it had become less salty and now tasted drinkable.

"I will turn us around. Fill the waterskins. Use the far side of the snekke."

We had the attention of the villagers who came from their lodges to view us. They could not see the sail but the mast, crosstree and the boat generally were a wonder to them. I wondered if they would board their boats to investigate. Brave Eagle did not seem worried. It took longer to fill the skins than I would have liked but when they had done so I took the reefs from some of the sail and headed back to sea. The fishermen had become more curious and as we entered the bay, I saw four or five of them heading to meet us.

"Erik, slow the snekke down and I will speak with them."

I was not sure for I had my family aboard. Laughing Deer said, "We must try to talk to people, Erik. They are curious and when they see you and your beard, they will want to ask Brave Eagle questions."

I reefed the sail and turned the snekke so that we were into the wind. The current held us still and the boats approached. I could now understand the language that even strange people spoke for they all had common words. It was like talking at home to someone who was a Rus Viking or a Danish one. Some words were different, but you could work out what they meant.

The Lenni Lenape warrior spoke first, "I am Grey Macaroo and I have never seen a boat like this."

"I am Brave Eagle from the Powhatan Clan of the Eagle and this is Erik, the Shaman of the Bear and his family. We are travelling back to my home on the Patawomke River. We hope you do not mind us using your river."

He shook his head, "You looked strange and we feared that you were Penobscot. They have made war on our brothers to the north."

Brave Eagle glanced at me, "And will the Lenni Lenape make war on them?" He saw the fisherman cock his head to the side, "I ask because the Clan of the Hawk holds my people captive."

"We will make war and our chief is gathered with other leaders to decide when we will attack them. They have taken Lenni Lenape women and children as captives. I will tell the chief of your visit when he returns."

"Then we will leave."

Grey Macaroo asked, "Where are your paddles?"

"We do not use them. I would move your boats out of the way for when Erik opens the wings of this boat you will think that we fly!" He nodded at me. I knew what he wished. He wanted a dramatic exit.

"Hold on! Moos Blood, when I loose the sail then turn to steerboard. I will take over as quickly as I can!"

I went to the sail and untied the reefs. I saw the bow turn and then the wind caught us. The sail billowed and the Lenni Lenape fishermen who were in front of it screamed with fear when they saw the dragon sail. And then we leapt away leaving a wake which had the birch bark boats bobbing up and down.

Brave Eagle laughed, "They will speak of this for a month!"

"And is that a good thing?"

"It is for it saves us having to repeat it. The word will spread amongst the Lenni Lenape and when I have enough warriors to rescue my family, we can use the story to ease our passage through their land."

Brave Eagle had been away from his family for so long that it had sharpened his mind. He had a plan to rescue his family and that was a good thing!

We did not see another island and I did not relish the thought of another night at sea. That meant we would have to risk landing on the mainland. We found the mouth of the river which Brave Eagle thought was the Lenni Lenape. There was a small spit of land with a hint of a beach, but the forest and undergrowth came right down to the sand. We pulled on to the sand and I waved Brave Eagle ashore. He soon returned.

"There are not many trees and on the other side is a swamp. There are no people." He held up a dead snake, "There appear to be more of these than anything else."

I pointed to what passed for a beach, "Then we will build a fire on the sand and sleep on the snekke."

He nodded, "And I will cook this. It is good eating!"

"I will stick to the fish."

We heard the insects that night, as they buzzed over the swamp, but the smoke from the fire kept them at bay. The beach and the trees looked to have collected driftwood and I had the boys gather it to save our kindling. I slept with my wife and two youngest that night. I felt safe and comfortable.

The next day we left the insect and snake-infested land as quickly as possible. I knew that we were getting close to the Patawomke river when Brave Eagle recognised more features of the water and the land. He became quite excited when he spied a small group of islands joined by sand which I suspected would disappear beneath the waves at high tide.

"I know this place. My people come here now and then to hunt and to fish. There are no villages here for the sea sometimes engulfs the land. It is called Gingoteague."

It was getting on to dark and so we pulled in. This time there was no swamp, but the air did not seem wholesome. The vegetation smelled unpleasant but we lit a fire and some of the wood we burned was fragrant and made the air seem cleaner and kept away the insects. The fish had bitten all the way south and we cooked all eight of them. We would not starve in this part of the world, but I had seen nothing yet which made me wish to live here. I wondered if Brave Eagle's home would be any better.

As we sucked on the bones of the fish he said, "It took three days to reach here from my village. That is how close we are. You can do it in two, can you not?"

"Perhaps but we have winds to contend with. Let us plan on two further camps and then you will not be disappointed."

He put his arm around me, "My friend, how can I be disappointed. I would never have reached my home travelling across the land of the Penobscot. If they are at war with the Lenni Lenape, then none will be able to cross their land without a battle. I owe you all and I cannot see how I will be able to repay you."

"If we can winter in your village then that will be payment enough. Come the spring we will decide where lies our future."

He looked disappointed, "With my clan!"

I shook my head, "That is not my decision to make alone."

"You are the man, and the head of your small clan are you not?"

I shook my head, "Laughing Deer and I were brought together by the spirits and we decide everything we do as one. We both knew that this voyage was the best for our family and when we see your village, we will decide then if our future lies with the Powhatan!" He looked crestfallen and to take his mind off our leaving, I asked him questions, "Tell me about your people. You said you were the chief of your clan?"

"We call the chief, werowance. Sometimes we have a female chief, and she is called weroansqua. Our homes are similar to the Mi'kmaq but sturdier for they are permanent. They are called yehakins and are made by bending saplings, burying them in the ground and placing woven mats or bark over the top."

"So the village should still be occupied, the ones who survived will not have left?" I made it into a question if only to make him prepare himself for disappointment.

"They should be for they would have harvested the crops and used the traps in the river to feed themselves. The old who were left would teach the young. That is why I was so keen to return home. I know not how many of the warriors survived the ambush. It may be that the ones who live there appealed to the mamanatowick."

"Who is he?"

He is the chief of the tribe and lives further upstream. Long Spear is a wise man. You will like him for he is like Wandering Moos. He lives at Werowocomoco which lies close to the Pamunkey River."

The next day we reached the mouth of a large bay and Brave Eagle pointed north. He was most disappointed when we did not manage to make the mouth of his river before darkness fell but the shore to larboard, he assured us was Powhatan. We would be able to camp there. It was at the mouth of the Pamunkey River where we stopped. There were heights above us but no sign of a village. He said that they lay further upstream. I liked the place where we had landed for it felt fresher than the last two campsites. The beach allowed both my youngest children to play and we collected a great quantity of shellfish. I was sorry to leave when, the next morning, we continued our passage up the great expanse of water seeking the Patawomke. We passed another river. Brave Eagle was like a chattering bird. He never shut up and he shouted, excitedly, "That is the Rappahannock River. My people fish and hunt there too! The next river we see will be mine!"

I suppose that had this been Larswick or Orkneyjar then I would have been just as irrepressible. My fear was that we would find a deserted village and he would be more than disappointed; he would be broken. We were moving too slowly for his liking but when he pointed to larboard, and I saw the river, his river, I could not believe how wide it was. It seemed to be wider than Fox Water. I guessed it was more than five or six miles wide. I had wondered if my snekke would be too large to navigate it and now I saw that we were perfect for it.

Moos Blood pointed, as we turned to larboard, to the smoke in the distance. There were villages. "Reef the sail a little. We have the wind once more."

Brave Eagle was leaning so far out that I feared he might fall in but then I realised this was his river. We passed many becks and burns. Brave Eagle called them creeks and named them all. It was late afternoon when he pointed to larboard. I saw the smoke rising from beyond the trees. I also saw a cultivated area with tall plants growing. Hanging from them were tasselled fruits or I guessed that they were a fruit of some kind. I learned later that the yellow fruit was the staple for the Powhatans. It was used much as we used wheat, barley and oats. It was sometimes cooked and eaten but often it was ground up to make a sort of bread. These were the first skræling I had seen who cultivated the land. The Penobscot did not and I now wondered if their raids were to steal the secrets of growing such crops.

Brave Eagle waved his arm to slow me down and I had Moos Blood reef the sail even more. I knew Brave Eagle was looking for a place to land. He now understood the needs of a snekke. He pointed to a tiny sliver of beach. It looked barely big enough for us but his judgement was good and we slid up it and bumped into the soft bank. He was ashore and had tied us up before I realised.

"Come, the village is less than a mile away! There is a creek that leads to it but I fear the entrance will be too narrow for this boat. Our birch bark boats are perfect for it."

I pointed to the snekke, "And will the boat be safe here?"

He frowned, "These are my people and this is my land! Of course, it will be safe!"

I was not so sure for he had been away a long time and much could have changed. "I will leave Moos Blood here for I would not want strangers or animals to damage the snekke." He seemed to accept that. We had a horn we had brought from Bear Island, "If there is trouble then sound the horn and I will come!"

He smiled, "I will be safe, and I will watch *'Gytha'*!"

I strapped on my sword, which I took from my chest and grabbed my spear, "Arm yourself."

Brave Eagle was already helping Laughing Deer and Golden Bear from the snekke. Brave Cub was waiting for me to aid Little White Dove.

"Here, hold my spear." Cub happily took the spear and I swept Little White Dove up into my arms, "Come little one. Let us see if we have a roof for you this night!"

I put her down on the ground and Brave Cub took her hand. Brave Eagle nodded and led us along a path next to the field. I would bring up the rear and watch for trouble. The path led through trees, but it was well worn and suggested that it was frequently used. We passed other tended fields, but they appeared to have different crops. I knew there would be people in the village for we had seen smoke, but I did not know who they were. I heard the noise of the village before we reached it and, as we left the forest the path passed two more cultivated fields and I saw, ahead, the village. Brave Eagle ran when we reached the fields, and I could only assume that he had recognised someone. That he was also recognised became clear when there was a shout from the village and the Powhatans ran to greet him. Laughing Deer, out of courtesy, slowed and we caught her.

"It seems the village still thrives."

I nodded and I saw that there were some warriors who yet lived and that was a good sign. One appeared to have an arm he could not use for it hung by his side and when he hugged Brave Eagle it was with one arm. By the time we reached the village, he had turned and pointed to us. "These are my friends and they have brought me many hundreds of miles from the sea. Make them welcome!"

Apart from the four warriors, everyone was old. The other exceptions were the four boys who looked to be a little older than Brave Cub. They all seemed to want to touch us. One old woman stroked Laughing Deer's arm and I saw that the woman was crying. It was then that I saw the four birch bark boats. They were drawn up on a beck, a creek. It looked to be quite wide, "Brave Eagle, does that lead to the Patawomke?"

"It does but I fear that it might be too narrow for your snekke."

I handed my spear to Brave Cub, "I will walk back to the river. If I can sail it here, I will do so."

"Do you need help?"

"No, Moos Blood and I will manage. You see to your people but if you could find a yehakin for my wife and children then they can rest."

"Of course. You can have mine and I will stay with my sons."

It was only when I reached the creek that I realised what he had said. His sons had survived! There was a path down the creek and there were cultivated fields. In places, it seemed to be a hundred paces wide, but I saw it shrink and knew why Brave Eagle had been cautious. It narrowed to just ten paces. I walked to the edge and saw that there were snakes and turtles swimming around the branches which had fallen there. The actual passage was just eight paces wide. It would be close but I thought we could do it. Getting further down the creek was tricky and I had to clamber over and through trees that barred my way. The snakes I had seen in the water made me wary of stepping into the water. Eventually, I made it around and saw, three hundred paces from me, my snekke. It took me some time but finally, I made the snekke.

"Come, Moos Blood, we can sail to the camp. We will sail under a reefed sail and you can steer. Watch my actions for we have a narrow passage to negotiate." I trusted my son who had become a skilled sailor. The worst that could happen would be if we struck a submerged branch but *'Gytha'* had new and strong timbers and we would not be travelling fast. I took an oar both to signal and to act as a fender. The entrance looked even narrower and was made even more constricted by a branch I had not seen. I dropped the oar and picked up my spear. In two strikes I severed the branch and waved to Moos Blood to turn to larboard. I picked up the oar again and used it to help my son to steer. The passage was two hundred paces long but the narrowest part was at the end. Had I not walked along the path I would have thought it impossible for us to pass along it, but I knew we could make it and I only had to use the oar once. Then we were out of the confining canopy and in wide, open water. I walked down the snekke and relieved Moos Blood. When time allowed I would take my axe and widen the channel.

"Go to the prow and enjoy the view. You did well, my son!"

I nudged us next to the boats and without being ordered Moos Blood leapt ashore and this time secured us fore and aft. "Do we unload the snekke?"

I nodded, "We need to examine the hull and your mother will need the things which are below the deck. We will put them on the bank and ask Brave Eagle for help to move the goods."

It took some time to remove the whole of the deck and by the time we had done so Brave Eagle had joined us along with two warriors, one of whom had the lamed arm. I could see that it was withered and scarred.

"Erik, Shaman of the Bear. These are two of my sons. This is my eldest White Fox and the one who has the wounded arm is Hides Alone."

I knew he had three sons but I said nothing of that. "I am pleased that you survived the battle!"

White Fox said, "And we are beholden to you for saving our father. Without Brave Eagle the clan is nothing."

Hides Alone nodded his agreement, "And now we can find our families for with the Shaman of the Bear all things are possible."

I looked over to Brave Eagle who had the good grace to look guilty, "I told them of your skill with weapons."

White Fox touched the gunwale of the snekke as though it might burn him, "And this is a magical creature. My father said that you need not paddle?"

"We use a sail. Brave Eagle, could we have some help to unload? I would like to examine the snekke for damage."

"Of course. Hides Alone, fetch the other warriors and the boys. They can carry."

"This is my son, Moos Blood. He will tell you what you need to do."

Moos Blood handed White Fox our one surviving barrel, "It is heavy!"

"I can manage."

Moos Blood picked up my byrnie and the rest of our weapons. "I will carry these, Father."

Left alone Brave Eagle said, "My other son, Black Owl, was killed in the battle. When I fell the three of them tried to rally the rest of the warriors but when Black Owl was killed the rest fled and my two sons barely survived. They went to the lodge of Long Spear and asked him to make war on the Penobscot, but he said they were too strong. It was what he said to me when I asked but now we know that the Lenni Lenape make war they may change their mind." He hesitated, "And if the Shaman of the Bear, dressed for war comes too then it may influence him."

Despite my plans, I was being drawn into war again! The Norns!

Chapter 17

It was after dark by the time we had finished emptying the hold and any examination of the hull would have to wait until a new day. There were only a handful of women in the clan and they were old, but they made Laughing Deer more than welcome. The fact that she was a mother with a babe in arms seemed to make her special and she was treated like a queen. When we carried the contents of the hold to the lodge, she handed Golden Bear to an old woman who beamed a toothless smile. Little White Dove was already enjoying the attention of two other old women from the clan. They had missed children and our arrival was like a breath of air. As soon as Brave Eagle had arrived then others had begun to cook a feast. Laughing Deer took out some of the salted whale meat and handed it to them. Any change in diet was welcome.

Laughing Deer said, "Sit in front of the lodge and smoke Wandering Moos' pipe. You have done more than anyone could have expected and the clan will wish to ask you questions. Brave Cub, fetch the bearskin and let your father wear that."

I tried to dismiss her idea but she insisted, and spoke quietly to me, "I have spoken to the women. Even when Brave Eagle's sons returned, they had lost all hope. It was our arrival which has made them smile. Play the part of the shaman, husband. You and I know the truth, but it will not hurt for them to think you and Brave Eagle might return the captives!"

I nodded and Brave Cub placed the skin over my head while Moos Blood, who had been listening intently, handed me my pipe and the pouch of leaves. I sighed and began to fill the pipe. Brave Cub brought a lighted brand and I sent clouds of smoke into the night sky. As I looked up, I saw that the women of the clan and the old men were smiling so broadly I thought their faces would crack. Some of the older men brought their pipes. They did not sit but looked as though they wished to. I gestured for them to join me and soon the eight old men from the village were seated on the floor on either side of me. None tried to question me but I knew that they wished to know about me and so I began to speak.

I used the sing song voice that my people used when singing sagas. I spoke in Mi'kmaq and I spoke slowly. They seemed to understand for they nodded at the appropriate times, "I am Erik the Navigator who sailed for many moons in a boat with more people than are in this clan, across a vast sea out of sight of land." As I spoke, I saw the old women, including the ones with my children draw closer to listen. "We found a land to the far north filled with ice and fire. The very earth boiled rocks and they poured down the mountains and into the sea to make more land. We left there and sailed to the land north of the land of the Mi'kmaq."

I saw Brave Eagle gesture for his sons and the other two warriors who had been speaking with him to come and listen too. "There I found the bear whose skin I wear and I killed him. We lived on an island and were happy. Then, one day, my brother made war on the Penobscot and he was killed. I fell from a roaring water and would have died had not Laughing Deer brought me back from the dead. When we returned to my home my clan had left to return to the east and I became Erik, Shaman of the Bear and a warrior of the Mi'kmaq. I fought and killed many Penobscot. When we rescued Brave Eagle who was far out to sea and could not see the land we decided to return him to his people. That is my story and that is all I have to say!"

The looks on their faces told me that I had given them what they wished to hear.

Hides Alone asked, "And now, Erik, Shaman of the Bear, will you help us to rescue our families? Will you use your magic stick to help defeat them?"

I looked up at Brave Eagle who shrugged. One of the old men said, "Magic stick?"

The bearskin cloak had hidden the sword. After laying down the pipe I stood and drew it. There were oohs, aahs and gasps as the firelight glinted off the blade. It was sharp and I saw a piece of kindling the thickness of my arm. I nodded to Brave Eagle who held it out in two hands. I swung the sword, and the wood was sliced cleanly in two. Brave Eagle held the two pieces so that the old men could see the clean cut.

White Fox gave a cry almost of victory and said, "With such a weapon none can stand before us! Truly you are a shaman!"

Thanks to Brave Eagle and my wife I was now committed to helping to rescue the captives. The looks on the old people in the clan would not let me do other. When we ate, I was offered all the best delicacies first and I was waited on as though I was a king. I saw Brave Eagle's face and knew that he had planned all of this. I did not blame him for I would have done anything to get my family back if they had been taken but in committing myself to the rescue, I was risking my family losing the head of their family. The sisters had spun.

At long last, we managed to extricate ourselves and seek sanctuary in our lodge. The lodges were solidly made and quite roomy. This one was particularly well made for it had been Brave Eagle's. The four children were exhausted for they had enjoyed the attention too and Golden Bear was laid on the bjorr skin so that Laughing Deer and I could cuddle.

"These are good people, Erik, and you must help them. I know we fled the Penobscot to avoid a fight, but I can see now that these three sisters of yours have plans for you and we are helpless to fight against them. This is a fight that must be fought for if we do not then the Penobscot have won and that is a world in which I do not wish to live. You came for me and Stands Alone when the Sisters sent you. If you had not come, then I fear that my sister and I might have taken our own lives such was our misery. I am the only one who can know what Brave Eagle's wife and the wives of his sons are enduring. They are held by a cruel people."

I kissed her gently, "You are right, and I had come to that conclusion myself. No matter what we do, we are pinned on this web. It means that we will be here for the winter, perhaps longer."

She snuggled into me and kissed my chest, "I know but this seems a pleasant place and we will not have to move home as we did in the north."

"Then we will stay, and the sisters have won." Even as I said it I knew there was no other outcome. The sisters always won.

The next morning I rose early and even before dawn had fully broken, I went to the snekke. The boys and I would have to work on her later, but I wanted to see that the mooring I had hurriedly made held. It had but as I was working on the boat, I felt the heat from the land. We had travelled hundreds of miles south and now I felt how hot it would be. Brave Eagle had told me on the way south how cold he had been in the north and now I saw why he felt that way. I had heard of lands to the south of Al-Andalus where it was so hot that it burned the skins of men to make them black. Was this land the same? I tightened the moorings and returned to the village. It was just coming to life. Brave Eagle emerged from his son's lodge and strode over to me. I saw both the question and the guilt on his face. He had created the situation the previous night and used his people to influence me. As Laughing Deer had said, I would have done the same had I been in his position and I did not blame him.

"I will come with you, Brave Eagle, but I know not what six warriors can do."

154

"Six warriors can do nothing but when we have visited Long Spear then we may have more warriors. We will leave tomorrow. Today is a day for settling you and your family into the village and for the steam hut. I went north once before to save my family and I failed. I saw the way you prepared for this last voyage. I saw the sacrifice you made and the care with which you planned. We made it here safely and I have learned from that. Before we leave on this quest we will purify our minds and our bodies. I will leave nothing to chance."

The old women helped Laughing Deer as though she was the matriarch of the clan. I knew when I had met her that Laughing Deer was special but now, seeing her with the Powhatans I saw just how special she was. It meant that the boys and I could work on the snekke. There had been, as far as I could tell, little damage to the boat. The ropes had inevitably worn and we had to replace one. The old rope was not wasted as the shorter lengths could be used in many ways on the snekke. The hold was dry. I had not seen any pine trees and that might be a problem should we need to make pine tar but that was in the future. After finding stones to replace the ballast we had left in the north we refitted the deck.

"We can step the mast and crosstree. I do not think we will be going to sea again soon."

Moos Blood stopped what he was doing and looked at me, "We are not going fishing? This river looks perfect for the snekke and when we sailed up the river yesterday, I saw that it teemed with fish. I thought we might make a net!"

"And that is a good idea. You and your brother can make a net while I am away. And you can paint the dragon."

"Away?"

"Yes, Brave Cub, tomorrow I go with Brave Eagle to see the mamanatowick, Long Spear. He goes to ask for help to recover his family."

"And you will go with them when he goes?"

"I will be going with the warriors to recover his family, Moos Blood, and you and your brother will stay here to guard your family."

"I could help!"

"I know but who would guard this camp and our family? The warriors will be coming with us. You, Moos Blood who is not yet a warrior, will be the one to defend the camp and you, Brave Cub, will have to help him."

The argument convinced them.

That afternoon I joined Brave Eagle and his sons in the steam hut. There were just four of us and this time we passed around a pipe that

155

had a very fragrant leaf in it. I normally felt lightheaded when I smoked and now, I felt even more so. It was as close to the dreamworld as I had come in a while. I had no visions, but my mind seemed to clear itself of all irrelevancies. My family would be safe and, as we would not have to fight a battle, I saw the chance to sneak in to a depleted Penobscot camp and retake the captives. It would not be easy, but I had completed far harder tasks in the past.

The next day we left for Werowocomoco. Brave Eagle told me that it was half a day away and we would probably have to stay there for the night. He insisted that I take my helmet, bearskin, sword, spear and hatchet. I refused to take the axe and left that with Moos Blood. I did not wear my skin but wrapped it and my helmet in my sealskin cape and wore it over my back with my shield.

The trail we followed was well made and clear but it passed through a forest that teemed with insects and the heat of the day did not help. As far as I could tell we were heading south and west. We came to a river which we had to ford.

Brave Eagle helped me to adjust my load when we crossed and pointed downstream. "There is another clan there, the Clan of the Aroughcun. If we receive no help from Long Spear, then we will ask them to send warriors to help us."

I nodded, "Is the bearskin necessary?"

He smiled, "I have had time to think about this. I will leave you and White Fox in the forest. You can don your helmet and skin and bear your shield before you. I will send for you so that when you and White Fox enter from the forest it will have a greater effect."

"Why do we need to do this? Surely your story should convince him that you have been wronged."

"The last time I came, when our families were taken, he was sympathetic, but he did not hear. This time I will make him hear. I will shock him with your appearance!"

I nodded my acceptance. It was not long after the sun was at its height. The shade from the trees helped but I knew that as soon as I entered the village I would be in the full glare of the sun and in my helmet and my cloak I would bake!

Brave Eagle and the others waved their goodbyes and left us at the place my friend had decided we would wait. White Fox had never seen my helmet and was fascinated when I took it out of the skin. I laid it on the ground while I slipped my cloak around my shoulders. He had a stone club in his belt and he looked at me. I knew what he wished to do. All the warriors I had met had done the same. "Of course. Strike it but not too hard eh? I do not wish it to be damaged."

He gave it a tap which was none too gentle and the metal rang making him leap backwards. "That is magic too!"

I nodded and donned it. There was a way to don the bearskin which allowed me to do it alone. I put the head on my helmet with my head forward and then threw both my head and cloak back over my body. Once again White Fox stepped backwards. It was, as Brave Eagle knew, a dramatic effect. I hefted my shield on my left arm and held my spear with my right.

White Fox had kept his distance, "If I had not met and spoken to you before then seeing you like this I would have fled and I would not wish to face you in war!"

"And that is what your father hopes. He wants me to terrify the Penobscot into fleeing, but the trouble is they have seen me before. The shock will not be there or, if it is, not as great as the first time."

He nodded as he took the words in.

Of course, the ones who had seen me had already fled from the battlefield and they would be afraid of me, but they would know that I could be hurt. White Fox believed that the skin was magic as were the helmet and shield. He thought me invincible. I knew that I was not.

It was Hides Alone who came for us and he stopped and clutched at his amulet when he saw me. White Fox said, "I know, brother, but it is still the man who saved our father. Erik, walk behind us so that when we part at the village you can continue to walk. It will have a better effect."

The heat was so great that I was already sweating long before we reached the open skies of the town. It was a town for when we neared it, I saw that it was the largest place I had seen since leaving Larswick. I saw it between the moving heads of the two sons of Brave Eagle and I could see a great crowd ahead.

Suddenly the two warriors parted, and I was hit by a shaft of light. There is no way that Brave Eagle could have predicted it, but the sun glinted off the freshly polished head of my spear and as I walked towards Brave Eagle and the tribal elders, I heard both men and women scream in fear. Weapons were drawn and it took all my courage to keep walking. Two warriors drew their bows and loosed arrows. I instinctively lifted my shield and the first arrow hit the boss and bounced off. The other struck my head and helmet. The arrowhead stuck in the fur and hung limply down.

Brave Eagle stepped before me and shouted, "This is not a demon he is a friend. This is the man who saved me from the sea and returned me here. This is Erik, Shaman of the Bear and he comes from a land many months across the sea."

The man whom I took, by his command and his dress, to be the chief, Long Spear, held up a spear with a large stone head. He shouted, "Do not send any more arrows on pain of death! I would speak with this shaman!"

I smiled, knowing that the smile was hidden by the bear's head for only Long Spear and Brave Eagle stepped forward. The rest had fear etched on their features.

Brave Eagle said, "Erik, take off your skin so that the people may see you are a man."

I needed to take off the fur for I was sweating profusely. I turned and handed my shield to White Fox and my spear to Hides Alone. I took the arrow from the fur and dropped it contemptuously to the ground. When I took off the helmet and the bright sun glinted off the helmet even Long Spear stepped back. I laid the skin at my feet and unfastened the sealskin cloak. Finally, I took off my helmet and placed it on the bearskin.

For the first time, the chief looked relieved and he stepped forward before poking me in the chest. "You are a man but what is this around your face?"

I smiled, "It is called a beard and all of the men in my tribe have one."

"And your hair? It is not black as night!"

"No, for we come from the east."

He turned and said, "Not that I doubted you, Brave Eagle, but all that you have said is proven to be true. If anything you said too little for those two arrows would have slain many a warrior." He turned to face the tribe, "This is a friend, and we would speak with him." He turned back to me, "Come, I can see that you are unused to this heat. We will go into the shade and you can tell me your story. I will then give thought to the words of Brave Eagle."

We sat under the shade of a large tree that was close to his lodge. Only the three of us sat while some of his tribal elders and Brave Eagle's sons stood within hearing of us.

"Tell me your story." I repeated the tale I had told Brave Eagle's clan and Long Spear nodded. "Had I not seen you I might have doubted you, but I see you speak true. Brave Eagle tells me that you have a magic stick."

I took out the sword and stood. "White Fox, find me a branch." Having seen the trick once before he knew what to do and he brought me a perfect piece of kindling. He held it out and I sliced it in two. The gasp was even louder than it had been when I had taken off my skin. I sheathed the sword.

158

Long Spear looked at Brave Eagle, "And if you have this shaman then why do you need warriors? Surely he alone could rescue your people."

They both looked at me and I knew what I had to do. I took out my seax, which was sharp and sliced across my palm. Blood dripped on the ground, "I am a man. If your warriors surrounded me and hit me with their weapons I could kill and hurt many of them but I would, inevitably, die. Brave Eagle hopes that fighting will be unnecessary, and my very appearance will drive away the Penobscot, but I have fought them before and they hate me, calling me a demon. They will fight. If you do not aid us, Long Spear, then we will still go but we will probably die. The Clan of the Eagle will disappear and the Penobscot will have the magic stick, the spear and," I tapped the helmet which White Fox had laid beside me, "and my helmet. Then the next time the Penobscot raid, and raid they will, they might come here and use these weapons to take your families into captivity. So, Long Spear, the choice is clear, you either help us or wait for the day when the Penobscot come back and take your family." I shrugged, "I am not of your clan, but I know what I would do!"

Brave Eagle's face told me that he was not happy about either my tone or my words, but they were out and I could not take them back. Long Spear frowned, "I had not thought of that, shaman and I can see that you are a clever man, as are all shamans. You use your words like weapons, and you make a threat, which I do not like but I looked into your eyes when you spoke and saw neither insult nor lie. You will stay this night for we have a yehakin for guests. I will speak with my elders and consider your words. Before you leave in the morning then I will give you my answer."

"That is all we ask, Long Spear," Brave Eagle sounded relieved that we had not been dismissed out of hand.

The chief nodded and said, "Prepare the yehakin and have food readied. I wish to speak more with this shaman." He looked pointedly at the ones who were stood around us and they all moved away. The chief wanted privacy. When they disappeared he said, "The part of your story I find hard to believe, shaman, is your journey across the ocean from this land of ice and fire."

I told him of our drekar and how we built it and repeated the story of the journey.

"You could not see the land?" I shook my head, "Nor the moss on trees?"

I reinforced my words with gestures, "Nor the sun when there were clouds. Neither could we see stars at night when they were hidden yet

159

we managed it and the proof of it is that I sit here now and speak with you. You can see that I am different. How else do you explain that I am here?"

"Yet you speak our words and know our customs!"

"I have been here for ten years and I have married a Mi'kmaq woman."

"I should like to see this boat which can carry a clan!"

I smiled, "Then if you return to Brave Eagle's village you can see a smaller version I built in the land of the Mi'kmaq. The design is the same, but it is smaller."

Brave Eagle suddenly asked, "Then you could build a bigger one? You could build one which would carry a clan?"

"If I had the wood and the tools then yes!"

"Then build one and we can use that to rescue my family!"

I shook my head, "It would take more than a year and I do not have the tools."

Long Spear had almost ignored Brave Eagle's words and he said, "I have decided that I will return with you tomorrow and see this boat. I would travel on it." He looked at Brave Eagle, "You were not enchanted after travelling through the seas on it?"

"No Long Spear."

The chief then spent the rest of the time asking me about the voyage and the Land of Ice and Fire. He was particularly interested in how the molten rock became land. "I have often wondered how the great spirit made this land. Perhaps that was how he managed it, eh, Brave Eagle?"

"Perhaps."

The chief nodded, "The news of the war between the Lenni Lenape and the Penobscot is interesting. The Lenni Lenape have ever been our allies. We share much with them, and perhaps we now see the Penobscot for what they are. They take rather than grow. We will talk in the morning. I will see my elders. This night we will take food together and welcome this stranger to our tribe."

We rose and Brave Eagle hefted my shield while I carried the rest. He led me to the yehakin. We knew which was ours for his sons and the other two warriors were there. I saw that close to the river were many fields. The people had hewn the trees and planted many crops. I asked Brave Eagle about the crops.

"The ones you saw by our river are mainly corn, but we have a field of squash and one of beans. We would normally have almost as many as you can see here but with so many of the clan taken that proved impossible. When they return, we will replant the fields." He suddenly smiled, "With your axe, we could even make new fields."

"Perhaps. In return are there any pine trees?"

He rubbed his chin and then nodded, "There are some, not as large as the ones you cut at Wandering Moos' camp but there are some. We call them the shortleaf pine."

I grinned, "Size is immaterial! It is their roots that I seek. Then when we return, if we return, from the hunt for your people I will cut down your trees and in return, you will help me to find this pine and to make pine tar."

He nodded and then said, "Pine tar? Then you are thinking of leaving us?"

"I need to coat the snekke with pine tar in any case but, yes, we may leave. The Penobscot raided here once and they could do so again. I would not wish to draw them to my family or to your people. We have made no decision and we will certainly be here for the winter."

White Fox was a curious warrior, "Where would you go? Back to the sea?"

"My snekke can get wherever your birch bark boats can. I have seen many rivers and perhaps one might take me west into the heart of this country!"

Hides Alone said, "I have heard that the Cohongarooton, which is the Patawomke above the falls travels for many miles and then is joined by another large, wide river, it is called the Schin-han-do, the spruce stream. You could travel far into this land and see places close to the mountains."

My heart sank, "There are mountains?"

They all nodded and Brave Eagle asked, "Why, is that a problem?"

"If there are mountains then there is no passage west and my journey would stop at the mountains!" Perhaps I should have gone north to the great expanse of water close to the roaring falls.

The feast was almost exactly the same as the one in Brave Eagle's village. I was questioned, politely, about my life and my homeland. At first, it was the elders and the braver warriors but once they saw that none was struck down by lightning or changed into a strange creature then many grew bolder and I was asked all sorts of things. The most amusing one was if our women had beards. The Mi'kmaq had done the same but that had been so many years ago and over a longer period of time. I felt exhausted at the end of it.

We slept well. In my case, it was because I knew I would be returning to my family and I would have a few days, at least, with them. If the chief agreed to help us, then in a few days we would head north and east to the camp of the Penobscot. We had better directions this time as the four warriors who had survived had seen where the captives

161

were held, and the winter camp was closer to Brave Eagle's. The journey would not be as long. If the chief did not agree to help, then Brave Eagle would seek help from the clans who lived within half a day of us. Even a few warriors who chose a glorious quest might be enough. We had worked out that the Hawk Clan had lost many warriors and we could use cunning rather than brute force to rescue them.

When I woke, Brave Eagle and his sons were not in the lodge. The two warriors were also missing. I rose and went outside. The three of them were waiting outside the lodge of Long Spear. I made water and then joined them. Long Spear appeared in no hurry to give his verdict.

"Whatever he decides Long Spear will return with us to view the snekke. I have sent the others back to prepare a yehakin for him."

Eventually, the chief came out of his lodge. He beamed, "You slept well, shaman?"

"I did and the food was well cooked. I enjoyed it."

"Is our food the same as yours?"

I shook my head, "We have bread which is made from a grain and baked in an oven. We also raise animals so that we do not have to hunt. We keep an animal which is like the moos but it does not have antlers and we can milk the cows. We make the milk into cheese and we feed the milk to our children. We eat the flesh of the animal which is like the moos."

"You grow crops as we do?"

I nodded.

"Then you are not like the Penobscot who just hunt, fish and steal from those who grow."

I decided to be honest, "No, but we do make war. Some clans take their boats and sail to other lands where they take precious metals and slaves."

"Precious metals?"

I took out the sword and pointed to the pommel which was made of bronze and had a blue stone in it, "Metals like this. We dig them from the ground as rocks and then make them into things we can use."

"You are all shaman then."

He turned to Brave Eagle, "The council has decided to help you. We will ask for warriors who wish to join you on this quest."

That was not exactly what Brave Eagle had hoped but it was better than nothing, "Thank you, Long Spear."

"I will return to see this boat and my sons will find warriors who wish to join you. They will come to your village in three days when they are prepared."

I knew the delay would not please my friend but, again, we had no choice.

"When I have eaten, we will leave!"

Chapter 18

Had I known that Brave Eagle was sending his men to our camp I could have requested to ask Moos Blood to fit the mast. As it was when I took Long Spear to see the snekke he was less impressed than he might have been.

He nodded as he looked at it, "I can see that it is sturdy and can carry more men but it would be slower than our birch bark boats."

I nodded, "Indeed? Moos Blood, Brave Cub, help me fit the mast." The wind was from the north and the inlet, which was very wide, ran north to south with a branch five hundred paces down stream which ran east to west. I pointed to the birch barks boat drawn up on the bank. "Could your warriors paddle those?"

"Of course."

"And beat me in a straight-line race?"

He was not a fool and he frowned as he thought to see the trick, "And who would be your paddlers?"

"Just me and my sons!"

He beamed. I had learned that the tribes loved competition, "And when I win, what will be the prize?"

I took out my hatchet, "How about this?"

His eyes widened. "Then let us begin."

I shook my head, "First I need to make my boat ready for the race and I need to know what I will receive if I win?"

"I will give you the skins from ten deer!"

I nodded, "Accepted. We sail to the end of this water and back!" I did not need the hides but if I had taken anything less he would have been insulted.

He chose his warriors who climbed into the boat and paddled it around. They were so busy, as was the chief, that we had the mast, crosstree and sail erected before they knew. When they saw it, they cocked their heads to one side. It was hard to see how we would sail faster."

Brave Eagle had watched it all with amusement. He knew what was coming. Long Spear said, "You are ready, like this?"

"Whenever you give the word, Long Spear." I nodded to my sons who untied us and then stood ready to loose the sail. I sat by the steering board.

"Your paddles?"

"We need no paddles!"

"Go!" He was a fair man, but he was trying to win and the four warriors dug their paddles in and soon had a healthy lead. The sail was loosed but the chief did not see the design for he was watching his men. However, he frowned as the wind filled it and it billowed. I put the steering board over and *'Gytha'* responded. Within a couple of moments, she had almost caught up with the birch bark boat. We were silent and the warriors did not look around. I did not want them to think I was cheating and so I took us to pass them well to their larboard side. We had overtaken them before we reached the east-west branch. The boys were squealing with delight. We reached the far end and I took my time tacking and turning. We would not be as swift on the return leg but what I had forgotten was the sight of the sail. The boys had managed, while I was away, to crush beetles to make the red eyes and even without the yellow root to colour its head it was effective and when the four warriors saw it, they threw themselves from the boat and tried to swim to shore.

I did not want to risk them drowning and so I said, "Reef the sail. Brave Cub, throw ropes for them." I cupped my hands, "There is nothing to fear, climb aboard and we will take you back!"

One grabbed a rope but shook his head, "You are a demon and that is a monster!"

Two others had righted the boat and clung to it. The third climbed aboard and began to bail. I shook my head, "Then paddle back. We will wait until you are all back on your boat."

They climbed aboard and began to attempt to empty the water. They had managed to secure two paddles but it would be some time before they reached the chief,

With our sail filling once more we sailed back, tacking to and fro to use the unhelpful wind. When we pulled into the bank my sons leapt ashore and tied us up. Long Spear looked shocked. He turned to Brave Eagle, "You knew?"

"We told you we do not need to paddle but instead use the wind. You did not believe us."

It was a delicate moment for the chief had lost face. I held out my hand, "Long Spear would you like to come aboard?"

"Will I become enchanted?"

Brave Eagle shook his head, "There is no magic for it is just the wind which makes it move."

He had brought other warriors with him and had he refused might have been accused of cowardice. He nodded and Brave Eagle held out his hand to help him aboard. I gestured for Brave Eagle to join us and I waited until they were seated before I said, "Cast off!"

165

As the sail filled, we raced south, and Brave Eagle had to support Long Spear. This time I headed for the branch so as to avoid the waterlogged birch bark boat. I saw the knuckles of the chief as he gripped the mast fish. When we neared the branch I shouted, "Prepare to come about!"

Brave Eagle's arm came around Long Spear's shoulder and we spun around and kept going. There was a slight hiatus as we went into the wind but the boys adjusted the sail and I put the steering board over. We reached the bank just as the four bedraggled warriors climbed ashore. The boys reefed the sail and we bobbed up and down next to the bank.

"If you wish we could sail to the Patawomke."

This was a test. Had we upset and offended the chief? He nodded and, in a voice a little higher than the one he normally used, he said, "Aye, let us try this beast!"

"Brave Cub and Moos Blood, take an oar each in case you have to fend us off going through the narrow passage."

I judged it better this time and having lopped off some of the overhanging branches the first time, we eased through and on to the Patawomke. After the channel, it looked like a sea and *'Gytha'* enjoyed the freedom. I used the wind to head diagonally across the river to the far bank. With no cargo in her hold, she flew. I was glad we had replaced the damaged rope. A dunking for Long Spear would have been a disaster. We must have sailed for an hour or more but when I saw the sun starting to set, I headed back to the creek. We nudged up the channel and tied up next to the birch bark boats and Long Spear's waiting warriors. The boys knew their jobs and I smiled as I remembered Arne, Siggi and myself when we had been ship's boys. The blood oath had bound us and the knife I had used had held us together until the falls. *Wyrd*.

I waited until Brave Eagle and Long Spear had stepped on to the bank before I had the mast taken down. Long Spear asked, as the three of us took out the pegs and slackened the ropes, "Why do you do this, shaman? Is it to stop this creature from running away in the night?"

I shook my head, "If the wind gets up then either the boat or the mast might be damaged. It does not take long for us to erect the mast." When it was done, we stepped ashore.

"That is a truly wonderful boat, shaman. What is it called?"

"The type of boat is snekke." He frowned at the word, "It means snake in my language. We named her *'Gytha'* after a wise woman who ruled our clan."

He nodded, "Like the Wampanoag." He began to head back to the village, "I can see how you could sail great distances without tiring and you say you sailed in one bigger than this?"

We had reached the village and I said, "Moos Blood, stand here, you are the steering board of the drekar." I led Brave Cub away from his brother and placed him, "You, Brave Cub are the prow." I pointed to the two of them, "It was that long!"

The chief said nothing, but I knew I had set thoughts racing in his head.

After we had washed, we ate the food prepared by the women of the clan. Long Spear had been quiet and his words after we had eaten told me his thoughts, "So there are many men like you in the east?" I nodded. "And they have large boats like the one you described?"

"Some are larger."

"Then they too could come here."

I shook my head, "They could but I doubt that they will for the only one who could bring them is my brother Fótr and I do not think that he would return."

The chief was like a wolf trying to get the last of the meat from a kill. "But others could come, and they would have weapons such as yours. They would be unbeatable, and my people would die."

I would not lie, and I said, "What you say is possible but I have been here these many years. The place we left, Bear Island, was known to those who left and they have not returned. What my clan did was difficult and there were many obstacles in the way."

The chief looked at me, "And what you are saying is that it is you who were the reason your clan reached here?"

I nodded, "My name amongst my people is Erik the Navigator."

"Then I am content that you are here and not back in your own land for others might have persuaded you to return and our world would end."

He was right, of course, Arne and those who had urged him to make war had been foolish. Had we simply made walls and a ditch, as we had at the bjorr camp then the Penobscot would have bled on our walls. If we had stayed with the Mi'kmaq, then we would have been able to control a large part of the land. If many more drekar had come we could have made the land of Wandering Moos' clan a haven of peace and prosperity but Arne had chosen the way of the conqueror. I doubted that I would see more drekar coming west in my lifetime but one day men would leave the Land of Ice and Fire and sail south. Then the fears of Long Spear might be realised.

167

The chief left the next morning and the visit had been useful for he and Brave Eagle were closer. The wounds which followed his refusal to help the clan the first time had been healed and Long Spear promised to encourage his warriors to come to our aid.

While we waited for the warriors to arrive, I sat with my sons and Brave Eagle's to plan the campaign. The Powhatans did not use miles but spoke of journeys in days. White Fox said that it had taken them seven days to find their way back. I knew that the people of this land could cover great distances on foot. They told us that the camp of the Penobscot was in a land of waters. From what they said, and after looking at the maps I had made on the way south I determined that it was fifty miles north of the huge island we had passed. We had to cross a great river which marked the boundary of Penobscot land, the Muhheakantuck. That made sense to me for the Clan of the Hawk lived at the southern end of the land controlled by the Penobscot. We had two ways to get there. We could sail north to the falls on the Patawomke and then cross to the north bank before heading northeast or, and this was my suggestion, we could cross the river here. Whilst it would be wider, we could use the snekke to ferry larger numbers across. Paddling the birch bark boats would take longer. Brave Eagle agreed to my suggestion, but I saw that Moos Blood had worked out that he would not be coming. I had already decided not to take my byrnie. We were not going to fight a battle. Brave Eagle and I had decided that if we chose the vengeance trail then we would lose men and that was not our intention. Brave Eagle had killed his enemy and, as he said, the ones who had fled were not worthy of the name, warrior. All that we wanted was to free the captives. Nor would I take my spear and axe. My sword, bow, seax and hatchet would suffice. Brave Eagle and his sons insisted that I took my bearskin and helmet. I agreed, reluctantly for it was a weight and I would be hot enough as it was. That meant I had to leave behind my shield.

By the end of the day, the first warriors had arrived. While Brave Eagle spoke to them, I was able to spend time with my wife. "It looks like we will be away for more than half a moon. The boys will have to fish." I turned to them, "I believe that you can use the snekke but if you think you cannot then just set fish traps."

Moos Blood said, "Do not worry, father. If we can sail the snekke across the Patawomke then we can sail the creek and catch fish. We will have the net finished before you leave."

I gave a word of warning, "Do not forget that there are both snakes and turtles in the creek. Brave Eagle has told me that all the snakes which live in the water are poisonous."

168

"We will be careful. If you are leaving your spear, then we can kill them without getting close to them." My eldest was getting close to manhood and it showed. He thought things through. That he had not complained about being left behind was a good sign.

Brave Eagle had decided that he needed no more than twenty warriors and as soon as sixteen had arrived we would leave. If more came then that would not hurt but we would not wait for them. The women of the clan were busy preparing pânsâwân which was a kind of dried meat. Some of it would then be mixed with berries and tallow to make pimîhkân. This was highly nutritious and lighter to carry than the pieces of salted meat we would otherwise need to sustain us. We would have neither the time nor the safety to cook food. Once we had left the land of the Lenni Lenape we would be trying to hide out as best as we could. Chief Long Spear had sent the hides, despite my insistence that he did not need to. As he told me, "You won and won well. It was a lesson to me in arrogance and from now on I will be humbler. Brave Eagle had told me of your skill, and I did not believe him."

As a result, I had spare hides and sewed a couple to make a sack in which I could carry my helmet, sealskin cape, and bearskin. I fashioned two straps so that I could carry it over my shoulders and leave my arms free. I used some of the trimmings to make loops for my bow and attach my arrow bag. I had decided to wear my bjorr hat; not because I might be cold but because it would protect my head from the insects. Laughing Deer had made a pungent-smelling salve to coat my face and arms for she knew that some of the insects could bite and those bites could cause illness.

Three days after we had returned to the village, we had sixteen warriors who wished to join us. We started to ferry them across at dawn. To reassure the new warriors that it was safe we took just the five Powhatan warriors first. After that, I would make just two trips. I left Brave Cub on the other bank. He would sail on the last trip and Moos Blood and he would sail the snekke back to the creek. I steered for the first trip but on the way back and for the rest I let Moos Blood be the navigator. He had a natural ability, and I was confident that despite the current and the width of the river on the last trip he would cope well.

The first snekke load of warriors were nervous but the presence of the old women of the clan and Laughing Deer meant that they had to board or lose face. It was like Long Spear all over again. Their knuckles were white as they gripped anything solid but by the time we were halfway across some had plucked up the courage to talk with others. The last trip was the most hazardous for the warriors were slightly bigger and I had to bring Brave Cub to help his brother sail the snekke back. We rode lower in the water and when we reached the middle some river water lapped over the gunwale. To be fair to the Powhatan warriors they showed no fear, but I was worried that I had exceeded the limits of the boat. We made the other side safely and they eagerly disembarked.

"You had better lift the deck when you return and dry out the hold. I do not want rot in the snekke."

"Fear not father we will watch the snekke and our family."

I nodded and watched as they turned the snekke around and headed back to the other bank. I was so proud of them I felt a lump in my throat. We had raised good boys.

Brave Eagle was keen to move and I waved him off, "Do not wait for me. You lead and I will bring up the rear."

He shook his head, "You are the most important part of this plan and you will run with my sons and warriors at the front. The others can bring up the rear."

My heart sank. Although my knee and my other wounds had healed, I was not as ready to run as these Powhatan warriors and they did run. I nodded and they set off. Hides Alone went before me and White Fox behind. I suppose that Brave Eagle was thinking that a lamed warrior would be more of my pace. They set off at a steady lope. This part of the journey was in familiar territory. There were Powhatan clans who lived on this side of the Patawomke and if we came across any hunters, they would be friendly. It would take us until the end of the next day to reach the land of the Lenni Lenape. I was not a runner and by the time we had run for an hour I had a pain in my side. I knew that I had to run through it, but it still hurt. I had spare mockasins in my bag and I knew that I would need them. I knew that when this quest was over my feet would be bloody and shredded! We stopped at noon and drank from a stream that bubbled white. We ate some of the pimîhkân which I found to be extremely filling. Then we began to run again. I had no idea how far we ran but I knew that at the end of it I would have been hard-pressed to cover the same distance in the same time sailing the snekke. The difference was that had we taken the snekke my feet would not have burned and my legs and back would not have felt as though I had carried a birch bark boat upon it! I was helped by Brave Eagle's sons who had seen or perhaps sensed when I was struggling and offered words of encouragement.

When we stopped to camp White Fox said, "If you need to stop running then just tell us and we will give you a rest."

I shook my head, "Your father pines for his family and we have delayed long enough. Each day that passes means that more of your people will suffer, perhaps even die and I could not bear that thought. I am a man, and I will keep up," I gave a wry smile as I placed my feet in the river where we were camped, "so long as my body holds out!"

When my feet had cooled, I lifted them out to examine them. Hides Alone produced a hollowed-out piece of wood. He took out the leather stopper and a finger of salve, "This might help." He began to smear it on my feet. It was an aromatic smell and as soon as the salve touched my feet, I could almost feel them thanking him for the gift.

I donned my mockasins knowing that the next day I would use my other pair. We ate pânsâwân for Brave Eagle said we should keep the pimîhkân for the day when it would keep us going for longer. While the Powhatan talked, I curled into a ball and fell asleep without even taking out my bearskin. It was not a comfortable night of sleep for the ground was hard and woke me now and then.

I was woken just before dawn by rain. It was a mixed blessing, while it woke me and made me damp, my bearskin had not been wetted. I knew that the next camp I would make a shelter from the sealskin cape! The second day was hard for me as I ached everywhere, but I gritted my teeth and tried to keep up with Hides Alone. I knew that without me they would have run faster and that spurred me on. The salve helped and changing my footwear also seemed to be a good thing. Making a bed from the bearskin also gave me a better night's sleep.

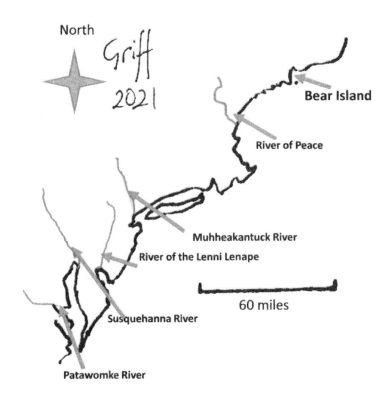

North

Griff
2021

Bear Island

River of Peace

Muhheakantuck River

River of the Lenni Lenape

60 miles

Susquehanna River

Patawomke River

The next day, in the late morning, we had a large river to cross. It was called the Susquehanna. Boats would have been easier but Brave Eagle and the others were not put out by the problem. There was an island in the middle, and they improvised a raft from some logs which I suspected had been left there by others to facilitate the crossing. We tied them with vines and with some warriors clinging to the side and kicking with their feet we crossed to the island, Lifting the raft we carried it to the other side and repeated it. We were not delayed by long and I was impressed by the warriors' ingenuity. I think the fact that I was on a boat, of sorts, lifted my spirits and I was able to keep hard on the heels of Hides Alone until we made our camp.

The next three days were almost identical days. My feet did not hurt as much as I had thought and, by the third day, my legs ceased complaining. It was at the end of the third day that we reached a Lenni Lenape village and another large river. It was the end of our journey. This one was called the Muhheakantuck and apparently led to the large island we had seen from the snekke. We were greeted, at first, with spears. The clan had been raided by the Penobscot and this was the borderlands. It was only when Brave Eagle spoke to them and told them of our quest that the spears were lowered. They too had been raided by the aggressive Penobscot and, indeed, they had lost captives to their northern neighbours. Many other villages had been raided and we were told that a vengeance raid was planned.

"We do not wish to warn your enemies, but we seek captives, and we know where they are kept. It is a village surrounded by water and belongs to the Hawk clan. My sons believe it is half a day from here."

Their chief knew of the clan, "The clan does not live far from here. You can be there in less than a day. They are not the warriors they once were. We heard that they went north to raid the Mi'kmaq and were defeated by a demon. Few warriors returned."

Brave Eagle turned to me, "I fought them that day, but it was no demon who slew so many of their warriors, it was this man."

I had been in the shadows and almost hidden. When they saw me and my beard they started with fear. Their chief said, "He is a monster! How did he defeat them for he does not look big enough!"

Brave Eagle nodded to me and I took out my sword and held it aloft, "With this!" I had seen the sun in the west and I made certain that the blade glinted and sparkled. This time they all fell back.

"Then with such a warrior, you might succeed. We will carry you across in the morning in our boats and all we ask is that you tell us, when you return, where the Penobscot warriors are gathering! If you can recapture your people then it means we can use your route to attack the others so long as there are no gatherings of warriors waiting for us."

"We will do so."

That night, as we ate hot food for the first time in many days, Brave Eagle held a council of war with the warriors from his clan. "We will spend the day getting close to the village. You say that the village is on the eastern side of the water?"

White Fox said, "It is in a clearing above the water. It is not a winter camp, but one used all year round."

"Then we scout out the defences first. I will not walk into an ambush as we did the last time."

I asked, "Where were you ambushed last time, Brave Eagle?"

He shook his head, "I was too angry and too confident. We did not cross the Muhheakantuck here but downstream. We cut down trees to cross it and it took a day. The noise we made alerted them and when we disembarked from the boats they were waiting for us. They lured us into the forest and attacked us. That was when I became separated from others. I fought my way back to the boats and although I slew many, I was struck close to the river and fell in. Swept downstream I reached the sea and the rest you know. Had I not had pimîhkân and my water skin I might not have survived."

"Then they are likely to have watchers by the river. Will they not see us when we cross?"

"You are right. We should cross while it is night."

He left to speak to the chief of the Lenni Lenape. Hides Alone said, "You think deeply about things, Erik, Shaman of the Bear. Are all your people like you?"

I shook my head, "I had a brother who was a great warrior, but he tended to act without thinking. He attacked the Penobscot and they ambushed him."

"Like our father."

I nodded, "The Penobscot are cunning fighters. They may not have as many warriors who are left but they will remember your father for he told them who he was. He told them he would come for his people and they will remember. What does it cost them to have warriors watching the river?"

Brave Eagle returned and his face told us that my warning had been a wise one. "The clan think it is a good idea for they have seen Penobscot in the trees on the other side of the river. We leave now and we prepare for war."

His words were intended for me and I unfastened my bag and took out my bearskin. I would leave the helmet inside but the bearskin would help to hide me in the woods. The Lenni Lenape were shocked when they saw me. The chief himself took me aboard the first birch bark boat. I was handed a paddle and Brave Eagle's own warriors were ferried across first. The sound of the river hid the noise of paddles. When we landed, Brave Eagle signalled for White Fox and me to follow him. Leaving the others at the bank we headed up the bank to the tree line. I held my seax in one hand and the hatchet in the other. There appeared to be no movement ahead, but we were vigilant until we reached the trees. Once there we stopped, and we listened. We used our noses, and it was White Fox who must have smelled the Penobscots for he pointed to our right. I saw nothing and I waited until Brave Eagle had moved into the trees and White Fox had also entered before I followed them. This was their land, and I was the least experienced.

I could now smell the Penobscot watchers as the wind was blowing towards us. I stepped in the footsteps of White Fox and we made no noise. I knew that upstream of us the other warriors were landing and they were waiting. I could see why the Penobscot had not seen us. There was a large rock with a scrubby shrub growing from the top. I doubted that it would survive a winter flood but it hid the crossing from

174

the scouts. The Lenni Lenape must have known that. We had been lucky. As we neared the watchers whom we could smell but not see I heard murmuring. They were talking and Brave Eagle and his son parted to come at the two watchers from two different sides. We had no idea how many others were further downstream. These men were a long way from their village. The chief of the Lenni Lenape had told us that it was more than half a day of running before we might see their lodges.

Then I saw one as he stood to stretch. Even in the dark, I could see that he was slightly built and that suggested a youth. I felt sorry for him for he would soon die. He would never become a man! I stopped to allow the other two to get closer. I would only get in the way. The two Powhatans were on the watchers so quickly that I heard little and saw less. It was a blur of movement and the two young warriors died without making a sound. The crack of the skull of the one hit by White Fox was the only noise I heard. Brave Eagle slid his dagger across the throat of the other.

Before anyone could say anything, a figure appeared from my right with a spear ready to ram into White Fox's back. There had been a third hidden watcher! I took one stride and hacked into the back of the Penobscot skull with my hatchet. The sound of the skull being crushed made White Fox turn around. Brave Eagle nodded and then made a sign to White Fox which, I assumed, was to check for any more. He seemed to take an age but eventually, he returned.

"There are no more."

Brave Eagle nodded and cupping his hands made the sound of a nightjar. While we waited for the others to join us, he checked the three bodies.

White Fox said, "I owe you a life, Erik Shaman of the Bear. I know not how my family will be able to repay you for all that you have done."

"It is nothing."

When Hides Alone brought the other warriors Brave Eagle pointed east, "Let us get as close as we can to the camp. Our plans have been upset and we need to change them." He pointed to the bodies, "First we throw the bodies in the river. Let us make their relief wonder what has happened to them."

After we had rid the bank of all trace of the three watchers we moved silently along the path which the Penobscot obviously used. It marked our passage, but we would need to be off it before dawn for the relief for the young warriors might well be heading down it. We were now in Penobscot land and we dared not speak. Once more I was between the brothers. We ran down the path. I was feeling the lack of

175

sleep. I was used to going without sleep but not doing so while running and I was weary. By my reckoning, I had seen more than thirty-five summers, and I was no longer a young man. Running at night slowed us down for there were animals in the forest and we startled some. The sudden sounds and movements made us stop each time in case it was an enemy. That and the rise and falls in the path made it a longer journey than it ought to have been.

One of Brave Eagle's warriors, Heart of the Fox, suddenly stopped and first held up his hand and then waved us to the side of the path. We all obeyed, and I found myself behind a large pine tree next to White Fox. I drew my hatchet. I saw no one but, as I sniffed, I detected, in the distance, wood smoke. That might mean a camp but as we had been running for many hours I took it to be the village. We had found the place where Brave Eagle's family were held. Would they still be alive and if they were, had we enough men to rescue them?

Chapter 19

Brave Eagle gave his whistle and pointed to the south. Heart of the Fox had been away for some time and now we followed him through the trees and down the slope to what I knew to be water. I saw light glinting from it and, as I peered east, I saw the light from fires. It was the village and we had to get around the water to be in a position to scout it out. This time the going was much harder for there was no trail and we all had to allow more distance between us. Our route was dictated by the water. We kept it to our left. I deduced that the path we had been following would go around the north side of the water. We were taking the longer route but also the one from which they would not, we hoped, be expecting us. As we neared the village the smell of woodsmoke became stronger. Heart of the Fox must have remembered more of the village for he continued to lead us. I knew from the talk in Brave Eagle's village that Brave Eagle's sons had been part of the fighting retreat. Heart of the Fox had been cut off and was forced to use his skills to evade capture. He had been the one who had come closest to the captives and he knew where they were kept. We began to climb, and I realised why. We were heading to a place above the village where we would be able to observe it better. I knew that dawn was not far away and we needed to be hidden before that time. That Heart of the Fox had a plan became clear when we found ourselves in a jumble of rocks and scrubby bushes and stunted trees.

Brave Eagle waved for us to sit. He, White Fox and Heart of the Fox disappeared. We did not speak. I saw some of the other warriors eating and drinking. One or two lay down to sleep. As much as I wanted, indeed needed, a night of sleep, I would wait until my friend and his son returned. The sun rose and still they had not returned. I looked at Hides Alone who did not appear unduly worried and gave me a reassuring look. Only the other warrior from Brave Eagle's village, Yellow Moon was on watch. The rest were now asleep. This was not really their fight. I suspected they had volunteered to come for the chance to fight and to kill Penobscot. They would not be bringing vengeance on their clan and they would have trophies of war to take back. All of them were very young warriors. Until that time they would allow Brave Eagle's warriors to do the hard work.

I knew when the three warriors were returning for Yellow Moon threw a stone to attract the attention of Hides Alone. The three stepped behind the rock and Brave Eagle spoke to Hides Alone and me. He put his head close to ours so that the words did not carry. I saw Heart of the Fox do the same with Yellow Moon." I have seen the head of my son and the other warriors on spears! The birds have been at them but I know my own son."

"I am sorry, Brave Eagle."

He nodded, "It is good that we have scouted out the village for we have seen that the captives are kept locked away and guarded at night. They have a long lodge for them with but one way in and out and two men watch. They also keep a good watch around the camp. If we tried to take them at night we might rescue some but I believe that some would be killed and I want none dead. It is clear to me that we cannot attack at night and the best time to make our attempt will be at dawn." My heart sank for by then they would know that their sentries had disappeared and would be on the alert. He looked at me and saw my face. He gave a sad smile, "Erik, we must use you and draw the enemy to you. We will sleep this day and then when it is night, you and my sons will make your way around to the other side of the village. There, the path we were on descends to the village. I need you to stand there so that when the sun rises and the captives are released from their long house, as we just saw, you can raise your sword, catch the sun and give a war cry. By then the rest of us will be in position and when their warriors race to get at you the rest of us will attack their guards and form a protective screen around them."

I nodded. I knew he had come up with the idea when we had met Long Spear. It made sense and, despite the risks to me was a good plan. I would have his sons to protect me and as soon as the warriors realised what was happening then some would have to turn to fight. "How many warriors did you see?"

His eyes dropped and he said, "More than thirty."

I nodded, "More than we thought."

"The village is larger than we thought and there are other warriors here. The warriors of the Clan of the Moos and their families have joined them." He held my eye again, "But we can defeat them."

"And your family?"

He turned to Hides Alone, "Your mother, your wife, White Fox's wife and Black Owl's widow live."

"Our children?"

"We did not see them, but we did not see all the captives either. They may be in a different lodge. That may be a way to stop the mothers trying to escape."

I had spoken to the brothers and knew that Brave Eagle had seven grandchildren. Three were White Fox's and two were Hides Alone. The fact that their wives were alive would not be enough to compensate for the loss of their children.

Brave Eagle said, "You three will need to rest. I will set others to watch. You will have to rise in the middle of the night to sneak into position."

I nodded and laid down. I would be able to eat when I rose, and I needed sleep!

I did not wake naturally. White Fox woke me and said, urgently in my ear, "Warriors have returned to the village. My father thinks they have discovered that their sentries are missing."

I had enjoyed enough sleep to make me feel rested and I rose to squat next to him, "What have they done?"

"They sent one warrior north, and they have set others as sentries all around the camp. There are two of them between us and the village now. We will have a longer journey to get to the place we need. We might have to kill them."

I nodded, "It is clear that we will have to kill them and silently at that. You have already shown you have the skill of silently slaying."

He smiled, "Thank you for the compliment. It would seem that you are right. The watchers will have to die."

I smiled at White Fox, "We knew there were dangers and let us look at this in a positive way. If they keep watch all day and all night, then their vigilance has to relax at some point."

"You are right, but they have placed guards closer to our families." He forced a smile, "We have seen all the children. They are alive."

I looked up at the sky. The sun still had some way to go to reach its zenith. I lay down again, "I will sleep and I suggest that you do the same. Let the Penobscot watch and we shall be the ones who are rested."

I wrapped myself in my bearskin. I did not fall asleep immediately for, despite my words to White Fox I was concerned. The only warriors we had who would be totally committed to this fight and rescue would be the Clan of the Eagle. The others had come to kill Penobscot. So long as we were winning then they would fight but they were not led by their own chief and if things went against us then they would simply flee and leave us. We had to win. I finally slept.

I had not dreamt of Arne and Siggi for a long time but that night they both came to me. Their forms were indistinct, but I knew it to be them from their voices. They seemed to be singing and each took a line. Perhaps they were in Valhalla and had made up the song whilst drinking at Odin's table.

179

You are the one who fights for the clan
Erik the Navigator, a warrior man
Fighting the Skræling it was he you slayed
The last one left of the brothers of the blade
You are the warrior who can be the bear
Be the Ulfheonar show no fear
The last of the brothers who swore in blood
You will win for your heart is good

Their voices faded and darkness came until there was a sudden flash of light and I was blinded. When I opened my eyes I saw Siggi and Arne, covered in blood at the top of the falls. In their hands, their swords were raised, and they flashed in the sunlight. Darkness enveloped me.

I felt a hand shaking me and I looked up into Brave Eagle's face. He was smiling, "You are truly a warrior for while others could barely keep their eyes closed you slept as deep a sleep as I have seen. It will be dark soon. You need to eat and prepare for battle."

I nodded, "They still have sentries?"

"Aye, but they have not ventured far from the village. Heart of the Fox chose this vantage point wisely. Fear not, Erik, I will lead these warriors to come to your aid as soon as you have their attention."

I leaned into him. "They will have sent for more warriors from other clans."

"I know and that means we have to hurry to reach the river. If we succeed, then I will send a warrior to run to the Lenni Lenape and ask them to bring boats across to carry the survivors to safety."

I made water and then drank from my skin. I took another piece of pimîhkân and chewed it. My dream had confirmed what I had to do. I had heard of the Ulfheonar. They were warriors who fought in animal skins and were terrifying because their enemies thought they had become the animal. Some fought as bears while others as wolves. They could hide, almost in plain sight and yet, like a berserker, on the battlefield they drew their enemies to them. That was what I would do. I would be so still that they could not see me and then I would rise like a wraith and give a Viking war cry which would instil terror in their hearts.

White Fox and Hides Alone came over to me as the sun set in the west. I peered through the bushes confident that I would be hidden in the dark. I saw the place we would stand and I fixed it in my head. I was a navigator and once I knew where I was going then I could find my way there in the dark. I turned and waved the two brothers to walk with me. We headed into the darkness some way from the others.

"I would change our plan." Neither questioned me but I saw the questions in their eyes. I will wait, as we originally planned, where the Penobscot can see me but I will make myself invisible." Hides Alone opened his mouth and I said, "Trust me." He nodded. "You two will lie down where you can see the village. Pick up some stones. As soon as the captives are brought forth then throw a stone at me. Do not worry I will only be invisible to the Penobscot. From that point on the plan is the same one. I will stand until they advance and when they do, then you two join me. I will have my sword drawn and ready to catch the sun and their attention. We will stand together and use our bows. When they close I will drop my bow and use my sword and hatchet."

I saw in their eyes that they trusted me. The brothers and their father had enjoyed little success as warriors. Brave Eagle's one victory had come when he fought alongside me in the Mi'kmaq village. I had a great responsibility resting on my shoulders, but it gave me some comfort to know that Siggi and Arne were watching me. Perhaps my father was too, and I hoped he would be proud of his son.

I put my bjorr hat on and then pulled the helmet over it. It was a tight fit, but it would give me a little more protection from blows on my head. I put my sealskin cloak over my shoulders and then donned my bearskin. I hung my bow from my shoulder and stuck five arrows in my belt. I doubted I would have time to loose more. I drew my seax. In the last rays of the sun, I saw the scar on my palm from all those years ago when I had sworn the blood oath with Siggi and Arne. I was still the same boy. I had just grown into a man. The other two awaited me and I saw the rest of the warriors staring at me. Only Brave Eagle was smiling. He said no words but clasped my arm and nodded. I knew his thoughts for the long voyage down the coast had allowed us to say all that there was to say. I set off through the trees.

We headed out to make a long sweep around the village. We wanted neither smell nor sound to reach them and we had hours to get into position. The one problem we had was that we did not know where they had placed sentries on the far side. White Fox had been told that sentries had left the village but their positions were unknown. If we found them then I would deal with them. I did not rush for the last thing we needed was to alert the Penobscot. My sense of direction came to my aid and I began to climb towards the place I had seen the sunset.

I smelled the sentry before I saw him. I stopped and laid my bow down. I took out my hatchet and sought the shape. He was hunkered down, and he was waiting at the exact place I had identified as the one where the sun would shine. I turned to the other two and gestured for them to wait. They nodded and I moved forward, studying the ground as I did so. This was no young warrior for I saw that he had placed twigs, leaves and branches behind him so that any who was doing as I was and creeping up would make a noise when they stepped on them. As his smell had come to me then I knew he would not smell me. I stepped over the trap and raised my hatchet. He was a veteran and somehow sensing me, he whirled around with his stone knife in his hand. I saw his eyes widen as he saw the bear before him. That made him pause and I ended his life. I smashed the hatchet into his skull as I ripped the seax across his throat. If he had intended a cry, then the seax ended it. As his blood sprayed me, he fell forward and I caught him. I dragged him back to White Fox and his brother.

After laying him down I picked up my bow and returned to the place he had been. I adopted the same position. If any looked up from the village, just two hundred paces below us, then they would see the shadow of the watcher in the same place. They would see what they expected to see and, in the morning, I hoped that they would not even look to see him. I watched the village. This was like being on watch on the drekar, staring into the dark for hours upon end. This was easier for I did not have to look at the sail nor feel for changes in the sea or the wind. The village was getting ready for night and the movements were predictable. The fires they had for their food would make them night blind and as they finished their tasks they would all go to their lodges and leave men to watch. I did not move for a couple of hours. I waited until I saw where they had placed their two sentries in the village. Then I stood to let my legs stretch. I stayed in that position. The sentry who turned to look at me was on the far side of the fire. He raised his hand to wave, and I raised mine to wave back at him. All that he would see was a shadow in the dark, but my waved hand was a reassurance that their watcher watched still. I squatted once more, and he and the other sentry sat on the log to chat.

My blood brothers had been right. I had to play the Ulfheonar.

The sentries by the fire were not doing their job properly for, after a short while, I saw them both hunched forward, they were asleep. All made sense for the best warriors, the diligent ones had died in the battle. The ones who had fled were not of the same quality and their training of the young would not have been as rigorous. It explained how White Fox and Brave Eagle had disposed so easily of the river sentries. I saw men rising from their lodges to make water. They would be the old men and were a sign that night was drawing to a close. The sentries by the fire roused themselves and they disappeared. I assumed they went to make water. When they returned, they brought firewood and encouraged the fire to flame brighter. That suited me as they would have no night vision. I watched them as they put their own food to cook and, in the east, I saw the first tiny sign that the sun was about to rise. I tipped my head forward so that there would be no flesh to be seen. The bearskin enveloped me and made me into a black shadow. I forced myself to keep still as I heard noise from the village. I had to trust that the brothers would be watching from their prone position and that they would choose the perfect moment for me to rise like a wraith. I felt the first hint of warmth from the sun which, I assumed, had begun to rise. I heard a shout from below me. I guessed it was a guard releasing the captives and then the stone hit the back of my head. I stood, drawing my sword and I looked down and saw the reason for the cry. One of the Penobscot was beating one of the women captives. It was fortuitous for the attention of all the village was on the two of them.

Raising my sword I shouted, in my language, "I am Erik the Navigator and I am of the Clan of the Fox. I am here to wreak vengeance on those who stole Brave Eagles' family!" I then gave a warlike scream which I hoped was blood-curdling. I did not care that my words were not understood.

I turned the blade so that the sunlight caught it and I saw it shine into the eyes of some of the warriors and they hid their eyes. The warriors' attention was on me and I saw, behind them, Brave Eagle silently leading his warriors towards the camp.

> *I am the one who fights for the clan*
> *Erik the Navigator, a warrior man*
> *Fighting the Skræling it was he I slayed*
> *The last one left of the brothers of the blade*
> *I am the warrior who can be the bear*
> *I am the Ulfheonar and show no fear*
> *The last of the brothers who swore in blood*
> *I will win for my heart is good*

My oath blade brothers had given me my war cry. I rammed the sword in the ground and picked up my bow. I drew an arrow, and the warriors all began to run towards me. I felt, rather than saw, the brothers run to flank me and I sent a metal tipped arrow to drive through the chest of the first eager warrior who was just one hundred and twenty paces from me and running as fast as he could up the slope. It drove through his body so far that the fletch was next to his skin. I nocked a second arrow as White Fox sent his stone-tipped arrows at the advancing warriors. I looked for the veterans, the ones with scars and battle honours. My second arrow hit my target in the forehead and pieces of his skull flew from the back showering the next warrior. My third was sent at a warrior who was less than thirty paces from me. I hit his neck and the blood sprayed those around him. I knew I had but one more arrow I could send, and it hit the warrior who was ten paces from me and pulling back his spear to skewer me. The fletch disappeared in his chest.

I dropped my bow and drew my hatchet and sword. White Fox had hit four warriors but only one had been killed. As I knocked aside the spear which was thrust at me and chopped into the neck of the Penobscot I heard a cheer and a wail from the camp as the captives saw their saviours and Brave Eagle and his warriors ruthlessly butchered the men who had been watching the captives. Their backs were to the Powhatans. The warrior before me made the mistake of turning to look and my hatchet split open the back of his skull. White Fox was wielding the sharpened antler axe with two hands while his brother used his spear to keep warriors from my side. More than half of the warriors who were advancing towards us turned to face Brave Eagle's threat. I saw two men trying to get around my side. The one-armed Hides Alone would struggle to fight two. I whirled to my left and hacked through the spine of one with my sword as my hatchet cracked open the skull of the other. Then I turned to face the warriors who were advancing. We had split them into two.

It was time to unleash the bear upon them and, screaming I ran down the slope towards the half who were advancing towards the demon. For two of the younger warriors, it was too much, and they turned and fled as the bearded bear shouted strange words and advanced with shiny, bloody weapons. I used my sword to slice into the men on my right while I used my hatchet like a shield, knocking aside the stone weapons. Its sharp edge sliced into flesh and wood equally easily. Inevitably I was struck but the stone spears caught on the fur and did not penetrate deeply. One of the clubs was thrown at me and hit my head. It did not hurt although it made my ears ring and the surprised warrior was speared by Hides Alone. One warrior managed to get behind me and he rammed his spear at my back. The hide bag, fur and the bearskin meant I was just pricked in the back and the scream from behind me told me that Hides Alone watched over me still.

Brave Eagle and his warriors were now facing good warriors and the battle was evenly balanced. There was no honour in this and as I stabbed one Penobscot in the back and split yet another skull I found myself behind the line of warriors fighting Brave Eagle. He had two fighting him and one had a fatal shock when my sword emerged from his chest. Brave Eagle used his seax to slit the throat of the other. That was the moment when the warriors who remained broke and then fled north. The Penobscot women and children from the village, as well as the old, were streaming up the slope. They feared a massacre. I saw that some warriors had died but they had been the volunteers. Brave Eagle's warriors lived.

I saw that many of the Powhatan were despoiling the bodies of the dead Penobscot. I pointed to the people streaming north, "Brave Eagle, get your people moving. Remember that they sent for help. We do not have time for this!"

He nodded and shouted out his orders. I sheathed my sword and rammed the hatchet in my belt. I ran up the slope to retrieve the arrowheads from the bodies. It was easier just to pull the arrows through the flesh and bone. I ruined the fletch but that was easy to replace. I reached my bow. I took off my bearskin and my bag. The bear had done its work and the day would be too hot to run in the skin. I put the helmet and skin in my bag and fastened the bow to it. By the time I reached the village Brave Eagle and the warriors of the Clan of the Eagle were moving towards the path which led, eventually, to the river. Some of the other warriors were guarding the captives but most were still busy taking trophies. I recognised the blood lust in their eyes.

I saw that the two brothers were hugging their wives as was Brave Eagle. "There is no time for that! Move!"

They nodded. I was the last one, apart from Brave Eagle's family, up the slope. Brave Eagle and his sons joined us. "I have sent Heart of the Fox to the river to warn the Lenni Lenape and Yellow Moon with the warriors who followed our orders to take our families to the river. They have been badly treated! I wish we could have hurt the Penobscot more!"

"Brave Eagle, I believe that the Penobscot sent for help. We must be a rearguard. Let us wait here and hide in the trees. We can always run after them. This way we will know the danger."

He smiled and said, "You see, my sons, he does not call himself one but this is a warrior."

I nodded, "And you, Hides Alone are a brave man and I owe you much, but you cannot fight with one hand. Better that you go with the families. We three are enough."

"But..."

"Erik is right my son. You have done more than enough already!"

He looked at White Fox who nodded, "They are right, and we will not be far behind you."

185

Hides Alone turned and led their wives to safety. He had been lucky in the fight. I knew why he had wanted to stay. He had a brother to avenge and a family to save but had I not been there then he would have been dead.

Just eight of the Powhatan warriors who had volunteered to come with us remained alive in the village. Another half dozen had obeyed orders and had gone with the captives and the rest lay dead. They were gorging themselves on taking from the dead. I had seen it before but normally it was Norse and Danish warriors who were drunk on ale. These were drunk with slaughter.

White Fox asked, "How long do we stay?"

Brave Eagle pointed north with his dagger, "Until the Penobscot come or noon. By noon, even the weakest of our people will be close to the river."

I knew we would not have the luxury of that for even as we peered north we spied movement. Brave Eagle shouted to the eight who were still hacking pieces from the bodies to take trophies, "Warriors, the Penobscot return! Run!"

They did not appear to hear and when I saw Penobscot filtering through the woods I knew it was time to go. I turned and loped off down the path. Brave Eagle and White Fox were reluctant to leave their fellow tribesmen, but I was anxious to make some traps to catch unwary Penobscot and to slow them down. I wondered if Brave Eagle and White Fox would follow me it was so long before I heard their feet pounding behind me. Brave Eagles said, "They will be dead men. When the Penobscot came they turned to fight them. The blood was in their heads. They had good deaths."

"And we need to find somewhere to lay a trap and then somewhere else to ambush them. The captives will not even be halfway to the river."

The Powhatan sacrifice would not be in vain for it would take time to kill them and then ensure that there were no more warriors hiding in the village. We found a place for a trap where the trail descended and there was a strong sapling just two paces from the side.

"Bend that over, I have some rope."

In my bag, I had a couple of short lengths of rope. We made a simple trap which we disguised with fallen leaves. Even if they spotted it, they would have to slow up to go around it. A little further down the trail, I saw two young trees which were close enough together for me to make a trip rope. Again, I knew they might see it, but they would have to slow and each time they did so the more it was likely that the captives would reach the river. We ran. Had this been the start of the quest then I would have struggled but the running of the last days had actually made me stronger and I was able to keep up with Brave Eagle and his son.

We caught up with Hides Alone, who was at the rear of the captives just a mile or so from the river. He was with the older four women who were struggling. Hides Alone said, "I think that Heart of the Fox will be at the river and should have the boats there."

Brave Eagle shook his head as he heard a shout down the trail, "They have tripped a trap. They will soon be upon us. Go and we will follow."

I saw him take out his stone club and I shook my head, "Here is not the place. Do you remember where we slew the sentries?" He nodded, "I recall that the ground fell away when we started on the trail. If we wait there with our bows, we will be able to see the progress of the crossing and the Lenni Lenape might be able to help. These are their enemies and they asked if we could find a stronghold. This might be better. If we anger the Penobscot and descend to the river we buy your people time and we might be able to shift the Penobscot's anger from your clan to the Lenni Lenape."

White Fox said, "I like that idea."

We turned and, running, followed Hides Alone. We then walked behind him. "Hides Alone, when you cross the river tell the Lenni Lenape that we have brought warriors for them to kill!"

I could hear the sound of the river and knew it was not far ahead but I could also hear, in the distance, to the north, the sound of pursuit. Our traps had, indeed, slowed them but they were coming and their war cries told us their anger. When we reached the river and looked down we saw that there were still more than fifteen captives to cross in the birch bark boats. Yellow Moon and Heart of the Fox saw us and ran up the slope to our side. We now had five warriors and four had bows. Brave Eagle spread us out amongst the trees.

I said, "Do not loose your arrows too soon for each one must hit a warrior. We will have an order. I will send the first arrow at the leading warrior and then White Fox, Heart of the Fox and Yellow Moon. Brave Eagle can deal with any who escape our arrows."

I nocked an arrow. I chose a stone-tipped one for I was loath to use and lose a metal arrowhead. The Penobscot appeared and, as I had hoped, their attention was on the trail as they sought traps. I waited until the leading warrior was just seventy paces from me and sent my arrow at him. I hit his shoulder. It was not mortal, but he was hurt. The other arrows had varying degrees of success and I sent my second arrow at a warrior who had darted to the left and thought to avoid our arrow shower. I hit him in the side. The Penobscot now left the trail and spread themselves out intent upon outflanking us. I used the last of my stone arrows and then drew my sword.

Hides Alone ran to his father's side, "The captives are across and the Lenni Lenape are now crossing to come to your aid. We can fall back!"

It was at that moment that a Penobscot who had crawled unseen to within a pace or two of us suddenly leapt up and smashed his stone club into the knee of Brave Eagle. My sword flashed and slashed at the warrior's head. I almost sliced the top off, "Get your father to the river!" White Fox and Hides Alone nodded and lifted Brave Eagle up. "You two walk backwards with me."

As we pulled back down the slope the Penobscot realised what we were doing and the thirty or so who remained ran at us. I barely had time to draw my hatchet before I was called upon to use it. The longest weapons the enemy had were spears and the wooden shafts were easily hacked but it was their sheer numbers that were a problem. I hacked, chopped, and slashed and when the two warriors fell at my feet I turned and ran knowing that I had left their bodies as an obstacle. Even though I had good weapons my legs and arms were bleeding from the cuts inflicted by spears and stone-tipped arrows. It was when we were just twenty paces from the river that the Lenni Lenape left their boats to fall upon the Penobscot who had managed to knock Yellow Moon to the ground. Before the shaven-headed Penobscot could crush his skull, I had thrown my hatchet to smash into the side of the warrior's head.

For us, that was the end of the battle but the Lenni Lenape did not return until the next day having chased the survivors to the village. We saw the smoke in the late afternoon as the home of the Clan of the Hawk was destroyed. The feud would be over for there were none of Grey Hawk's warriors left!

Epilogue

The wounds to Brave Eagle and Yellow Moon were not serious but they meant we had to delay for almost a week before we could return to Brave Eagle's home. It allowed the captives to recover some of their strength and for the warriors to speak to their families.

The journey back took four days longer than the journey out. I stayed at the rear of the column with the last of the volunteers. They saw me as some sort of lucky charm. The wild ones had died and these would return to their clans better warriors. I camped with them at night. We acted as the sentries. Although we were not worried about pursuit it made sense to take precautions and I got to know them. It was they told me about the lands to the north and west of Brave Eagle's home and I discovered that I could travel more than a hundred miles until the mountains stopped me. I began to formulate a plan. Brave Eagle was keen for me to stay with him and while I was happy to do so for a short time, I wanted to sail my snekke as far as I could.

When we reached the Patawomke I saw that my sons had worried so much about us, for we had taken longer than they had expected, that they had taken to fishing in the river so that they could see us arrive. So it was that by the time I reached the bank of the river *'Gytha'* was there. I smiled when I saw that they had painted the head yellow and the captives were fearful as the fierce dragon came towards them. I forgot about them as my sons leapt ashore to embrace me.

I nodded to the snekke, "You have not sunk her yet then?"

They laughed and Moos Blood said, "We have worked hard, father, for Brave Cub can now steer. The family has three navigators!"

I felt so proud of them, "Good, then I will wait here while you ferry the rest across and I will judge your skill!"

It took all afternoon for the captives were fearful but eventually, all were safely in the village and I crossed the river with my sons. I sat by the mast fish. My days of standing a watch alone were over. Now, once we had explored this land, we could sail further south and find some of the rivers I had been told reached deep into this new world. My family of navigators would be the clan who mapped this world, and I was content.

The End

Glossary

Alesstkɑtek-River Androscoggin, Maine
Aroughcun -Raccoon (Powhatan)
Beck- a stream
Blót – a blood sacrifice made by a jarl.
Bjorr – Beaver
Byrnie- a mail or leather shirt reaching down to the knees.
Chesepiooc- Chesapeake
Cohongarooton- The Potomac River above Great Falls
Fret-a sea mist
Galdramenn- wizard
Gingoteague - Chincoteague Virginia
Lenni Lenape- Delaware- the tribe and the land
Mamanatowick - High chief of the Powhatans
Mockasin- Algonquin for moccasin
Muhheakantuck - The Hudson River
Natocke – Nantucket
Njörðr- God of the sea
Noepe -Martha's Vineyard
Odin- The 'All Father' God of war, also associated with wisdom, poetry, and magic (The Ruler of the gods).
Onguiaahra- Niagara (It means the straits)
Østersøen – The Baltic
Pamunkey River -York River, Virginia
Patawomke – The Potomac River below Great Falls.
Pânsâwân- Cree for dried meat
Pimîhkân – Pemmican
Ran- Goddess of the sea
Skræling -Barbarian
Smoky Bay- Reykjavik
Snekke- a small warship
Tarn- small lake (Norse)
Wapapyaki -Wampum
Wyrd- Fate
Yehakin – Powhatan lodge

Historical references

I use my vivid imagination to tell my stories. I am a writer of fiction, a storyteller, and this book is very much a 'what if' sort of book. We now know that the Vikings reached further south in mainland America than we thought. Just how far is debatable. The evidence we have is from the sagas. Vinland was named after a fruit that was discovered by the first Norse settlers. It does not necessarily mean grapes. King Harald Finehair did drive many Vikings west, but I cannot believe that they would choose to live on a volcanic island if they thought there might be better lands to the south and west of them. My books in this series are my speculation of what might have happened had Vikings spent a longer time in America than we assume.

I have my clan reaching Newfoundland and sailing down the coast of Nova Scotia. The island I call Bear Island is Isle Au Haut off the Maine coast. Grey Fox island and (Horse) Deer Island can also be found there. The Indigenous people, the Mi'kmaq, inhabited the northeastern coast of America. In the summer they would migrate to the coast and in winter, when there were fewer flies, they would retreat back to the hinterland. The maps are how Erik might have mapped them. Butar's deer are caribou and the horse deer are moose. Both were native to the region.

I have no idea what names the Algonquin speaking tribes used a thousand years ago. I have used names that follow the structure of the Norse. The names are used just to identify individuals. I am not writing this as a historical treatise on the people at the time. The tribes I use lived roughly where I placed them but as the European colonists did not arrive for another six centuries then much could have changed. I confess that I had fun with the names and if I have offended anyone then I apologise. I hope that the names I use help you to follow the story.

I have used maize, squash and beans even though I know that they were not the names the tribes used. It is for the simplification of the story.

The Powhatan confederacy of tribes came about in the 17th Century and I confess that I do not know the names they would have used in the 10th century. Due to Covid, I have not been able to travel to the area for more detailed research. I apologise to the purists. The tribe I use was not the powerful one of Chief Wahunsunacock, that came later. As with all my writings about the North American indigenous people, it is 90%

speculation. This is not a historical treatise but a story that I hope will entertain you.

Pinus echinate or shortleaf pine is native to Virginia and grows both in swamp plains and mountains. For the purposes of this story, I have the Powhatans call it the shortleaf pine.

I used the following books for research:

- Vikings- Life and Legends -British Museum
- Saxon, Norman and Viking by Terence Wise (Osprey)
- The Vikings (Osprey) -Ian Heath
- Byzantine Armies 668-1118 (Osprey)-Ian Heath
- Romano-Byzantine Armies 4th-9th Century (Osprey) - David Nicholle
- The Walls of Constantinople AD 324-1453 (Osprey) - Stephen Turnbull
- Viking Longship (Osprey) - Keith Durham
- The Vikings in England Anglo-Danish Project
- Anglo Saxon Thegn AD 449-1066- Mark Harrison (Osprey)
- Viking Hersir- 793-1066 AD - Mark Harrison (Osprey)
- Hadrian's Wall- David Breeze (English Heritage)
- National Geographic- March 2017
- Time Life Seafarers-The Vikings Robert Wernick

Griff Hosker
February 2021

Other books by Griff Hosker

If you enjoyed reading this book, then why not read another one by the author?

Ancient History

The Sword of Cartimandua Series
(Germania and Britannia 50 A.D. – 128 A.D.)
Ulpius Felix- Roman Warrior (prequel)
The Sword of Cartimandua
The Horse Warriors
Invasion Caledonia
Roman Retreat
Revolt of the Red Witch
Druid's Gold
Trajan's Hunters
The Last Frontier
Hero of Rome
Roman Hawk
Roman Treachery
Roman Wall
Roman Courage

The Wolf Warrior series
(Britain in the late 6th Century)
Saxon Dawn
Saxon Revenge
Saxon England
Saxon Blood
Saxon Slayer
Saxon Slaughter
Saxon Bane
Saxon Fall: Rise of the Warlord
Saxon Throne
Saxon Sword

Medieval History

The Dragon Heart Series
Viking Slave
Viking Warrior
Viking Jarl
Viking Kingdom
Viking Wolf
Viking War
Viking Sword
Viking Wrath
Viking Raid
Viking Legend
Viking Vengeance
Viking Dragon
Viking Treasure
Viking Enemy
Viking Witch
Viking Blood
Viking Weregeld
Viking Storm
Viking Warband
Viking Shadow
Viking Legacy
Viking Clan
Viking Bravery

The Norman Genesis Series
Hrolf the Viking
Horseman
The Battle for a Home
Revenge of the Franks
The Land of the Northmen
Ragnvald Hrolfsson
Brothers in Blood
Lord of Rouen
Drekar in the Seine
Duke of Normandy

The Duke and the King

New World Series
Blood on the Blade
Across the Seas
The Savage Wilderness
The Bear and the Wolf
Erik the Navigator

The Vengeance Trail

The Danelaw Saga
The Dragon Sword

The Reconquista Chronicles
Castilian Knight
El Campeador
The Lord of Valencia

The Aelfraed Series
(Britain and Byzantium 1050 A.D. - 1085 A.D.)
Housecarl
Outlaw
Varangian

The Anarchy Series England
1120-1180
English Knight
Knight of the Empress
Northern Knight
Baron of the North
Earl
King Henry's Champion
The King is Dead
Warlord of the North
Enemy at the Gate
The Fallen Crown
Warlord's War

Kingmaker
Henry II
Crusader
The Welsh Marches
Irish War
Poisonous Plots
The Princes' Revolt
Earl Marshal

Border Knight
1182-1300
Sword for Hire
Return of the Knight
Baron's War
Magna Carta
Welsh Wars
Henry III
The Bloody Border
Baron's Crusade
Sentinel of the North
War in the West
Debt of Honour

Sir John Hawkwood Series
France and Italy 1339- 1387
Crécy: The Age of the Archer
Man at Arms

Lord Edward's Archer
Lord Edward's Archer
King in Waiting
An Archer's Crusade

Struggle for a Crown
1360- 1485
Blood on the Crown
To Murder A King
The Throne

196

King Henry IV
The Road to Agincourt
St Crispin's Day
The Battle for France

Tales from the Sword I

Conquistador
England and America in the 16th Century
Conquistador (Coming in 2021)

Modern History

The Napoleonic Horseman Series
Chasseur à Cheval
Napoleon's Guard
British Light Dragoon
Soldier Spy
1808: The Road to Coruña
Talavera
The Lines of Torres Vedras
Bloody Badajoz
The Road to France

The Lucky Jack American Civil War series
Rebel Raiders
Confederate Rangers
The Road to Gettysburg

The British Ace Series
1914
1915 Fokker Scourge
1916 Angels over the Somme
1917 Eagles Fall
1918 We will remember them
From Arctic Snow to Desert Sand
Wings over Persia

Combined Operations series
1940-1945
Commando
Raider
Behind Enemy Lines
Dieppe
Toehold in Europe
Sword Beach
Breakout
The Battle for Antwerp
King Tiger
Beyond the Rhine
Korea
Korean Winter

Tales from the Sword 2

Other Books
Great Granny's Ghost (Aimed at 9-14-year-old young people)

For more information on all of the books then please visit the author's web site at www.griffhosker.com where there is a link to contact him or visit his Facebook page: GriffHosker at Sword Books

Printed in Great Britain
by Amazon